Praise for

Florence Gordon

"[A] smart, funny, and compassionate book . . . It's a treat."—*People*

"You wouldn't want to be [Florence's] friend or family member; rather, you're deeply grateful—at least I was—to meet her in the best way possible: in the exquisitely crafted pages of Morton's witty, nuanced, and ultimately moving novel . . . *Florence Gordon* is one of those extraordinary novels that clarifies its readers' sense of things . . . Morton's ending is straight out of a Chekhov story: it's up in the air and brave, a closing vision of a life in all its messy contradictions."—**Maureen Corrigan**, *Fresh Air*

"Angular and comic."—*The New Yorker*

"What a treat it is to read Brian Morton's latest novel, populated with the prickly, civic-minded liberal intellectuals we've come to expect from him . . . Morton doesn't insult us with cheesy, sentimental breakthroughs, but he does offer this comfort—characters who are so believable you expect to run into them ordering from the deli counter at Zabar's."
—**NPR.org**

"Morton . . . writes with a refreshing lack of irony about the little disappointments and consolations that no one is above caring about. His work is the kind of old-fashioned that happily endures."—*New York Times*

"Admirers of Elizabeth Strout's Pulitzer Prize–winning novel *Olive Kitteridge* will see traces of Olive in Florence . . . Morton has artfully constructed the novel in scenes with perspectives shifting among characters."
—*Chicago Tribune*

"It's such a cliché to say a book makes you laugh and cry, but this one does, in the deftest way. Morton is that rarest of birds: a dude who's really, truly a feminist. His characters live and breathe, and I still miss hanging out with them."—**Emily Gould**, *Paste*

"What makes *Florence Gordon* a crucial book is the way that it engages with truths that we're living through but don't get the chance to talk about on a daily basis . . . This book is vital in the way that it looks at several generations of women, canny with insight."—*Flavorwire*

"Hilarious and addictive . . . [Morton] manages to be moving without ever being sappy, showing how people can affect each other deeply while remaining stubbornly—wonderfully—themselves."

—*San Francisco Chronicle*

"Combining a rigorous intellect and a deep humanity, this is the story of a feminist hero, a family coming together and apart, and the ways we interpret the past and attempt to face the future. Most of all, *Florence Gordon* shows how passion—of one type or the other—shapes a heart."

—**Alice Sebold, author of *The Lovely Bones***

"Florence Gordon is a marvelous creation. Like many great characters in English literature, she is a sacred monster, fully realized and richly present in the pages of this thoroughly enjoyable book."

—**Vivian Gornick, author of *The Odd Woman and the City***

"A marvelously wise, compassionate, funny, rueful, and altogether winning novel. Brian Morton knows inside-out this tribe of witty, thoughtful people who, for all their decent values and good intentions, can't seem to narrow the unbridgeable distance between men and women, young and old, pride and compromise, solitariness and community. *Florence Gordon* is his most generously ample, humane, and vital book."

—**Phillip Lopate, author of *To Show and to Tell* and *Against Joie de Vivre***

"*Florence Gordon* is one of contemporary literature's most wondrous characters: flawed and brilliant, funny and serious, totally unforgettable."

—**Darin Strauss, author of *Chang and Eng* and *Half a Life***

"*Florence Gordon* belongs on the very short list of wonderful novels about older women. Florence, the brilliant, cranky, solitude-craving feminist writer, is an indelible character, and her New York—the fading city of books and writers and melancholy oddballs—lives on in these immensely pleasurable pages."

—**Katha Pollitt, author of *Learning to Drive and Other Life Stories***

"[Morton] has consistently demonstrated a respect for the humanity of even his most flawed characters . . . Witty and sophisticated."—*Haaretz*

"Morton treats the material with a light touch and a dry sense of humor . . . He is compassionate without being sentimental, even when his characters face life-changing challenges . . . Morton creates individuals, not types, and makes what could be a familiar story fresh."

—*Columbus Dispatch*

"Warm, funny, and always deeply human . . . Florence Gordon, for all her fine qualities, never ends up being lovable. But Brian Morton's novel certainly is." —**Margaret Sullivan,** *Buffalo News*

"Morton is a quietly confident writer, who imbues even throwaway lines of dialogue with crackling wit, and whose characters banter like actors in a screwball comedy . . . This is one of the most terrific novels you will encounter this fall. With *Florence Gordon*, Morton has written a heartfelt paean to a 'gloriously difficult woman.'" —*Christian Science Monitor*

"Deliciously sharp and deeply sympathetic . . . [Morton] is one of the most unostentatiously intelligent novelists at work today . . . A truly gifted novelist." —**Adam Kirsch,** *Tablet*

"Morton views the New York literary community through the lens of an Austen-esque irony . . . The energy of *Florence Gordon*, the heat that keeps a reader turning pages, comes from the spark lighted between Florence and Emily." —*Los Angeles Review of Books*

"The author is as iconoclastic as his heroine, and his characters remain true to their nettlesome selves right up to the very last page."
—**Fernanda Moore,** *Commentary*

"Perhaps readers will pick up this book for the audacity and intrigue of straight-shooting Florence. But they will want to keep reading thanks to Morton's high-stakes scenes . . . Memorable, poetic, and pitch-perfect."
—*Washington Independent Review of Books*

"A treat for anyone keen on literary fiction. Always a pleasure to read for his well-drawn characters, quiet insight, and dialogue that crackles with wit, Morton here raises his own bar in all three areas."
—*Kirkus Reviews*, **starred review**

"A fascinating family . . . Morton's characters are sharply drawn, vivid in temperament and behavior, and his prose smartly reveals Florence's strength and dignity." —*Publishers Weekly*, **starred review**

Also by Brian Morton

The Dylanist

Starting Out in the Evening

A Window Across the River

Breakable You

Florence Gordon

Brian Morton

Mariner Books
Houghton Mifflin Harcourt
BOSTON   NEW YORK

First Mariner Books edition 2015

Copyright © 2014 by Brian Morton

www.hmhco.com

Library of Congress Cataloging-in-Publication Data
Morton, Brian, date.
Florence Gordon / Brian Morton.
pages cm
ISBN 978-0-544-30986-9 (hardback)   ISBN 978-0-544-57024-5 (pbk.)
1. Older women—Fiction. 2. Authorship—Fiction. 3. Psychological fiction.
I. Title.
PS3563.O88186F58 2014
813'.54—dc23
2014011676

Book design by Brian Moore

Printed in the United States of America
DOC 10 9 8 7 6 5 4 3 2 1

For Heather

Florence Gordon

1

Florence Gordon was trying to write a memoir, but she had two strikes against her: she was old and she was an intellectual. And who on earth, she sometimes wondered, would want to read a book about an old intellectual?

Maybe it was three strikes, because not only was she an intellectual, she was a feminist. Which meant that if she ever managed to finish this book, reviewers would inevitably dismiss it as "strident" and "shrill."

If you're an old feminist, anything you say, by definition, is strident and shrill.

She closed her laptop.

Not much point, she thought.

But then she opened it up again.

She didn't *feel* strident or shrill. She didn't even feel old.

And anyway, old age isn't what it used to be—or at least that's what she kept telling herself.

This was her reasoning. Florence was seventy-five years old. In an earlier era, that *would* have made her an old lady. But not today. She'd been a young woman during the 1960s, and if you were young in the sixties—"bliss was it in that dawn to be alive"—there's a sense in which you can never grow old. You were there when the Beatles came to America; you were there when sex was discovered; you were there when the idea of liberation was born; and even if you end up a cranky old lady who's proud of her activist past but who now just wants to be left alone to read, write, and think—even if you end up like that, there's something in your soul that stays green.

She wasn't—this seems important to say—a woman who tried to look younger than she was. She didn't dye her hair; she had no interest in Botox; she didn't whiten her teeth. Her craggy old-fashioned teeth, rude and honest and unretouched, were good enough for her.

She wasn't a woman who wanted to recapture her youth. In part this was because she found the life she was living now so interesting.

So she was a strong proud independent-minded woman who accepted being old but nevertheless felt essentially young.

She was also, in the opinion of many who knew her, even in the opinion of many who loved her, a complete pain in the neck.

She was writing a memoir that began with the early days of the women's movement—the modern women's movement, her own women's movement, the one that had been born in the 1970s. If she could finish it, it would be her seventh book.

Each book had posed its own difficulties. The difficulty with this one was that she was finding it impossible to bring the past to life. Her memory was efficient; she could recall the dates and the acts and the actors. But she was finding it hard to remember the texture of the past.

Tonight she had finally begun, she thought, to crack the code. She'd remembered a moment that she hadn't thought about in years. It was just a moment, not important in itself. But precisely because she hadn't thought about it in so long, she was able to remember it now with a sense of freshness, and she was hoping she might have finally found the door that would lead her back into the past.

She was free for the rest of the night. She'd had dinner plans with friends, but with a secret glee she'd canceled so she could stay home and work. It was seven o'clock on a Friday in early May; she was through with her academic obligations and her mind was clear.

And this evening, in which she'd finally, finally, finally begun to make some progress—this evening was the happiest one she'd had in a long time.

Except that Vanessa kept calling.

Her friend Vanessa kept calling, and Florence kept not picking up. After the fifth call, she thought Vanessa might be in some sort of trouble, and on the sixth, she finally answered.

"Thank God you're home," Vanessa said. "I've got a problem."

"What's wrong?"

"Nothing big. Nothing terrible. It's just that I got pickpocketed, evidently, and I don't have anything except my phone. I need some money to get back home."

"Where are you?"

"That's why I called you. I'm three blocks away."

She named a restaurant.

"Well I'm right here," Florence said. "Just come up."

"That's nice of you. But it's a little bit complicated."

"Why?"

"Ruby and Cassie had to run, and I stayed to pay the check, and that's when I found out my purse was gone. So the owner doesn't want me to leave. He wants to be sure I'm not going to skip out on him."

"Vanessa, you're a very respectable-looking woman. You're a very *old* woman. You're obviously not skipping out on him. Tell him you're not Bonnie Parker."

"That's just what I told him. That's exactly what I told him, in fact. I told him I'm not Bonnie Parker. But he's not being very understanding. I think he thinks I *am* Bonnie Parker. I'm really sorry. But it'll just take a minute."

People, Florence thought as she put on her shoes. What do I need them for again?

He's afraid she'll skip out on him. As Florence waited for the elevator, she was muttering to herself. She reminded herself of Popeye the Sailor Man.

She crossed the street, still muttering. Muttering, and clenching and unclenching her fists.

She was doing this with her fists because she'd been having some trouble with her left hand. Carpal tunnel syndrome. Her fingers sometimes jumped around as if they had five little minds of their own. A neurologist had told her to get an ergonomic keyboard and an ergonomic mouse and an ergonomic splint for her wrist; she'd gotten all of it, and she'd faithfully done the exercises he prescribed, but none of it was working so far.

Muttering, clenching, unclenching: I must look, she thought, like a madwoman.

4

The restaurant was on Sixty-seventh Street, between Columbus and Central Park West. She went inside, couldn't see Vanessa.

It was a fancy, expensive, somewhat full-of-itself restaurant. It didn't seem like the kind of place where the owner would hold you hostage.

The greeter, a somber-looking man, asked her if she needed help.

"I'm looking for a friend. Woman my age? Couldn't pay her bill?"

"Oh, yes. I know who you mean. She's in the back room."

They've got her in the back room, Florence thought. They're working her over.

He led Florence down a hall and gestured toward an entryway, behind which the room was unaccountably dark. She stepped in, and the lights went on, and the room was filled with people shouting "Surprise!"

Surprise.

Friends from NYU, friends from the movement, friends from

the writing world. Even her family was there: her daughter-in-law, her granddaughter.

Vanessa was embracing her.

"This was the only way we thought we'd be able to celebrate you."

"It's not my birthday."

"I thought if we did it too close to your birthday, we'd lose the element of surprise. You'd know what was coming and you'd never show up. It was a delicate operation. Like trapping the mythical yeti. We wanted to celebrate you. And we wanted to get you out of your apartment so you could have some fun."

It was astonishing how little people know each other, even old friends. I *was* having fun, Florence thought. I was having fun sitting in my apartment and trying to understand our life, our collective life. I was having fun trying to make the sentences come right. I was having fun trying to keep a little moment in time alive.

And now that was gone. She had been so close to seeing things clearly, but it had felt so precarious, so fragile. Who could know whether that little flicker of clarity would still be there in the morning.

Janine, her daughter-in-law, and Emily, her granddaughter, were at her side. They'd been in New York for months now, and she hadn't arranged to see them. She felt guilty for a moment, then realized that the guilt was merely a sort of tribute she was paying to convention—in fact, she simply hadn't wanted to see them—and she stopped feeling guilty.

"Happy birthday, more or less," Janine said.

"Not that you look that happy," Emily said.

"I wish someone had nipped this in the bud."

"I tried. I tried to nip it," Janine said. "I told them it was a bad idea. But . . . Vanessa. She's almost as much of a force of nature as you are."

Oh Christ. Even Saul was here.

He put his arm around her shoulder. He seemed to be half drunk.

"I couldn't not be here," he said. "And I mean that literally. Your friend wouldn't take no for an answer."

Someone Florence half remembered materialized at her side and told a long story about how hard it had been to get there from Rockland County. Someone else told Florence a story about how hard it was to tear herself away from her adorable but not yet housebroken puppy. As Florence smiled and nodded and pretended to listen, all she was trying to do was hold on to the moments of clarity she'd experienced at her desk, and all she wished for was to go back home.

In the women's room, she looked at the window. It was ten feet off the ground. Maybe if I stood on the toilet seat I could lift myself up to the top of the stall . . .

No. Too craven. Too undignified.

She returned to the room where the celebration was in progress, picked up a glass, and tapped a knife against it until she had everyone's attention.

"My friends," she said, "I'm touched that you decided to do this. I'm touched, and I'm honored. What was it Yeats said? Something like 'Think where our glory begins and ends, and say my glory was, I had such friends.'"

There was a murmur of appreciation.

"One of the things that I find beautiful about you all is that you understand me. I know I'm not easy to be with. I'm a difficult woman."

"You're a gloriously difficult woman," Vanessa said—she always gushed too much—and others made noises of agreement.

"Well, thank you. But whether I'm gloriously hard to get along with or just plain hard to get along with, each of you has found ways to get along with me. Which is a tribute to your generosity, tolerance, and ingenuity. Because I've asked you to put up with a lot.

"And now I'm going to ask you to put up with one more thing. I'm delighted by this surprise party, but I'm going to leave you now, because I need to get back to my desk. I hope you know that I truly do appreciate this, and that I'll be here in spirit. And I hope you have a wonderful evening."

She turned and left. It would have been nice to avoid meeting anyone's eyes, but it was more important to keep her head up, and therefore she saw the faces of several friends as she passed them. They looked as if they weren't sure whether she was serious.

She'd left her computer on, and as soon as she got home she sat back down in front of it. It took a while for the fog to burn away—the fog of embarrassment or ambivalence or whatever she was feeling—but after a time she found that she was not so far from where she'd left off. She worked for the rest of the night with satisfaction, and didn't give her friends and well-wishers another thought.

After she left, no one knew what to say. Nobody even seemed to want to look at anyone else.

"Now you understand why I divorced her," Saul said.

People laughed, and went back to eating and drinking.

"What the hell," Vanessa said. "Let's have a party. Let's celebrate Florence in absentia."

"I think I'll 'celebrate' her some other time," Saul said. "I'm out of here."

"Did *he* divorce *her*?" Emily said to her mother.

"Other way round," Janine said.

"That's what I thought. I can't even imagine them married."

"Why?"

"She's so independent. And he seems like he needs somebody needy."

Janine was constantly surprised by the things her daughter came out with. But parents always are.

For a parent, time is not a one-way street. In Janine's mind, the nineteen-year-old Emily was accompanied, shadowed, by the infant Emily, and the toddler Emily, and Emily in all her other incarnations. So when she came out with a shrewd perception or a sophisticated thought, it was always something to marvel at, because it was as if the five-year-old Emily were saying it too. A parent is perpetually thinking, "Where did she learn that?"

"We've got the evening free, at least," Janine said. "Wanna go to the movies?"

"But can we not see anything self-improving tonight? Can we go to something fun?"

"Only if you promise . . ."

But Janine couldn't think of anything to make her daughter promise. There was nothing she wanted Emily to change. This hadn't always been true, and wouldn't always remain true, but it was true right now.

The next time Janine and Emily saw Florence, it was in an even less intimate setting.

The two of them were in the audience at Town Hall, waiting for the panel discussion to begin.

"Is it unhealthy to have an intellectual crush on your mother-in-law?" Janine said.

"Not if it's only an intellectual crush," her daughter answered.

Janine's relationship with Florence was an unusual one for a woman to have with her mother-in-law. It was an unusually strong relationship, though it existed mostly in Janine's mind.

Janine had heard of Florence before she'd ever met Daniel, and when Daniel told her who his mother was, she couldn't believe it.

Not that Florence was in any sense famous. She was a feminist writer—an essayist and, as she called herself, a seat-of-her-pants historian. She'd had a little flare of literary glory in the seventies, which had vanished, as flares of literary glory tend to do, and since then she'd continued, calmly and patiently and entirely out of the limelight, to do her work.

But though she wasn't famous to the world, she was famous to

Janine. Janine had read a book of essays by Florence in college. She read them for a class in modern American feminism, and Florence's voice on the page was unlike anything that Janine had encountered before. By turns eloquent and chatty, confident and self-questioning, it was the voice of a real person. It was a style Janine later encountered in other writers—Vivian Gornick, Ellen Willis, Katha Pollitt—and though all of them were better known than Florence was, Florence had been the first member of this tribe whom Janine encountered, and, maybe for that reason alone, Florence had always meant the most to her.

Janine had never wanted to be a writer—after a few years spent "finding herself" after college, she went to grad school in psychology—so Florence wasn't a role model for her in any direct sense. But Florence remained an inspiration. She continued to represent Janine's idea of a free woman.

The collection of essays that Janine read in college was called *Opportunities for Heroism in Everyday Life*, and the idea that there *were* such opportunities—the idea, in the words of a psychologist whom Florence quoted, that one is constantly confronted by situations in which one must make either a growth choice or a fear choice—conferred a new significance, first, on Janine's life, and then, the longer she thought about it, on the lives of everyone she knew or came in contact with.

Janine and Daniel were on their third or fourth date before she found out who his mother was. She couldn't believe it. She tried to tamp down her excitement—she limited herself to saying something like, "Your mother's Florence Gordon? I've heard of her," and when Daniel seemed surprised, she said, "Yeah. I've read some of her stuff. I liked it." The funny thing about all this was that because she was determined to play it cool when she first found out (it seemed weird and somehow risky to let a new boyfriend know that she had an intellectual crush on his mother), Daniel never understood, and probably still didn't understand, how important his mother was to her. She'd told him about it since, but she had the feeling that he'd never really revised his first impression.

"Here she comes," Emily said, as the lights went down.

The event was a panel discussion commemorating the revolutions of 1989, on their twentieth anniversary.

What revolutions of 1989? Emily thought.

Florence was seated at a table with two men, both much younger than she was. One of them had a gleaming shaved head; the other had luxuriant brown locks that obviously received a lot of tending. Both of them radiated testosteronely confidence. Emily felt almost afraid for her grandmother, a bony, brittle woman in her seventies, flanked by these cocksure boys.

Emily was there to keep her mother company. She had no interest in listening to people theorize about revolution and social change. She had once heard a psychologist give a long, ponderous talk about why jokes are funny; theorizing about revolution had the same appeal.

She didn't mind being here, though. She had her copy of *Middlemarch*; she had her keychain flashlight. She had everything she needed.

The gleamingly bald man pulled the mike closer and began to speak.

Lately Emily had been thinking about writing a novel. She knew she was a little young for it, but a lot of her friends had participated in National Novel Writing Month, and she was thinking that when it came around again this year, she might participate too.

If I were writing a novel, Emily thought, I wouldn't want to write a description of a panel discussion. I'd just skip over it.

After the panel discussion, Emily and her mother joined Florence and two of Florence's old friends at a restaurant.

"How'd I do?" Florence said.

"'How'd I do?'" one of her friends said. "You sound like Ed Koch."

"Do I really?" Florence said. "Jesus."

Emily smiled (to look as if she knew who Ed Koch was) and looked down (to avoid being called on).

Emily had no idea who Ed Koch was. Normally she would have asked, but there was something about her grandmother that made her reluctant. Emily couldn't remember Florence scolding anyone for not knowing something, yet she felt certain that Florence was the kind of person who would.

Florence's old friends were Vanessa, whom Emily had met, and Alexandra, whom she hadn't. Florence introduced them as "two fifths of my study group." They'd been in a study group together for thirty years.

As she ate her salad and listened to the conversation, Emily was feeling very meta. On the one hand, she was just listening to a few older women talk. On the other hand, she was witnessing the miracle of Women's Friendship.

One of the few things she'd ever read by Florence was an article about women's friendships. Florence wrote it in the 1970s, in the early years of her career. Florence had pretty much made the case that the term "women's friendship" was redundant, because only women really knew what friendship *was*. Men, from what Emily remembered, were described as being roughly on the level of apes or moose: they could stand around and grunt together, or they could compare antler size, but they could never experience, to the degree that women could, the pleasures of sympathy and compassion and conversation.

Emily had no idea whether Florence still stood by them, but she couldn't help but listen to the conversation in the light of the arguments Florence had made back then.

The grown-ups were on their second pitcher of sangria. Emily, below the drinking age, had ordered a Shirley Temple—partly as a joke, partly because she liked Shirley Temples.

"Would you put that down?" Florence said.

Alexandra was looking at her BlackBerry, thumbing the keys rather haplessly.

"Billy's coming in tonight, if he . . . He's bringing Alison."

Something about Alexandra's voice made Emily sure that she was talking about a son and a granddaughter. How do we know these things? Somehow, we know.

"They should ban texting in restaurants," Florence said. She tapped Alexandra on the knuckles. "Put it away."

"Some restaurants do," Vanessa said—and they were off. Florence and her friends and Emily's mother started talking about the Internet, and the conversation grew ever more predictable. Why was it that at every grown-up function, the exact same conversation had to take place? Sometimes Emily felt as if she could hand out scripts, to save everybody the trouble of thinking, except that there would be no point, because they weren't thinking—they were just saying the same things they'd said the last time. The adults would talk about how silly Twitter was, and then one of them would speak up for it, saying that Twitter had helped people organize protest movements around the world, and then they would talk about Facebook, and some of them would talk about how useless it was, and then most of them would guiltily admit that they were on it. At about this point Emily would usually go to the bathroom, because she knew what was coming, namely that someone was going to turn to her and ask her, as if she were a representative of the Young, if she had any attention span for reading, or if she was on Twitter, or if she was on Facebook (they would actually ask her that), or if she used Gmail—it was enough to make you scream.

Emily was a generous person, but it was hard to put up with the fatuousness of older people sometimes.

"So how'd I do?" Florence said, after they had exhausted the Facebook/Twitter conversation. "No one is answering my question."

"You did brilliantly, Florence," Alexandra said.

"You did," Vanessa said. "And did you see how many nose rings there were in that room? You're a hero to the young."

Florence looked like a cat in the sun. It was strange, Emily thought, to see someone who was so old and so supposedly wise fishing for compliments like this. But the fact that she was doing it so openly and cheerfully made it endearing in its way.

"You surprised me, though. For a minute there you sounded like a cockeyed optimist," Vanessa said.

"The doom-and-gloom stuff annoys me," Florence said. "Have you read *The Country and the City*?"

For some reason she was looking at Emily, who had never heard of it.

"Raymond Williams," Florence said, as if that meant anything. "Williams quotes a contemporary of his—I think it's Leavis—saying that life was better thirty years ago, when England was a real community. Then he quotes someone from thirty years earlier, saying that the sense of community in England had died out thirty years before *that*. He keeps going back, all the way to the Roman Empire, with Pliny or somebody, who's pining for the way things used to be when *he* was young."

"That's not really relevant," Vanessa said, and she said something about Raymond Williams, and Florence countered with something about Joan Scott, and Emily was lost.

"Would you stop that?" Florence said.

Alexandra was peering at her BlackBerry again.

"Just a minute. I need to . . ."

That seemed to be the end of the sentence. Whatever she was looking at had sucked her in.

"My God," Florence said. "What are we coming to?"

Florence leaned across the table and slapped her friend's hand—slapped the BlackBerry out of her hand. She picked it up and dropped it in the pitcher of sangria.

Emily was the quickest person there: she plucked it out of the pitcher, turned it over on her napkin to dry it off, and passed it back to Alexandra.

"You're going to have to expect that sort of thing," Florence said. "Until they extend the anti-texting laws, concerned citizens are going to be taking matters into their own hands."

The conversation went on. Somehow Alexandra forgave her, with not much more than an exasperated shake of her head.

If it were me, Emily thought, I would have just left, but I guess they've been friends so long that they can forgive each other for everything.

Emily wanted to find her grandmother lovable. But it wasn't easy. Florence seemed proud of herself for vandalizing her friend's phone, and her friend seemed to accept it. Evidently you tolerated her quirks for the privilege of knowing her. But Emily kept thinking of how excited Alexandra was about her son and granddaughter's visit. Maybe she was using the thing to check the arrivals at the airport.

On the street, Florence declined Janine's offer to share their cab uptown.

"You look great, both of you," Florence said. "Emma, I can't believe how tall you've gotten."

In the cab, Emily said, "Emma."

"She was in the ballpark," Janine said.

Getting rid of her daughter-in-law and her granddaughter was a production. Janine kept trying to get her to share their cab, insisting that it wasn't safe to walk home at that time of night—as if Janine knew anything about New York—but finally Florence was able to peel her off and insert them in the cab and close the door.

Emily, as usual, had been inquisitive, ironic, and distant. Florence wasn't sure she'd ever seen anybody hold her cards as close to the vest as her granddaughter, whom she uneasily thought she might have called Emma when they said goodbye.

It was a joy to be alone. It was fun to play the social role, it was fun to play the old lion at Town Hall, but it was far, far better to be alone again. She walked uptown, twenty-five glorious blocks in the rain-washed streets, feeling like a representative of all the glamour of the city.

The strain of being with other people was sometimes close to unendurable. The strain of other people's need. She could feel it radiating off her daughter-in-law, and she didn't understand why. What do I have to do with *her*? Doesn't she have Daniel; doesn't she have her own parents; doesn't she have her kids? What does she need me for?

No matter how hard-boiled you think you are, thought Daniel Gordon, you're never quite prepared for New York.

Out of cop's habit, as he walked toward Grand Central, he assessed everyone for troublemaker potential—after more than twenty years, it wasn't even conscious anymore—and instantly he was on overload. Everyone in New York seemed like a miscreant. Even the little old ladies—most of them looked as if they were running some scam.

The bus from Kennedy takes you as far as midtown; Emily had insisted on meeting him when he got in, so they'd arranged to find each other in Grand Central. When he got there, she was already waiting, standing near the information booth in the middle of the great vaulted space. He saw her from fifty feet away, and he had the same feeling he always had when he saw her, that mix of heartlift and worry. The world is never safe enough, if you have a child.

At nineteen, she was a dark, skinny beauty—at least she was beautiful to him.

He put his two bags down and they embraced.

"Did you miss me?" she said.

"Not that much."

His answer made her smile, because she knew it was his way of saying yes.

"It's weird to see you in New York," she said.

"Thanks. You too. Where's Mom?"

"She's got a cold. Didn't she tell you?"

"I haven't talked to her since Tuesday."

Emily started telling him about Janine's cold. He couldn't really pay attention, because he was too happy to see her.

As they were nearing the exit, a man sprinted past them and out the door. Ten seconds later, four cops bolted by. Emily kept talking.

"You've become a New Yorker," he said, but since she hadn't even noticed the incident, she didn't know what he was talking about.

"You wanna take a cab?" he said.

"Let's walk awhile. I can pull one."

She reached for one of his bags but he wouldn't let her take it.

They went out into the bright day. At a corner she took his arm and turned him gently north.

Even walking was different in New York. The afternoon streets were crowded, and people kept stepping impatiently around him. A woman his mother's age stepped around him and gave him an irritated look as she passed.

He'd have time to get used to it all again. Taking off just one week a year, he'd been accruing vacation days for more than two decades, and he had enough to take him from Memorial Day to the end of September.

"How's your class?"

She was taking a literature class through Barnard's summer general-studies program.

"It starts next week. It's gonna be great. Jane Austen. George Eliot. Virginia Woolf. What could be bad about that?"

"And what have you been eating?"

"Excuse me?"

"What have you been eating?"

"The interrogation begins."

"I'm just asking what you've been eating. Is that such a difficult—"

"*Why* are you asking what I'm eating?"

"I just want to know whether you've been eating real food or whether you've been eating that birdseed you eat at home. I don't see why that's such a difficult—"

"All right! I admit it! I've been eating birdseed."

"Seriously. Are you still being a vegan?"

"Vegan. Yes. I'm still being a vegan."

"Why? Vegetarianism I can understand, but why do you have to take it to such an extreme?"

"You want to know the reason?"

"Yes. I do."

"The real reason?"

"Yes."

"I do it because I like to annoy you."

He shook his head, supposedly in exasperation, but he was having a good time.

He had asked her to explain her veganism about a thousand times, and he didn't really care about it—she was obviously in good health—but he liked to keep asking, because she expected him to.

She had the same light, easy walk in the middle of Manhattan that she had in Seattle. That was good, because it meant that wherever she was, she was at home. That was bad, because in New York you should be on your guard.

He worried about her safety; he worried about her happiness; he worried about her resilience. He hadn't been pleased when she decided to take time off from college; you might even say he'd been panicky. Janine had had to talk him down.

But somehow all the worries felt like matters of the surface alone. In the deepest places, he was confident—about who she was and who she'd become.

You expect to love your children; it brings a different kind of joy to realize you admire them. Emily was a young woman of great decency. He remembered an afternoon when she was six or seven; she had a friend over and they were playing in the living room. The two of them were throwing a ball or something, and her friend said,

"I'm much more bad at this than you are," and Emily had said simply, "You're learning." That was Emily.

"Have you been in touch with the eternal wanderer?" he said. Her brother, Mark.

"Of course."

"How's he doing?"

"I don't know. He seems groovy, as you would say."

"What's he up to?"

"How should I know?"

"You know. You never miss anything. Is he reading? Is he inventing things on the Internet? Is he dating? What's he up to?"

"I don't really know. He hasn't changed his status. That's all I know."

"That's all you'll say. How's Mom?"

"She hasn't changed her status either," Emily said.

"What's she been up to?"

"Reading. Inventing things on the Internet. Dating."

"I want facts, damn it. Facts."

"I don't have any facts. I never see her. By the time I get home at night she's sleeping. By the time I get up in the morning she's out for her run."

Janine was a devoted runner and swimmer. She pursued these pastimes not in a grim effort to battle the aging process, but in a spirit of ebullience, because she had so much energy to burn off.

At home he liked to swing by the Y and pick her up from swimming. He liked to see her emerging from the water.

"Have you seen my mom?" he said.

"We've seen her maybe one and a half times."

"How'd she seem?"

"Splendid. We went out to dinner with her the other day. She destroyed somebody's BlackBerry. She called me Emma."

"She didn't."

"She didn't which?"

"She didn't call you Emma."

"Of course she did. Last year she called me Amelia."

"She's not that good with names. But she loves you."

"She loves me in a very special way," Emily said.

"And my dad?"

"Even less. Half a time."

Men, men of all ages, were checking out his daughter as they passed. Daniel wanted to punch them.

The sublet was on the Upper West Side. It came with the fellowship that had brought Janine to New York. By coincidence, it was just a few blocks from the building where Daniel had grown up.

The neighborhood had changed, and hadn't changed. It was weirding him out to be up here, but he didn't say anything to Emily. He was not in the habit of admitting to being weirded out by anything.

The lobby had an indefinable but unmistakable smell: boiled potatoes, cleaning liquids, old, tired marble, and the sadness of elderly Jews. It was a smell he knew from all the Upper West Side apartment buildings of his youth.

The elevator was an ancient affair; as it slowly rose, he had the most peculiar sensation of being drawn back in time. It was as if he'd been his forty-seven-year-old self when he'd stepped in off the street, and now, by the fifth floor, he was a boy.

He shook that off quickly. He was wearing a sport jacket. His teenage daughter was at his side. He was a grown man.

"I wonder what you'll think of this place," she said.

She opened the front door to an apartment with shabby furniture, faded walls, wooden floors that hadn't been polished for decades, and, compensating for all this, a view of the late-spring greenness of Riverside Park.

He put his bags down, and felt peaceful. He was where he belonged, not because he was back in the city of his youth, but because his wife and one of his two children were here.

"Where's the woman?"

Emily tilted her head and he went that way.

Janine was on the couch in the living room. She was in her bathrobe, with a pile of wadded-up tissues beside her.

"You look like hell, darlin'," Daniel said.

He said it quietly, and Emily, watching them, felt embarrassed. Though her father hardly ever put any of it into words, the intensity of his feelings was sometimes close to unbearable. The way he was looking at her mother now made Emily retreat from the room.

The next few hours were a strain. Janine felt strained, at any rate. She couldn't be sure how anyone else felt.

She and Daniel had been married for twenty-three years. She considered their marriage to be happy; she considered their marriage to be successful—not in superficial ways but in real ways. But they'd been apart for months, and whenever they spent even a few days apart, the experience of coming together reminded her of the simple fact that he wasn't her type.

He was so *male*, she thought, as he stalked around the kitchen, breathing on things. She and Emily had spent two months in a rapport so intuitive that they weren't even aware of it. But now Daniel was here, smearing his maleness over everything.

She was at the kitchen table drinking tea and he was going through the cupboards. He was looking for something to eat, ostensibly, but as she watched him, she began to be possessed by the idea that even if he was hungry, the desire to eat was secondary right now, and that his primary desire, even if it was an unconscious one, was to mess up her arrangements. He looked in the refrigerator and moved things around; he looked in the cupboard and moved things around. Supposedly just looking, he put the sugar where she kept the tea and the tea where she kept the raisins and did God knows what with the raisins.

He wasn't really messing things up, just moving things around. It was as if, in setting up the place, she'd played a white pawn, and now he was playing a black pawn, and the game was on again, the great game of marriage.

"Let's take a walk," she said.

They walked up Broadway. She started to feel better now that they were out and about.

"How's everything been?" Daniel said. "How's the girl?"

"She's doing well. She looks good, don't you think?"

"She looks great. What's she been up to?"

"She's excited to be starting that class. Women writers, from—"

"Has she talked about going back to school for real?"

"Only when I bring it up. But yes. She wants to. She's been look-ing at catalogs on the computer."

"She doesn't want to go back to Oberlin?"

"Probably not. She says sometimes she thinks she wants some-place bigger, sometimes she wants someplace artsier. She says she likes being a student, but she prefers to approach it at a slant."

"What the hell does that mean?"

"I have no idea."

Unhappy during the first semester of her sophomore year, Em-ily had decided to take the second semester off and work at the bookstore where she'd worked for the last three summers. When it abruptly went out of business in March, she'd accepted Janine's invitation to spend a few months with her in New York.

"Have you heard from the boy? He never answers my phone calls."

Their son had graduated from Reed a year ago and was now in Portland, living hand to mouth.

"The boy is doing just fine," she said. "The boy is reading and writing. Or so he claims."

"Or so he claims. What is it he's supposedly writing?"

"I don't know. Beat poetry. The Great American Novel."

"It's funny," he said. "Without having read a word, you know exactly what it's like. If he's writing it."

She nodded but didn't smile, because she didn't want to be disloyal to their son. She knew exactly what Daniel meant, though. If their son was writing a novel, it would be adolescently Kerouacian, a series of stream-of-consciousness whooshings about drugs and sex and travel, and it would be close to unreadable.

"But maybe he *will* write the Great American Novel someday," she said. "Maybe whatever he's writing now—"

"If he's writing now."

"Is just something he needs to get out of his system."

"Of course. I shouldn't be so hard on him. Of course he's writing juvenilia now. He's a juvenile."

"You're probably one of the few police officers who use the word 'juvenilia.'"

"Actually, that's a misconception. Many of us do. There's a whole movement."

"A movement to use the word 'juvenilia.'"

"A movement to increase our vocabularies."

"I read about that somewhere. You use—what was it—*Word Power*?"

He smiled when she said this, because it was only people of a certain age who remembered the elementary-school vocabulary book *Word Power.*

"*Word Power.* That's right. We get together once a week, on Fridays, after lunch, and learn new words. One new word a week."

"I was going to ask if it was just a word a week. Because that *is* the *Word Power* philosophy."

"It is the philosophy, and that's how we do it. There were some who thought we should move more quickly, but the traditionalists held sway."

"You're probably one of the few police officers who use expressions like 'held sway.'"

"Actually, that's a misconception," he said, and she laughed.

This was always the way they came back together; this was always the way they healed the rift after being apart. They played. Ever since she had met him, they'd been able to play together, in a way that she simply didn't do with anyone else.

It all came back to her now: who he was, what they had.

15

But this was a little different from past occasions in which they'd come together after spending time apart. This was different because rather than having to wrench herself back from the pleasures of traveling alone or the pleasures of parenting the children alone (parents will rarely admit this, but most of them find it easier to take care of their children by themselves, without meddling from the spouse), today she had to come back from the pleasures of having met another man. She had hoped that when she saw Daniel, her infatuation with Lev would disappear, and at first she thought it had, but as the day wore on, she admitted to herself that it hadn't.

16

"Would you put that thing away?" Daniel said.

"I don't know if I can," Emily said.

"Can't you turn it off for just one hour?"

"But I never know when I might get a text message from Grandma."

They were at an Italian restaurant, where they were meeting Florence and Saul for dinner.

"Are we sure this is a good idea?" Janine said. "The two of them together?"

"I'll get back to you on that," Daniel said.

When Daniel went outside to return a phone call, Emily said, "Dad seems nervous."

"He does?"

"You haven't noticed?"

"No. I haven't. What have you noticed?"

"I've noticed he seems nervous."

"What's he been doing that makes you think he's nervous? Has he been biting his nails; has he been—"

"No. Nothing like that. But I can tell. And you can too."

"It's understandable that he's nervous," Janine said.

"Why?"

"He's got a lot on his mind."

"Like what?"

"Whether to quit his job, for one thing."

"He had that on his mind six months ago."

"But now it's six months later. So it's a different kind of question. And, you know, his parents."

"What about his parents? They're nice old people."

Janine wondered if her daughter was being cagey. There were a lot of valid ways to describe Florence and Saul, but "nice old people" wasn't one of them.

"His parents are a trip," Janine said. "His parents are two different trips. You know that."

"They're not that much of a 'trip' to me."

"Lucky you."

"Anyway," Emily said, smiling, "whose parents aren't a trip?"

They were sitting near the big plate-glass window, and they could see for blocks.

"Here she comes," Emily said.

Florence was crossing the street, a trim and businesslike and wholly intimidating seventy-five-year-old woman. She was leaning to the side because she had a heavy laptop bag hanging from a strap over her shoulder.

She was, as usual, lost in her thoughts. She walked past Daniel without seeing him.

Janine watched him: he was still on the phone, but he lifted his hand to wave to his mother, and smiled wryly after she passed him.

"It's good to see you again," Florence said, as Janine got up to embrace her.

If she hadn't been a polite person, Janine would have laughed at this. She and Florence had talked on the phone just after Janine got to New York, and they'd exchanged pledges about getting together soon, and then neither of them had been in touch with the other until Janine saw a notice for the Town Hall panel discussion and wrote to Florence to say that she and Emily would be there.

Janine had often thought about calling her, but she stopped herself each time, remembering at the last minute that being with Florence was never what you hoped it would be. Florence never let you relax. She was always asking Janine if she'd read this or heard of that, and the answer was usually no. After it was over, Janine would feel as if she'd endured a sort of intellectual pummeling. Florence was vaguely insulting even when she didn't mean to be. She always made Janine feel as if she hadn't lived up to the promise of feminism. Janine couldn't quite understand how she was being made to feel that way, since she was about as feminist as you could get without being an actual activist. She had her own career, which had kept her fascinated for almost twenty years; she'd earned a living at the same time as she'd raised two kids. She didn't know what the problem was, but evidently there was a problem.

During her first few years of being married to Daniel, Janine used to try to engage Florence in conversation. She had so many questions she wanted to ask. Are you working on a book? What did you mean by that line in your last book of essays where you seemed to be insulting Susan Sontag? Did anybody ever give you a hard time about the fact that in that essay about the people who've influenced you the most, more than half of them were men? But she had found that questions like these invariably met with impatient responses. A few times Janine had asked Florence about key passages in her work—passages that Janine considered key—and Florence didn't remember them or didn't think they were important. Janine started to feel like a pathetic fangirl, like one of those people who show up at sci-fi conventions wearing Vulcan ears, so finally she stopped asking Florence anything about her work at all.

She never fared any better with other subjects. Once or twice, during the early years of their marriage, Janine had been by herself in New York and had given Florence a call, and when they went out to dinner she tried to use Daniel as a conversational icebreaker. But whenever she told Florence something about what Daniel was up to, Florence seemed remarkably uninterested.

When Daniel got back to the table, Florence started in on him.

"So how are you, my son? Have you locked up any perps lately?"

"That's not really what I do, Mom."

"Really? Aren't you still with the police force?"

"Yes, Mom, I'm with the police force. But I don't lock up perps."

"Do you lock up mopes?"

"Mopes?"

"Mopes. That's what you call the perps if you're a po-lice."

"Someone's been watching *The Wire*," Emily said.

"Vanessa gave me the DVDs for my birthday," Florence said.

"It sounds like you know more about police work than I do," Daniel said.

Florence seemed to feel a perpetual urge to needle her son. Janine didn't understand it, but she had a theory. Her theory was that Florence — both of Daniel's parents, really — still couldn't comprehend how he, the child of two certified New York intellectuals, had become a cop. Her theory was that after all these years, they still couldn't really accept it.

"So you're here for how long?" Florence said.

"Long as I want. I've got twenty-two years of vacation days to use up."

"They let vacation days roll over? You've got a good union."

"Yep."

"And you've seriously never taken a vacation in twenty years? That can't be right."

"He took a week a year," Janine said. "You could set your watch by it."

"You never wanted to take some real time off and go somewhere?"

"I did," Daniel said. "I did want to. I kept meaning to stop by at a travel agent's."

"And then there were no travel agents anymore," Emily said.

"Well, all right. So you've finally gotten out of your rut. How do you like being back in New York?" Florence said.

Daniel slowly finished his drink and put the glass down.

"I couldn't be more thrilled."

There was an awkward pause, and then Emily said, "He's acting like he's joking, but he's not. We're all very excited. We're happy to be in New York, and we're super happy to see you."

She spoke with an obvious sincerity that Janine found touching. Like every other member of her generation, Emily had been infected with the virus of irony, yet she remained capable of emotional directness. She didn't feel the need to look cool at all times.

"We are," Janine said.

Florence smiled approvingly, probably more because of their affection for New York than because of their affection for her. She was like the ambassador of Manhattan. She seemed to believe that a life that took place elsewhere couldn't truly be called life. She probably held that it was all well and good for Parisians to live in Paris and Londoners to live in London, but she could not comprehend how any thinking person from the United States could choose to live anywhere other than New York.

Florence looked at Janine steadily. She looked like someone examining a bill to see if it was counterfeit.

"I don't think this one is going back home," Florence said. "Watch out, boy."

Janine felt guilty, as if Florence had seen through her.

At that moment, the worst possible moment, Janine's cell phone went off. It was in her purse, which was on the floor next to her; it was buzzing and throbbing and writhing. Really it was just on vibrate, but it seemed to be unusually buoyant just then.

"You won't want to go back either," Florence said to Emily. "I can see it. Where are you going to college again?"

"That remains to be seen."

"No it doesn't. Obviously you'll be transferring to Barnard or NYU."

"Why do you think?"

"For the same reason your mother wants to stay. Both of you hunger for the life of the mind."

"I hunger for the life of the mind," Daniel said mildly, as his second drink arrived.

"You," Florence said.

Janine's cell phone had gone back to sleep, but now it shook one more time, trembling with joy about having taken a message. She was hoping that she wasn't blushing.

"Isn't your father supposed to be here?" Florence said.

"I spoke to him yesterday," Daniel said. "He said he'd be here. With bells on. Whatever the hell that means."

"He probably can't tear himself away from his work. You know Saul. His pen has not yet gleaned his teeming brain."

This was a not-nice thing to say, as Saul had evidently gleaned his teeming brain a long time ago. He still called himself a writer, but he hadn't published anything of significance in twenty years. Though he always claimed to be working, though he always claimed to be in contact with "two or three publishers" who were interested in his work, nothing was ever finished, nothing ever appeared.

"Let's just order," Florence said. "The smart money never waits for Saul to show up."

After the waiter went away, Emily said, "So you're working on a memoir?"

"How did you know that?"

"Your surprise party. I heard you say something about it to someone before you disappeared."

"The famous surprise party," Daniel said. "Good going, Mom."

"Thank you," Florence said.

Janine thought she saw a hint of embarrassment in Florence's face, but she was probably wrong. I'm probably only thinking that because I'd feel embarrassed if I'd done that.

"'Thank you all for coming,'" Daniel said. "'Now leave me the hell alone.'"

"Isn't that what people usually say at their birthday parties?" Florence said.

"Those could be your last words," Emily said. "'Leave me the hell alone.'"

"What'll be your last words?" Florence said.

"Emily's?" Janine said. "'Give me another minute to finish this page.'"

"So about this memoir," Emily said. "Are you going to write about my dad?"

"Maybe in a footnote," Daniel said.

"Maybe in a footnote," Florence said.

"She's got a much bigger story to tell," Daniel said. "She can't be troubled to write about distractions like her son."

"And you just got a medal, right?" Emily said.

"Right."

Florence had received a medal from the American Academy of Arts and Letters that spring.

"That must've been exciting."

"It was," Florence said. "It's not that you sit around hoping for that kind of recognition. But it's nice when it comes."

Janine, though she was aware that she analyzed her mother-in-law's every utterance too eagerly, found something refreshing in this—in what she said and the way she said it. If any other woman Janine knew had been honored in this way, and were asked what she thought about it, she would profess herself unworthy, downplay her own achievements, downplay the honor itself—she would find some way of denigrating herself. She admired the way that Florence simply allowed herself to enjoy it.

"You're my mother's hero," Emily said, with that frightening way she sometimes had of reading Janine's thoughts.

"I hope not."

"You are. She thinks you're the very model of a feminist intellectual. She thinks every woman should be more like you."

"That's enough," Janine said.

But after she finished her glass of wine, she couldn't help herself. She'd been excited to learn that Florence was working on a memoir, and, now that her tongue had been loosened, she couldn't stop herself from asking about it. Would she write about the Town Hall debate between Norman Mailer and Germaine Greer? Would she write about the year she spent in England in the 1970s? Was it true that she got into a quarrel with Juliet Mitchell? No? Because—

Florence, who'd been answering in monosyllables, cut her off.

"What about you?" she said. "How's *your* work? I mean, do you feel like you're a member of a dying species?"

"Why?"

"Psychology. Isn't psychology as we've known it pretty much over? Everything comes down to brain chemicals. Doesn't it?"

"Does it?"

"That's what I keep reading. The talking cure is finished. You can spend thousands of hours on a couch talking about all the terrible things your mommy and daddy did to you, and it won't help you half as much as taking a pill."

Florence, obviously, didn't have the slightest idea of what Janine's work was all about. The curiosity that had brought Janine to pursue a fellowship in New York was precisely about the complicated relationship between our intentions and our impulses, between the parts of ourselves that seem to be under our control and the parts of ourselves that don't. Janine *was* a believer in the talking cure—in the end she believed that there was probably no substitute for the classical analytic relationship, in which one person talks and another patiently listens—but the entire reason she was in New York was to explore the question of how newer and more scientifically based ways of looking at problems of will and motivation and self-control might supplement the classical approach.

But Florence wasn't interested enough to find out about any of this. And if that was the case, Janine didn't care to enlighten her.

"You might be right," Janine said. "It may be that I'm a member of a dying species."

"Oh, come on. Aren't you willing to fight with me? A little?" Florence said.

"I'll fight with you," Emily said.

"Oh, good."

"She might be a member of a dying species, but isn't the pot calling the kettle black? You're a *writer*. You write *books*."

"And?"

"Who reads books anymore?"

"Plenty of people. Did I tell you that they're putting out a Kindle edition of my last one? People will be reading me on Kindle."

"Are you going to find out where they live and dunk their Kindles into puddles and stuff?"

"Not if they're reading my books."

"What are you talking about, nobody reads books?" Daniel said to Emily. "You're reading—what are you reading?"

"*Middlemarch*," Emily said.

"Well?" Daniel said.

"I'm an unusual girl."

Janine ordered another glass of wine and stole a look at her watch. Seeing Florence was always unpleasant. The remarkable thing was that it was always unpleasant in a new way. Maybe this was a tribute to Florence's character. She always found a way to surprise you.

17

For hours that night, as she sat at her computer, writing in a state of carpal-tunnel-y churlishness, Florence kept thinking about Daniel and his family. Wondering why she didn't feel more goodwill toward him. It was as if they weren't related. There he sat, whenever she saw him, solid and stolid and impenetrable, getting drunk but never showing it, safely moated away from any questions about what the hell he had made of his life.

And his wife was worse: the eternal ingenue, panting with worshipfulness. Florence, do you write on a computer or a typewriter? Florence, do you write in the mornings or the afternoons? Florence, what did you mean by that colon on page thirty-two of that book you wrote thirty years ago? Why a colon instead of a dash? Really? 'Cause this is what I think it means . . . Florence, did you know Gloria Steinem? Florence, did you know Norman Mailer? Did you ever have an affair with him? I thought all the feminists of your generation had secret affairs with him. Florence, did you meet Emma Goldman? Ulysses S. Grant? Socrates? Jesus? Really, Florence, you never met Jesus? I could've sworn he refers to you in the Sermon on the Mount. Not by name, of course, but I thought the reference was pretty obvious. It's here, on page thirty-two of the New Testament. I mean, why would there be that colon if he wasn't thinking of you? Have I told you what I think that colon means on page thirty-two of your book?

The only way to deal with someone like that is to avoid her, and if you can't avoid her, the only way to deal with her is to attack her. Florence felt slightly bad about going on about brain chemistry—she hadn't believed a word she was saying—but she needed to do *something* to wipe that oppressive look of adoration off the woman's face. The look of bafflement and hurt that replaced it was preferable. Florence always loved to talk to intelligent younger people; she was glad that a lot of younger women had liked her books; but she'd never wanted followers, groupies, acolytes, worshippers, "mentees." Why did my son have to marry such a suck-up?

The granddaughter wasn't so bad. She had a little bit of spirit, at least.

18

Florence was having breakfast with her longtime editor.

"I'm sorry I had to miss your birthday party," he said.

"You didn't miss much."

"It sounds like I missed a lot. I heard about your performance. You're a new species of human being, Florence. The outrageous old fogey."

"What's new about that? There's nothing new. I've become one of those horrible women who goes around saying things like, 'Now that I am old, I shall wear more purple.'"

There was a polished silver pot of coffee on the table. Edward poured some into her cup. He was a gentleman of the old school—she didn't know if she'd ever seen him without a tie and jacket—and, with his courtly formality, he'd always struck her as somehow timeless. He'd always been a reassuring presence in her life.

"Do you have exciting news for me?" she said.

She was half joking. She had published a book two months earlier, called *How to Look at a Woman*. A collection of essays about intellectuals and activists from Mary Wollstonecraft to Elizabeth

Cady Stanton to Rosa Parks, it was her sixth book, and the fifth that she had done with Edward.

Her question was a joke because when a book has been out for almost two months, nothing exciting can happen. One of the sad little secrets of the writing life is that it's become like the movie business, where a movie has to "open big"; if a book hasn't caught anybody's interest in the first two weeks of its life, it's not going to. It was hard to bring herself to walk into a bookstore, because she knew that her book was already about to disappear from the shelves, like milk that has reached its expiration date.

But it was also not a joke, because you never stop hoping.

He didn't even bother to answer.

They'd planned to meet for lunch two months ago. It was supposed to have been a celebratory lunch, to mark the publication of her book. But Edward had been ill, and then Edward had been busy, and now it was less like a christening than a wake.

After they ordered, she took a large manila envelope from her bag and slid it across the table.

"On to the next thing," she said.

Weeks ago, he'd asked her to give him whatever she had of her memoir.

"This'll be a treat," he said. "But . . . well, it brings me to what I wanted to tell you about. I'm afraid I'm going to be reading it as a civilian."

She didn't understand.

"I didn't want you to hear about it from anyone else, and I didn't want to tell you on the phone. I'm afraid my condition has returned, and I'm finding it harder and harder to do my job and fight my cancer. I've given notice. I'm retiring at the end of next week."

"Jesus, Edward. I'm sorry."

"I'm sorry too," he said.

"How have you been feeling?"

"I usually have about one good hour a day. Which isn't that much of a change, really. Before I got this thing I used to have about two good hours a day."

"Are you going to do more chemo?"

"Chemo, radiation, some experimental stuff. They're going to do everything they can and one or two things they can't. They'll be carpet-bombing me. I'll be North Vietnam."

He smiled, as if he'd said something witty, so Florence smiled too, but he hadn't said anything witty, of course. Carpet-bombing as a figure of speech to describe chemotherapy had been around forever. She had a moment of engulfing sadness about this, about the way that even when we're living through tragedy, the language we reach for, the only language available to us, is secondhand.

But it probably wasn't a moment to be mourning the way we use language.

"How's Susan?"

"Susan is being brave. Susan is being great."

Florence had known him, worked with him, in that peculiar intimacy in which a writer and an editor can sometimes work, for twenty years now, but she barely knew his wife, and she had no idea how happy he was in his marriage.

"Don't start preparing your eulogy, though. Even if this round of treatments doesn't stick, they're telling me I can hope for five more years. I haven't started pricing funeral plots. I just don't want to spend the time I've got left behind a desk."

"What'll you be doing?"

"Traveling. Gardening. Visiting my grandchildren. Too many things to count."

She nodded, trying to appear as if she were still in the room, still spiritually within his reach, but she wasn't. She was thinking about herself. She was thinking that he was the only editor in the world who would be interested in publishing her memoir, and now he was going to be gone.

She needed to get back here, out of her thoughts and into the room. In what was surely a moment of need for Edward, she had it in her power to give him a gift—the gift of her full attention—but she was squandering the moment by getting tangled up in worries about her career.

She had always felt protected by Edward's presence in his publishing house. Her books had never sold that much, and there were people in the company who questioned his loyalty to her, but as long as he was there, she'd felt sure that nothing she wrote would be judged solely by its potential to earn a profit, and that everything she wrote would have a fighting chance of being published. And almost as important, she was sure that everything she'd published would stay in print. (Having one of your books go out of print—it's not like having one of your children die, but it's the closest that an experience in the world of letters can come.)

As she struggled to put her worries about him ahead of her worries about herself, she wasn't condemning herself; she wasn't wishing that she could be some saintly creature, composed entirely of concern for other people. But at the same time, she wished she could be a little bit better than she was.

"My writers are already being redistributed," he said. "They've got you lined up with one of our younger editors. He's eager to meet you. He's an admirer. He's read all your stuff."

She didn't quite believe this. She couldn't quite buy the picture of a young male editor who had read all her stuff.

"What's his name?"

"Kevin. Kevin Cleaver."

"Kevin Cleaver. Jesus Christ. You're kidding, right?"

"You know him?"

"No. But the name."

"It *is* a frightening name. But he's a good editor, and he's a comer. He's a good person to have in your corner."

Florence already didn't like him. She was too old to be impressed by comers.

She saw him as some swaggering cocksman, pulling out his iPhone to check *Gawker* so he could keep track of who was up and who was down.

It was hard to believe that Kevin Cleaver, the ninja of the late-night literary scene, the *Gawker* checker, would give a damn about anything she had to say. Her memoir, which had seemed a solid thing in her mind when she had thought that she would eventually be sending it to Edward, seemed flimsy and ignorable when she imagined it arriving on Kevin Cleaver's desk.

It wouldn't arrive on Kevin Cleaver's desk, though. She'd have to email it to him. He probably never even looked at his regular mail. Kevin Cleaver, master of the new.

She asked Edward about his next round of treatments, and when it seemed as if he had said as much as he wanted to say, they talked about Obama — it was his first year in office — and then they talked about Edward's summer house in Rhinebeck. He and Susan hoped to move there full-time. Florence had no interest in his summer house — hearing about other people's houses was as boring as hearing about other people's dreams — and in other circumstances she would have told him so, but today she smiled and nodded as he told her about repainting and finding a roofer and redoing the floors.

After she left the restaurant, she thought that the struggle she'd been having — the whole internal drama that had been playing out as she'd sat there trying to look as if she were listening to him — was something she could have told him about. He would have understood; he would have offered her the implicit reassurance that this kind of struggle is simply one of the things that come with being human. He might have even been relieved. When you're facing death, people start to treat you with caution — caution and a kind of superficial reverence. He probably would have gotten a kick out of hearing that she'd been assailed by selfish thoughts. But she could no more have told him than she could have traipsed around in a miniskirt and a nose ring. His illness had sealed him off from normal conversation. It was one sign that illness was taking him away.

She felt dismantled as she walked to the bus stop. There was something wrong with her balance. Her left foot kept flapping or flopping or something. She briefly wondered if she'd had a stroke—when you're in your seventies, this is what you think whenever you feel a little strange. But she knew she hadn't had a stroke. She knew that the world was tilting because she was upset about Edward.

The nature of time baffled her, just as much as it had on the morning of her ninth birthday, the first occasion on which she'd tried to grasp the fact that the moment she was experiencing would, a moment later, be in the past. Edward was alive; she could turn around and go back and embrace him if she wanted to. But soon he'd be gone.

When she was nine, and newly reflecting on these matters, she'd earnestly thought that if she could just concentrate hard enough, just cherish the moment strongly enough—this wasn't the language she had used at the time, but this had been the thought—she could stop time.

Five days a week, Janine walked twenty blocks from the apartment to her job. She'd been doing it for months now and it hadn't grown stale.

Sometimes she thought she was drunk on New York. She'd been in love with the city when she went to college here, and she was even more in love with it now.

The city was overwhelming, in all the best ways. On a crowded street, you felt as if worlds were hurtling past you: men, women, and children, unknowable, with exaltations and miseries of their own. Each of them looking both battle-hardened and hopeful in that distinctly New York City way.

She stood on the corner, waiting for the light to change. In New York, even this was an event. She loved the way no one in the city stayed on the sidewalk during a red light. No matter how old or how young, everyone moved out into the street, impatient, looking for an edge.

It was a beautiful Tuesday morning, the day after Memorial Day, and, as always, she was happy to be going to the lab.

At first she'd attributed her happiness to the work itself. For years she'd been interested in matters like self-control, willpower, decision making, attention—how we can cultivate those faculties and why it's so difficult for many of us to cultivate them—but she'd been interested as an amateur. These were things she read about and thought about on her own, but she'd never found a way to integrate any of it into her practice.

When she learned she could apply for a research fellowship at Columbia, she was excited and hesitant in equal measure. She enjoyed seeing her clients—she worked with students at the University of Washington—and she'd miss them if she took time off. She was nervous about picking up and going to New York, nervous about being without Daniel. But it came at a perfect time. The kids were out of the house—she didn't yet know that Emily would soon be back. And Daniel had been talking about taking all the vacation days he'd saved up, since the right to take them was unlikely to survive the next municipal budget. So it wasn't as if she'd be away from him for an entire year.

And she was eager to learn more, eager to do more with the learning she had. At a conference about "executive function" in adolescents in San Francisco last year, she found that she knew as much about the literature as some of the people who were lecturing there. The opportunity to work day by day alongside other people who were thinking about these things was finally too good to pass up.

Lev, at first, was like a pleasant background hum. It was a piece of good fortune that the director of the lab was such a nice guy—that's how it felt at first. That's all it felt like.

One day in March, though, walking down to the lab with the eagerness that had come to feel customary, she'd found a song going around in her head, one she hadn't heard or thought about in years. Actually just a line. It was called "The Dresses Song," and the line was simply "You make me want to wear dresses."

What she was thinking taught her what she was feeling. It was only when she thought about the song that she understood that as much as she liked the work, it wasn't just the work that was making her so happy.

21

Lev was already there when she arrived. No matter how early she got to work, Lev, if he was in town, was always already there. Although she hadn't witnessed this, she knew he was sometimes there at six in the morning.

He was a divorced man whose children were on their own and far away, and he could arrange his life as he pleased. When he wasn't traveling—giving talks and meeting with funders—he worked long hours during the day and spent the evening at concerts or lectures or in restaurants, with colleagues and students and friends. He had an endless appetite for conversation, conviviality, city life, but his work at the lab came before everything. When he spoke about the place, he looked as if he were speaking about a person he loved.

He was a disheveled, overweight older man, but as someone once said, exuberance is beauty, and in this way, at least, he was beautiful.

"You're here," he said when he saw her. "I'm so glad you're feeling better."

Whenever she showed up, he made her feel as if the party had finally begun. But he greeted everyone this way. His secretary was a woman in her seventies, and Lev brightened up when he saw her too. The old and the young, the hobbled and the swift: he was an overweight, male, middle-aged Statue of Liberty, shining on all.

"Daniel get in safe?"

"Yes. Yes. He was very safe."

"I hope I can meet him sometime soon."

"That would be great," she said.

His hair, as always, was Einsteinishly uncombed. He was wearing a nice suit, but it was hanging all wrong; it was as if the suit were embarrassed to be seen with him.

"You chose a nice set of clothes to sleep in," she said.

Lev had been engaged in the same research for thirty years, and he continued to be fascinated by it. Long ago, as a graduate student, he'd been an assistant to Walter Mischel, the psychologist who, researching self-control in children, had come up with the now-famous Marshmallow Test. A child would be told that he could have one marshmallow now or two marshmallows later, and would then be left alone in a room with a marshmallow. Some children couldn't hold out and ate the marshmallow immediately, some devised strategies to help themselves wait. Mischel eventually found that the children who could wait at the age of four or five were doing better ten years later, by a variety of measures, than the children who couldn't.

Lev had pursued similar questions, and now, in the age of the Internet, when no one seemed to be able to resist its opportunities for distraction, the subject had become hot. Research funds were pouring in; Lev was being profiled in magazines. *U.S. News & World Report* had run an item in which, citing his work on perseverance and goal-oriented behavior in adolescents, Lev had been dubbed "The Guru of Grit." He was glad to get the additional funding, but he didn't seem to care about the profiles. All he seemed to care about was the work.

At the lab, Janine was doing talk therapy with students from Columbia and other colleges in the area, who were also receiving training in "behavior management." It was part of a study to see if talk therapy plus behavioral therapy was more effective than either of them alone. So she was doing what she'd been doing at home—listening to young people—but learning things that she never would have learned at home.

Today she saw six students, went online to do research for a paper she was writing, and tried to get caught up on her email. If she had just two and a half more hours of free time today, she thought, she could finally get her inbox down to a reasonable level, but she'd been thinking the same thing every day for the last five years.

Normally she enjoyed every moment at the lab, but today she was conscious of a feeling of constraint. Now Daniel was here. She hadn't done anything she needed to feel guilty about, and yet she felt guilty. She had had a secret little crush, which might be seen as the most commonplace thing in the world, except that she hadn't had a secret little crush in years.

At 6:30, Lev was at her door. They were going to a retirement party for someone who'd worked at the lab for decades.

She'd asked Daniel if he wanted to come—spouses were welcome—but he had looked up from the TV and said, "Believe me, darling . . ."

It was a reference to a line they'd once read in a review of Dennis Rodman's autobiography: supposedly, after Madonna gave him detailed instructions about how to pleasure her in bed, Rodman replied, "Believe me, I won't do that, darling." Daniel liked to quote the line from time to time.

22

"Are you sure this is okay?" she said to Lev on the way. "I hardly know her."

"Doesn't matter," Lev said. "You're part of the team."

He was the strangest man in the world to have a crush on. He wasn't young, he wasn't handsome, he wasn't particularly masculine.

What he was, was warm. He was warm, warmer, warmest. When she fantasized about being with him, she rarely fantasized about sex. She fantasized about cuddling. She fantasized about lowering herself slowly into a warm bath of Lev.

The lab — formally the Center for the Study of Motivation — was a distant outpost of the Columbia University Department of Psychology. It took up all five floors of a converted townhouse on Seventy-fourth Street near Central Park West.

The party was in a rented space on Seventy-second Street. When they got there, Janine drank a glass of punch too fast, and it went to her head.

The room was too crowded and the music was too loud. She leaned against a wall watching Lev talk with people, watching him transporting his benevolent portliness around the room. Emily had seen Lev once, just after she got here, and had taken to referring to him as Santa Claus. This wasn't completely on target, but it wasn't completely off.

He made a circuit of the room, and then he came back to her.

"People-watching?" he said.

"Not really."

"Then what? You look like . . ."

"Jim Thorpe?"

"That's not what I was going to say."

"It's funny," she said. "Getting used to someone again. Even if you've lived with him for twenty years."

"You mean Daniel?"

She raised her eyebrows, which somehow meant yes.

"I know what you mean," Lev said. "I used to feel that way sometimes when I was away from Rachel for a week or two. It was like, 'Who are you again?'"

To what other man could she have said that it felt a little strange to reacclimate herself to Daniel? None. Not because it was too intimate, but because most men wouldn't know what she meant.

He had a quality of mind that she couldn't help but think of as womanly. He was tall; he was heterosexual (even if she hadn't known anything about his life, she would have known this: you can feel these things); but there was something about him that was best described as maternal. And thus, her friendship with him felt dizzyingly genderbenderish. Daniel occupied the masculine space in their relationship so obdurately that she felt as if she had no choice but to occupy the feminine space. With Lev everything seemed to be sliding around. It was the psychosexual equivalent of Twister.

She'd spent all too much time trying to figure out if he was flirting with her. She was still trying. A week ago he'd invited her to attend a conference in Pittsburgh with him later in the summer. Did that mean something? Or did it just mean he thought the panels would interest her? Sometimes a conference is just a conference. She hadn't said yes and she hadn't said no; eventually she'd have to say something.

"Why do you even like me?" Janine said. She was perhaps a little drunk.

"Why do I like you?"

"It's a simple question."

"It's a simple question, but there's not a simple answer."

"Oh, there must be. I must remind you of someone. I must remind you of your beloved . . . I don't know . . . some girl you liked in third grade."

"You don't remind me of my beloved anybody. Which is the point. You don't remind me of anyone I've ever met."

This was not what she expected, and she felt herself blush.

"Oh, come on. I'm not even a person."

"You are a person. But I think I know what you mean. You have an unfinished quality that in a person of your age is an achievement."

Maybe he was a little drunk too.

"Uh . . . thank you," she said.

"I know it sounds strange but it's true. I mean that you're open to life. You're open to being surprised. You're open to being changed by life. Most of us lose that quality in our twenties. I don't know how you've managed to hang on to it, but you have."

The music was loud, and the people were loud. Even weirder than the fact that he was saying all this was the fact that he was shouting it.

"Oh, that's just . . . I'm from Seattle. Everybody else you know has New York City armor on."

"Well, that could be. It could be that I only like you because you're from Seattle."

"That's what I thought," she said.

23

She walked back to the apartment instead of taking a bus, because she wanted to spend some time torturing herself about how untrustworthy she was.

The thing is, this had happened before, and it had happened before that.

The first time was with Trotsky. He was the assistant research librarian at the university when she was getting her master's. She'd thought of him as Trotsky because he was always reading the Russians and because he had an aggressive little goatee. He was a beautiful boy, unkempt, uncombed, uncouth, unguarded, and he was always thinking about matters of great moment, such as who was more right about the soul, Tolstoy or Dostoevsky, and he recalled her to a set of questions that she thought she had forgotten, and for a few months she used to enjoy daily fantasies of running off with him and living a life in which they pondered the great mysteries together. One stupid night, at an end-of-the-year party, she and Trotsky had kissed in his car, and one even stupider night not long after that, she'd told Daniel, who hadn't responded in the amused and unthreatened way that she'd somehow imagined he would.

They'd had a series of conversations that had made things worse and worse, and it had taken months for their marriage to heal.

Five years later, there was Chips Ahoy. He was her thesis supervisor when she was getting her Ph.D.; he was a scholar, a thinker of distinction, and a mindfucker: he liked to open you up and climb around inside your head with his psychic flashlight and leave you with the feeling that he was the only person who had ever truly understood you. He liked to get to that part of you that was loyal to nothing and no one, and convince you that that place, where he alone had joined you, was your most sacred chamber. He became Chips Ahoy one night when Janine and Daniel were shopping at Safeway. They ran into him in the snacks and cookies aisle, and she dropped a box of Chips Ahoy! cookies as they were talking, and Daniel took another box off the shelf and handed it to her, and she dropped that one too. Daniel, obviously, realized something was up, and every once in a while after that, he asked her how things were going with Chips Ahoy.

One kiss marred by bad beer and bad breath, and two dropped boxes of cookies, over twenty-three years. It didn't add up to much in the scale of marital divagations. But this felt different.

24

She found Daniel at the kitchen table, reading a book about the robber barons.

"How's it going?" he said, barely looking up. "How's the motivation biz?"

She leaned over and kissed him.

"It's all very exciting," she said.

"My God, you smell of cigarettes. Have you been smoking?"

"Of course I haven't been smoking," she said, feeling as if she were lying, although she wasn't.

"Then you've been kissing somebody who has."

They rarely talked about anything serious, with the exception of their children, and yet he was completely tuned in to her. He didn't really think that she'd been kissing anyone, and yet . . .

"Yes, I have. I've been making out with Humphrey Bogart."

"Well, that's not so bad. I was afraid you'd been kissing Christopher Hitchens."

"Christopher Hitchens doesn't like girls."

"He likes girls. He just doesn't think girls have a sense of humor."

"If you don't think girls have a sense of humor, you don't like girls."

"So that's why you didn't kiss him?"

"That was one of the reasons."

"What were the others?"

"Well, his views."

"His views on what? Surely it wasn't his atheism."

"I don't mind his atheism."

"Is it the things he said about Mother Teresa?"

"Only partly. I agree with a lot of what he said about her, actually."

"So what was it?"

"It isn't his views I don't like. It's his contempt for anyone who doesn't share them."

"So you would have kissed Christopher Hitchens if he weren't so snarky to believers?"

"Yes. In a word, yes."

"So who did you kiss?"

"Mother Teresa."

"And she was smoking?"

"I wouldn't say she was smoking. She had a few puffs on a cigar."

"Mother Teresa. Who would have guessed she was a smoker?"

"Well, that's the thing. She considers herself a statistical non-smoker."

"What does that mean?"

"If you have just a few puffs."

"I get it."

"She smokes pot like a hound, though."

"Like a hound."

"Yes. Like a hound."

"Are you too hot?"

"Why do you ask?"

"Because you're fanning yourself."

"I just fan myself sometimes. It's something I do."

"I've never noticed that before."

"I've been fanning myself forever. I was fanning myself the night we met."

"I do remember, now that you mention it. I found it very appealing."

"I thought you found it appealing. I noticed."

"Break it up, you two," Emily called from the next room.

25

Florence's new editor wanted to meet her. He volunteered to come to her, on the Upper West Side, which was a display of deference that she appreciated.

But the reason he wanted to meet her, obviously, was to tell her that her literary services would no longer be required. She was fully aware that her books, with an impressive consistency, had lost money; she was fully aware that Edward had kept publishing her work out of personal loyalty, not because it made any business sense. With Edward gone, she knew she was gone as well.

She had tried hard to avoid the dreadful Kevin Cleaver. What was the point of meeting him in order to learn she was being dropped? He probably thought that telling her to her face was the humane thing to do. She didn't want any part of it—send me an email, was her feeling—but he was intent on meeting her, and after three voice mails she'd decided that it wouldn't be so bad. She would get to observe a human type that was unfamiliar to her, an experience that was always of interest; and she'd get a free lunch.

They met, at his suggestion, at Gabriel's, a restaurant she liked but rarely went to, a friendly and relaxed and expensive place on West Sixtieth Street.

"So this is the great Florence Gordon," he said.

"Florence Gordon," she said.

She was thinking: Don't mock me. If you're going to drop me, just drop me. Don't humiliate me too.

He was so hip that she didn't have words to describe him. She couldn't even describe what he was wearing. He was wearing jeans, of course, but she couldn't have given a good account of his shirt, or his earring, or his shoes. Especially his shoes. They were hipster shoes, shoes that proved that he was in the know, shoes you could probably purchase only in Williamsburg.

"Why?" she said.

"Why what?"

"Why are we getting together?"

He laughed at this.

"I've heard about how direct you are," he said. "I would have been disappointed if you weren't."

"Thank you. So. Why?"

"Sorry if I've been badgering you. But I've been badgering you for two reasons. First, I wanted to meet you. Second, I read the beginning of your memoir the weekend before last, and I wanted to tell you how beautiful it is."

Edward must have passed it on before he left.

She waited for the next sentence, which would inevitably start with "But . . ." But it isn't really marketable. But we're looking for a different kind of thing right now. But we're not the best publisher to do justice to your work.

"It's just wonderful. It's everything I hoped it would be and more."

It took a while for his words to reach her. He seemed to be speaking with a five-second delay.

"I'm glad you feel that way," she said.

She was still waiting for the "But."

"Those were my two reasons, as of last week. But as of yesterday, there's a third reason."

He produced two pieces of paper and slid them across the table. A blurry fax. A blurry faxed copy of the front page of the *New York Times Book Review*. With a review of *How to Look at a Woman*.

"Is this a prank?"

"If it is, it's a prank that's about to be perpetrated on a few million people."

It was real. It was a copy of the book review section that would come out two Sundays from now.

"Read it."

She read it. She was having trouble focusing—maybe I'm having a stroke, she thought—but it contained phrases like "a national treasure" and "an unsung heroine of American intellectual life."

The review was by Martha Nussbaum, the University of Chicago philosopher, an author of books on every subject from Greek tragedy to disability theory to educational reform to the idea of religious tolerance in American life to—well, to everything else. Nothing human was alien to her.

She seemed to have read everything Florence had ever written. From the review you might have thought she'd spent her life doing nothing but meditating on Florence's work.

"Jesus," she said. "When did you get this?"

"Got it yesterday. I'm sorry I waited, but I got greedy. I wanted to show you in person. I wanted to see your face."

"Did you get your money's worth?"

"You seem remarkably calm, actually."

"Well. Maybe not."

"Maybe this is the way you look when you're elated."

She thought of Edward, poor dear Edward. He had been so loyal to her for so long. It was unfair that it wasn't he who was giving her this news. She'd called him twice since their breakfast, but he hadn't felt well enough to come to the phone.

She looked at the review again. It went on and on and on and on. Martha Nussbaum had always been a woman with a lot to say, and now she had a lot to say about Florence.

"It's going to take some time to sink in. I can't really understand it. I mean, why?"

"Depends on how you want to look at it. You could say it was long overdue. Or you could say you got lucky. Sometimes the *Times* likes to throw everybody a curve. Whatever the reason, it's going to change your life. You've been declared a national treasure."

He took out his iPhone or whatever the hell it was and read a few messages, and then wrote a few messages. It was remarkable, the way people interrupted their conversations with you to do this sort of thing, without a word of apology. It had become as natural as taking a sip of water.

"So now can we talk about your memoir?"

"Sure. Of course."

She made an effort to get the review out of her mind. Wasn't sure she was going to be able to do it.

"The main thing I have to say is that it's brilliant. I think this could turn out to be the best thing you've ever done."

She reached for a poppy-seed roll. The floor was tilting. They were onboard a ship, and the ship was listing. The national treasure reached for a poppy-seed roll.

"Why?" she said. "Why do you like it?"

"You're not hearing me. I don't like it. I love it. I'm sure you've needed to write it for your own personal reasons. You're writing it for yourself, and you have no idea what it will mean to other people. You've been thinking you're writing a memoir, but what you're writing is the story of your generation."

The story of her generation. Of course she'd been telling herself much the same thing, hoping other people would see it that way, but now that he was saying it, it sounded glib and superficial.

"You thought you were someone who'd made a home for herself in the cozy little ghetto of feminist literature. But it turned out that wasn't your destiny. It turned out that your destiny was to write the inner history of your age."

She had always found it curious, the way that even sophisticated younger people liked to speak of "destiny," liked to tell themselves that "there's a reason for everything." The way they married a quirky individuality with a passive acceptance of things as they are.

Why am I so hostile to this man? He's bringing nothing but good tidings, and he's saying nothing but nice things.

Am I, she thought, one of those dreary people who won't join any club that will have them for a member? She hoped she wasn't.

"This has been quite a meal," she said. "I walked in here thinking I was going to have to find a new publisher, and I walk out of here . . ."

"You walk out of here an American classic."

She made a face.

"That's what you are," he said. "Get used to it."

26

After she said goodbye to Kevin Cleaver, she didn't know what to do with herself. She wanted to tell her friends, of course, but not yet.

She wandered over to West End Avenue and walked north. At first she thought she wasn't headed anywhere in particular, but by the time she passed Seventy-ninth Street she realized that she'd walked this way for a reason. Soon she was standing outside the building of a woman whom she'd known a long time ago.

Her name was Simone. She had been Florence's French teacher at the Bronx High School of Science. She was the first woman who'd taken a special interest in her. Florence remembered Simone once telling her that she thought she was going to have an interesting life.

Florence and Simone had stayed in touch after Florence went to college, but Florence had withdrawn from her sometime after that. During the decade in which Florence had been little more than her husband's helpmate, she'd been too embarrassed to stay in contact with Simone. She felt too much as if she'd let her down.

Simone had died before Florence started on her writing career;

she'd never had the opportunity to be proud of her student's successes.

Florence stood outside Simone's building for another minute or two, looking up at what used to be her window.

Thank you.

Then she started back home.

27

"This is a little different," Janine said.

"All of a sudden my mother is a legend," Daniel said.

"It's damned strange," Florence said. "I'm not really sure I like it."

"Trust me," Daniel said. "You like it."

Florence had come to their apartment. It was Sunday afternoon. The review was still a week away, but word had begun to trickle out. A woman from *Time Out New York* had called to arrange an interview. *O* magazine had asked for an essay. Florence had been booked for something on NPR, and her literary agent had been in conversation with someone at *Charlie Rose*.

Emily, on the couch, was watching everyone, or trying to. It was like watching a game where the action is taking place on three parts of the field.

Florence seemed different, but in a way Emily couldn't define.

Or maybe she wasn't different at all. Maybe it was just that Emily was seeing her differently, now that she was a national treasure.

Emily's grandmother might or might not seem different, but her mother definitely did. She seemed kind of shellshocked. But why should she be shellshocked by Florence's success?

Her father seemed the way he always did.

He was astonishingly statuelike. What the hell was he? She was convinced that nothing would really change him, ever. If you slipped E into his coffee, she believed, he wouldn't act any differently. No matter what was going on inside his mind, he would remain unperturbed, unswayable, undiverted, doing his duty to the last.

It was clear that he was happy for his mother, in his low-key way. Among the three grown-ups, he was the only one who did seem simply happy.

"They want to send me on a book tour," Florence said.

"Do you like going on book tours?" Emily said.

"I'll let you know after I've been on one."

"You've never been on one before?"

"When I did the history of struggle, they got a car and drove me around to different bookstores in the city. They took me all the way to Park Slope. That was my book tour."

"Where do they want to take you now?"

"All the major markets."

"What does that mean?"

"I have no idea."

"Of course you know what it means," Daniel said. "It means Los Angeles, San Francisco, maybe Boston, maybe Chicago. Where the hell else is there?"

"Seattle, maybe, Dad?" Emily said. "Portland?"

"New Yorkers don't know Seattle and Portland exist," Daniel said.

"That's not true," Emily said. "They're big book-buying markets."

"How do you know this?" Daniel said.

"Your daughter knows a lot of things," Janine said.

"I do. Anyway, the point is that Grandma is a literary lion now. You know what this means, don't you, Grandma? It means you're going to have to start tweeting."

"My publisher has already broached the idea."

Because her mother seemed oddly immobile, Emily went to the

kitchen and got some snacks and brought them back into the living room. Nobody seemed to have moved.

"Will success change Florence Gordon?" Daniel said.

Emily was surprised when it seemed that Florence was taking the question seriously.

"If you make a big splash at *her* age," Florence said, looking at Emily, "then it changes you. I'm too old to change."

"I don't know, Grandma," Emily said. "I don't think it would have changed you even if you'd been my age."

"You don't think so?"

"I think you're made of iron."

"I'm glad you think of me that way."

"Are you going to do anything differently now?" Emily said.

"What should I do differently?"

"My dad said you said the review got everything right. Right?"

"I have nothing to complain about."

"So now you can rest assured that people understand you. So I was wondering if there were other things you might want to say, now that you know you've said your piece and people have understood you. Maybe it's a chance to change your life."

"I never had any doubt that people understood me. And I didn't need Martha Nussbaum to come along and help people understand my meaning. I think I've managed to make it plain enough myself."

"Okay."

"And I have no need of a chance to change my life. My life is just fine as it is."

"She wasn't trying to offend you, Mom," Daniel said. "Don't jump down the girl's throat, for God's sake."

"She wasn't jumping down my throat."

"Exactly," Florence said. "I wasn't jumping down her throat. And you stay out of this."

Emily couldn't quite tell whether her grandmother had been jumping down her throat. Florence always made you feel as if you'd just said something dumb. It was impossible to tell whether she was more irritated than usual.

28

Janine felt oddly . . . what was the word? Not exonerated, but something like exonerated. Passed over? Let off the hook? She was usually the object of Florence's scrutiny, but life was coming at the old
lady so fast now that she didn't have any spare energy to conduct
her usual inquisition.

But this didn't leave Janine feeling relieved. She was infected
with a spirit of restlessness. She couldn't wait for Florence to leave,
but when Florence did leave, Janine felt lonely, even though her
husband and daughter were still there.

In the evening, she and Daniel went to the movies downtown.
After that, he wanted to walk around in the East Village, where
both of them used to live.

She'd visited New York often enough in the years since they'd
moved to Seattle, but she hadn't gone back to the East Village. She
hadn't set foot here in more than twenty years. By the time they got
to Cooper Square, she felt like a ghost, haunting her own life.

Here was the street where she'd spent her first summer in New
York, just before she started at NYU. Here was the bar where she
met that sad, sweet boy she'd once thought she was destined to spend

the rest of her life with. What was his name? Here was the bench where she'd kissed that girl with the purple hair. She'd thought of herself as such a daring soul back then.

Here was the spot where she made that desperate and humiliating phone call to that boy she had a crush on in her sophomore year. The phone booth, of course, was gone. Here was the club where she used to listen to her friend Spider play guitar. It was a shoe store now. And here was the spot where she met Daniel.

"What do you think?" she said to Daniel.

"That was the place, right?"

"That was the place."

Each of them had been traveling with friends that night. Some of her friends knew some of his friends. They'd met on the street corner, and while their friends were talking about what to do that night, the two of them launched into an argument about the country versus the city. Pure flirtation. He, who had grown up in the city, was denouncing it as prisonlike; she, who'd come from a suburb, couldn't understand how anyone could ever be unhappy or bored here. She had pointed to some random apartment building and said, "Every brick in that wall is alive with human intention!" Later he had told her that when she'd said that, he'd decided that he wanted to go out with her.

They went out for a year, broke up after they graduated, and got together again a few years later.

"I wonder what we would have turned into if we'd stayed here," she said.

"You would have become exactly what you are. Questing, self-questioning, deeply involved in your work. And I would have remained a snot-nosed would-be poet."

"You think so?"

"I'm not sure I would have had the guts to give up."

29

The young man finding the courage to live the life of an artist: that's an oft-told story, a story people are fond of. For Daniel, it had been a question of finding the courage not to. During his childhood, living with two obsessed parents, the background music was a duet for typewriters, and he took it for granted that he'd become a writer himself. In high school he'd seen himself as Byronically romantic; during one spring, besotted with poetry and marijuana, he strode around in a cape. In college he studied literature and writing. During the week before commencement, his poetry teacher, an ex-marine who wrote poetry marked by a sort of burly anguish and who seemed to regard the academic world with a genial contempt, asked Daniel what he planned to do next, and when Daniel said he didn't know, the teacher suggested that instead of bumming around aimlessly, he should spend a few years in the military and see how the other half lived.

Normally, this was the kind of suggestion Daniel would have laughed off—his teacher probably expected him to—but it came at a time when he was feeling rigorously critical of both of his parents, and within a few weeks he went to a recruiting office and signed up. When he looked back on this decision in later years, his only question was whether he had done it to spite them or merely to baffle them. He served for two years, and although he saw no action and never even left the States—he was posted to Fort Lewis, Washington, where, having been recognized immediately as a bookish type, he was assigned the job of editing a veterans' newsletter—by the time he got out, he felt thoroughly liberated from his parents. Not just from his parents: he was liberated, also, from their world.

Florence and Saul, long divorced by then, were united only in this: neither of them could understand why the hell he'd done what he'd done. They were comfortably cloistered in the worldview of the Upper West Side; they wouldn't have called themselves pacifists, but they'd been against every war the United States had waged in their adult lifetimes. If he'd joined a revolutionary organization dedicated to overthrowing the government by force, that might have made a little sense to them; joining the U.S. Army made no sense to them at all.

Later, when he became a cop, one thing he felt clear about, and felt good about, was that he hadn't become a cop to spite them. He'd known that it would leave them both aghast, but that wasn't why he did it.

He'd hated most of the things he encountered in the army. He hated the rigidity, he hated the hostility to thought, he hated the way you get turned into a machine programmed to inflict harm. But the thing that he loved about it was that it gave him his first real experience of democracy. The institution as a whole was hierarchical, but the enlisted men lived in a condition of stripped-down equality: nothing from your past, nothing that you'd been or done or had, meant anything now. The only thing that meant anything to the people you bunked with was not being an asshole, not doing your job so poorly that it made everybody else look bad, and not doing your job so well that it made everybody else look bad.

When he joined the police force, his parents thought that he'd rejected them twice. What they failed to understand was that under his unfamiliar aspect, he was not very different from the person he'd been all his life. He still had the same social conscience that had led him to make posters for an Upper West Side anti-littering campaign when he was eight and to go door-to-door for Jimmy Carter when he was fourteen. He still wished to be of use.

He'd rarely regretted his decision to become a cop, but, even after working for the Seattle PD for more than twenty years, he'd never really fit in. Early in his time there, one of his colleagues had spotted him reading a book on his lunch break, which was apparently a signal event in the history of the police force, and this led to someone's calling him "the professor," a name that had stuck with him since then — mostly because he was a reader, and partly, he suspected, because he was a Jew. Nobody hazed him or gave him a hard time, but he never stopped feeling like an outsider.

After a few years he found his way into the Crisis Intervention unit, which is a little world within the world of the police force, with its own culture and its own values. He spent most of his time working with people who were mentally ill, trying to make sure they didn't get swallowed up by the criminal justice system. (Crisis Intervention kept getting funded every year only because the city had found that it was cost-effective in keeping the violent mentally ill from clogging up the courts.) When you're in CI, most of the other cops don't think of you as a cop anymore; they think of you as a social worker with a badge. And for Daniel, at least, the description was accurate.

His parents didn't know anything about all this. As far as they understood, he was a cop now, through and through. They didn't know that he still read, doggedly and intently — they probably assumed he'd stopped reading. Sometimes, he wasn't sure why, he got the feeling that they didn't even think of him as Jewish anymore. They apparently held to the Lenny Bruce theory that if you live in New York you're Jewish, and you're a goy if you live anywhere else.

But though he was more like his old self than his parents realized, he wasn't simply the same old Daniel in disguise. He'd been changed by his experiences, and he'd wanted to be changed by them. He had a different idea of what was important. He didn't believe you could be judged by the number of books you'd read or the number of articles you'd written; he didn't believe your worth was based on your attainments or your erudition or even your intelligence. Just about the only thing he valued was simple decency.

Janine had been with him through all of this. She had watched him grow into manhood. Year by year she had been more and more impressed—with his steadiness, his compassion, his gentleness with and interest in the children. But she couldn't tell herself that all of his changes had pleased her. When they were young, he'd seemed ambitious—or maybe she'd just assumed that he was—but it had been years since he'd shown any signs of wanting to improve himself in any way. Maybe there was nothing wrong with that. Maybe she should have felt nothing but appreciation for his ability to treasure the life he actually had. But she'd always believed that if you weren't striving, you weren't alive, and she couldn't understand his complacency.

The life they lived was far from the life she'd always dreamed of living—a life of cultural excitement, a life of conversation, a life in which you kept meeting people who made you think. To the extent that she'd had that life, it hadn't been one that Daniel had been interested in sharing; it had been one she'd had to find for herself.

Sometimes she thought that Daniel's rival wasn't Lev, it was Manhattan. It was coming here that had made her feel alive to her own possibilities. She hadn't been unhappy in Seattle; her job was absorbing, and she'd found a balance between being a mother, which she loved, and being a woman at work in the world. But on coming back here she'd discovered how little she'd trained herself to live with. Everything was richer here: work life, cultural life, street life—even her dream life. She didn't know if it was even possible for her to go back.

Tonight she couldn't shake off her restlessness. Before they'd left the apartment, she'd felt as if she were in the wrong clothes, and she'd changed twice, but she still felt as if she were in the wrong clothes.

Florence's success had shaken something loose inside Janine. Florence was a woman who had never compromised. And now, at long last, she was reaping the fruits of her courage. So the question, Janine thought, is this: If I exercised a bravery in my own life equivalent to that which Florence has exercised in hers, what would I be doing? What would I be doing differently?

30

"You think you could live here again?" she said.

"Saint Mark's Place?"

"You know what I mean. New York."

"We'd never be able to afford it. We'd have to live out in Brooklyn, with my father. Cozy times around the fire with Saul. We could read his masterpieces as soon as they came out of the typewriter."

"Wherever. You know what I mean. Could you see yourself coming back east?"

They could do it, if the will was there. Daniel was growing increasingly tired of his job, as budget cuts kept making him feel less like a social worker with a badge and more like a clerk. He'd be eligible to retire at half-salary in a few years, and she was confident of his ability to find something here — much more confident than he was, but she was certain that she was right. And she'd been all but assured that she'd be able to make her position at the lab permanent if she wanted to. Nothing was stopping them, except, perhaps, his mixed feelings about being back in the place he'd once felt the need to escape from.

"You ever see that show *McCloud*?" he said. "This cop from out west moves to New York, walks around wearing a ten-gallon hat, outsmarting the city slickers."

"I never saw that," she said, and heard a heart-sunk inflection in her own voice.

"Maybe it's on Netflix. I think I'd have to watch a few episodes. Get a sense of whether I could make it work."

"Sounds like McCloud made it work," she said.

"Well, he did. But I'm not sure I have his talents. You should see the way he could ride a horse. The bad guys would jump into a getaway car, but McCloud . . ."

She didn't listen to the rest. She took his arm and they continued their ramble.

31

"You must be hating all this," Vanessa said.

"Why?" Florence said.

"It must be upsetting all your routines. It must be hard for you to clear out your inbox every day."

Florence grunted. She was vain about the tidiness of her inbox.

"Seriously," Vanessa said. "Is it overwhelming? Or is life pretty much back to normal now?"

Florence was having dinner with five friends whom she'd known for more than forty years. Three of them were in her study group; they'd been meeting once a month to talk about books and politics since the seventies. (Back then they used to call it a consciousness-raising group, but none of them had used the term in years.) Tonight her friends had taken her out to celebrate what Vanessa had called her "coronation."

"It never stopped being normal. You know that. You get a few phone calls, you get a few emails. Life goes on."

"I don't know about that," Vanessa said. "Success can make you crazy."

Vanessa was a psychotherapist who worked with people in the

arts. She proceeded to give a few examples. A painter who, after selling one of his works to the Whitney, began to speak of himself in the third person. A writer who'd so long suppressed her desire for fame, so long suppressed the narcissism near the root of every creative life, that when she finally achieved a bit of recognition, all her hunger for it had come bursting out—a ferocity of hunger that no degree of success could satisfy—and she was plunged into a depression from which it took her months to recover. Another writer, a woman who'd always seemed a model of tolerance and tact, who, after finally writing a book that brought her a degree of acclaim, felt nothing but anger toward all the people who were celebrating her. Late recognition, Vanessa said, was the stage for the return of the repressed.

Alexandra too believed that success could make you crazy, and she too had a theory. Buried deep in the psyche, she thought, is a sort of lump, a creature that craves nothing except stability, and as far as the lump is concerned, change for the better is just as bad as change for the worse.

The conversation wandered away from its starting point, the revolution in Florence's fortunes. And Florence was thankful for that. Her experience had been very different from the kind of thing they were talking about, and she was glad to be relieved of the necessity to explain this or to pretend otherwise.

For Florence, this moment in the limelight hadn't been disorienting in the least. It hadn't been disappointing, or vexing, or complicated in any way. It had been that rare thing: an unmixed pleasure.

Ever since the voluble philosopher had anointed her, Florence had been enjoying herself. She felt as if she'd been preparing for this all her life: preparing to be appreciated. She hadn't been hungering for it; she'd never really felt the need for anyone's applause. But now that she was getting it, it was a delight.

But flaunting your happiness is no less vulgar than flaunting your wealth, so she was happy to avoid the subject of how she was feeling these days.

The conversation meandered further, and she grew more and

more relaxed. She was more comfortable with these women than with anyone else in the world. Their lives had gone in different directions over the years; some of them had seemed to go from success to success, some through decades of bad choices and bad luck. But when they were together, none of this seemed to matter. What mattered wasn't what any of them had achieved or had not achieved. They knew one another well enough to see beneath the vicissitudes of the moment.

Their get-together lasted for hours, and the subject of Florence's success came up only once or twice more, and that was only when her friends teased her about it.

She enjoyed being teased, by these women. These were the people she trusted. This was her tribe.

32

It was strange, though, that your close friends are rarely the people who ask the questions that mean the most to you.

Florence was still turning over the questions that her granddaughter had asked her: "Are you going to do anything differently now? Isn't this a chance to change your life?"

None of her friends would have ever thought of asking her questions like this.

Maybe they'd never ask because they knew her so well. They knew she wasn't interested in changing.

Or maybe they'd never ask because our ideas about our friends and loved ones congeal over time. We see them in a fixed and limited way, so we come to imagine that they themselves are fixed and limited.

When Emily had asked, Florence had hardly even bothered answering. She wanted to make it clear that the line of inquiry was beneath her.

But the questions had kept scratching at her.

She could see what Emily meant. Nussbaum's article had summed up her life's work sympathetically and clearly. Florence didn't need to repeat herself, because it had all been understood. So maybe it was time to say something new.

But what?

A few days after her little exchange with her granddaughter, Florence had taken out a box of old notes. Years ago, she'd flirted with the idea of embarking on a grand project, a synthesis of feminism and radical social theory—*A Vindication of the Rights of Woman* meets *Das Kapital*. She'd imagined writing a volume that would be gnarled, daunting, exhaustive; it would be filled with footnotes and thick as a canned ham. Now she unearthed the notes she'd made, to see if she might want to revisit the project, and spent a few days looking through them.

It was a clarifying experience, because it helped her understand why she'd put the project aside in the first place. More than that, it helped her understand who she was. She had put it aside because she wasn't a grand system builder. She wasn't, and she didn't want to be. She was a guerrilla fighter, a saboteur, a master of the sneak attack. Her métier was the long essay. Of the books she'd written, most had been essay collections, and even the ones that weren't essay collections were essay collections in disguise.

After a few days of looking over the old notes, she threw them, with a tremendous feeling of satisfaction, away.

Emily's question had been important because it helped Florence remind herself what she wanted. She didn't want to do anything differently. She didn't want to change her life. She wanted to keep going. Maybe the shot of public approbation would help her become more reckless, more slashing, more licensed to assault and insult and offend. But probably not. She felt free to assault and insult and offend already.

All I want to do, she thought, is to keep doing what I'm doing, as long as I can.

33

At the age of seventy-five, Florence embarked on her first book tour. It had been thrown together hastily, and it didn't take her to all the major markets, but it still felt lavish to her. She visited Miami, D.C., Philadelphia, and Boston, stayed in nice hotels, and spoke in one bookstore and three synagogues. Kevin had explained to her that this was what a book tour was. "Jewish women," he said, "are all that stand between us and the death of the publishing industry."

Florence's friends expected her to be curmudgeonly about her book tour, but she enjoyed it. You travel around and you talk to women who've never been part of any social movement of any kind, women for whom the word "organizing" probably refers to nothing more radical than redoing their closets, and you find that not only have they felt the stirrings of feminism throughout their lives, they've often acted upon them, struggling out of hostile and constricting circumstances in the effort to breathe a freer air.

What delighted her most was that women in their twenties were showing up. A new online magazine, the *New Inquiry*, run by a circle of feminists just out of college, seemed to have adopted Florence as an honorary grandmother—they'd run an interview with her and a review of her work in the same week—and in both D.C. and Philadelphia, confident and well-read young women showed up, most of whom said that they'd first heard of her because of the *New Inquiry*. It might not have been true, as Vanessa would have it, that Florence was a hero to the young, but this kind of attention from the young was more than she'd had in a long time, and it was flattering.

34

The last stop of her tour was Hartford, Connecticut, where she was going to speak at another synagogue. She took a train from Boston, where a summer storm had limited the audience at Newtonville Books to four or five old friends and email acquaintances. She was tired, and the weirdness in her hand and foot was flaring up again—her fingers wanted to jump around and her foot wanted to scrape against the pavement—and all she wanted, the whole woman as distinct from her parts, was to be back home.

She was met at the train station by a young woman—was she young? Florence couldn't tell. Everyone seemed young to her now—named Dolly.

Dolly had organized this event. "I'll be your chaperone, your bodyguard, your guardian angel, and your groupie, all mixed in one," she said.

Dolly's car was not what Florence would have expected, had it occurred to her to expect anything. Most of the people who picked her up for this kind of engagement had cars that were professionally spotless. You could have eaten off the floors. But this one was redolent of a large and—somehow Florence sensed this—not particularly happy family.

A family, she quickly realized, with dogs. The car was doggish. It was the car a dog would own if a dog could own a car. Dog hair on the seats, the smell of dog food, the smell of dog breath, the smell of rain-soaked dog fur locked in by airless heat.

It was also filled with the detritus of childhood: boxes of apple juice, wrappers from cheese sticks, potato-chip bags. After a minute in the car Florence thought she knew this woman and her family too well.

"I thought you might like to read this while we're driving," Dolly said. She handed Florence a stapled brochure, which turned out to be this week's edition of the synagogue newsletter. There was an article about Florence's talk that night, by someone named Alice Tyler. Florence looked through it quickly.

"It's amazing how they can never get a damned thing right. If this chucklehead didn't feel like putting down a dime to make a phone call, you'd at least think she'd go on the Internet to check her facts. I wasn't born in 1937; I never got a doctorate; I'm not retired."

"I wrote that, actually," Dolly said. "That's my pen name."

"That's you? It's a good thing you have a pen name, so nobody finds out what a terrible writer you are. You need to get your facts right. You also need to get your grammar right. 'A New Yorker whom I think is one of the savviest thinkers around . . .'? It's 'who,' not 'whom.' 'Whom' is phony elegance, and it's grammatically incorrect. 'She's not adverse to calling herself a democratic socialist.' It's 'averse.' You might try finding out what a word means before committing it to print. This is appalling."

Dolly had a beatific smile on her face. "This is just so awesome. To get insulted by Florence Gordon on our first encounter. Within, what, five minutes of picking you up. I feel like I made it to the big leagues."

"You don't make it to the big leagues by writing with such bad grammar that it makes Florence Gordon want to insult you."

"I know, I know, I know. It's just that I'm so stressed lately. My husband—he's the associate dean of students at Trinity—my husband has back problems and he hasn't been able to help me at all around the house. He can't even get comfortable on the couch. Sometimes he'll come home at night and turn on the TV and lie on the floor."

"Sounds like the assistant dean of students has a nice thing going for himself."

"No, Ronald would never—you're teasing. And both of my kids are in a gifted and talented program, and the amount of homework they get every day is whack. I swear, I spend three hours a night doing homework with them."

"If you're doing their grammar homework, God help them."

Dolly let out a loud, horsey laugh. She seemed unoffendable. There was something appealing about her resilience, at least, or her ability not to take herself too seriously.

As they drove, Florence took in the passing streets. Domino's pizza, Starbucks, Subway. Everything here was the same as everything everywhere else. This was something that Florence felt she was supposed to deplore, but she found it comforting. These were all businesses you could find on the Upper West Side.

She'd once spent a week in the country, during a brief relationship with a nature-lover, and it had been the most horrifying week of her life.

"Why a pen name?"

"Excuse me?" Dolly said.

"Why do you use a pen name? Do you have something to hide?"

"I do have something to hide. Myself. I have to hide myself from my mother."

"Why?"

"Because she's a mountain. My mother the mountain. She terrifies me. She looms over my life."

"That must be difficult for you."

"It *is* difficult. It's very difficult. Even though I can recognize irony, and I understand that you don't really give a damn, it's nice to talk about it anyway. I'm writing a memoir of my family life, actually. I'm not sure if I should try to publish it now under Alice, or wait until my mom is gone and do it under Dolly. I'd rather publish it now, but when I go on TV, that would be the end of my secret identity."

"When you go on TV?"

"I have a lot to say. I'd expect it would be a hit. I don't know if they'd want me on *Charlie Rose* or anything, but I'm sure some of the morning talk shows would be interested. I've really got a fascinating story."

"How old is your mother?"

"Sixty-seven."

"You might have to wait a while."

"I know."

Dolly kept glancing over at her, smiling shyly.

"What is it?"

"I know this is going to sound weird, but you remind me of my mother. She even kind of looks like you. It's amazing the way she's kept her figure. She's always emailing me these articles about diet plans. And she has this . . . she seems angry all the time. Not that you seem angry. Or if you do seem angry, it's about the injustices of the world. She just seems angry because, you know, I don't call her enough."

"I promise not to get angry at you because you don't call me enough," Florence said.

At the synagogue, there was a nice crowd. Florence gave her talk, read a little bit from her book, and answered questions. There were some intelligent women there, asking intelligent questions, mostly about Elizabeth Cady Stanton, the subject of the longest essay in her book. They seemed to dislike her—Stanton, not Florence; they seemed to see her as essentially masculine in her insistence that each of us is fundamentally alone.

After the event Dolly drove her to her hotel.

"I can't tell you how moved I was by your reading. I really can't tell you how much it meant to me to have you up here."

"Thank you, Dolly."

"A lot of the things you said really resonated with me on a personal level. Some of the things you were saying were just like things I say in my memoir."

"That's a nice coincidence."

"I think you'd really love my memoir. I really think it would move you. I showed part of it to Cynthia Ozick when she was up for a reading last year, and she loved it. She told me I should publish it right away."

"Did she?" Florence said.

"Yes. I know that you and she probably don't get along because of your opinions on the Middle East, but she possesses a first-rate literary mind. Wouldn't you say that?"

"Yes. I would."

"I also showed parts of it to Alice Munro. She's—I can't believe I even met her. She's like the Meryl Streep of literature. She didn't have time to take it home and read it, but she read a little bit in the car, and she said I should keep going. You know, I have a copy in the trunk. I keep it with me so I can keep revising it—if I get to the dentist's office and they tell me that he's running late, I can just run out and get it and work on revising it. So it has some stuff in pencil in the margins, so it's sort of precious to me, because it's the only copy that has all my latest revisions, but I'd love for you to borrow it and tell me what you think. I could send you postage so you could mail it back."

The literary critic Edmund Wilson, near the end of his life, had a supply of preprinted postcards stating that "Edmund Wilson regrets that it is impossible for him" to read manuscripts, judge literary contests, make after-dinner speeches, supply photographs of himself, and so on. Florence needed a postcard like that.

"I think it would be really interesting for you to read," Dolly said. "I feel like it would be a treat. No offense, but I feel like you're one of my ancestors."

"Excuse me?" Florence said.

"I know this is silly, but sometimes I have this fantasy. It's silly, but I can tell you, because I feel close to you. I've read so much of your work that I feel close to you. I fantasize that someday people will write biographies about me, and that they'll talk about you in those biographies, and they'll talk about how important you were to my development.

"In my fantasy—I know it's just a fantasy—but in my fantasy, that's the reason you'll stay alive in people's minds. Maybe your own work will be forgotten for a while, but when people find out how much you meant to me—you know, when they read my biography—they'll start reading your books again too."

They were moving through the silent, empty streets of Hartford. It was nine o'clock, but everything was darkened and locked. Florence longed to get back to the city, where you could go out at two in the morning for a bowl of hot-and-sour soup. Not that she ever did, but how comforting to know that you could.

"I know it's kind of a crazy fantasy," Dolly said. "But it's a way of imagining giving something back to you. That's what I'm saying. I like to imagine giving something back to you, because you've given me so much."

"Is that what it is?" Florence said. "It sounds like a fantasy of destroying me."

"No. No! It's not that at all. I mean I can see what you mean, but . . . I'm sorry. I didn't mean to offend you."

"It's all right. I'm not offended. I'm not offended because it has nothing to do with me. Whatever we may think of Freud, it seems pretty clear that what you're fantasizing about is destroying your mother's power over you and bringing her back as a dependent. Wouldn't you say?"

Dolly was silent for half a block.

"No one has ever talked to me like this. That was so rude. No one has ever talked to me like this before."

"Do you know why that is? It's because no one has ever taken you seriously before. Most people probably tune you out, because you say such foolish things. I'm taking a chance here on the possibility that you're not as foolish as you seem. But when you invite someone for a reading and then tell her that you have this fantasy that someday everything she's done is going to be forgotten—well, Dolly, if you expect anyone to be pleased by that, you're out of your mind. All I can really tell you is that you might have more in you than this. Maybe not. Maybe you're just as crazy and thoughtless and oblivious to other people as you seem to be. But maybe you're putting on this ditzy, poor-little-me act because you're afraid of who you'll be if you really let your aggression flow. That would be my advice to you, if I were a shrink. Let your damned aggression out. The way you're acting now, you're trying to be this little Yiddishe Pollyanna, but your hatred of that role is leaking out of every pore. So let your real aggression out and see what happens. Things might get interesting if you do. And while you're at it, you might find a real name. *Dolly?* Really? Is that the name you were born with?"

"I was born Dora. Everybody's always called me Dolly."

"Well, for Christ's sake, use Dora, or find another name that befits a grown woman. Dolly might have fit when you were five, but isn't it time to get a name that isn't so confining?"

They were at a traffic light. It turned green, but Dolly didn't take her foot off the brake. She just sat there, gripping the wheel, looking stunned. Stunned, but, it turned out, not offended.

"I really, really, really want to thank you. I think you're right. No one's ever talked to me like that before. No one's ever taken me this seriously before. It just goes to show what makes you *you.*"

Now there was a car behind them, and the driver leaned hard on the horn, and Dolly quickly put her foot on the gas, lurching through the intersection just after the light had turned red again.

"It's just so great that you're willing to talk like this to me," Dolly said. "I feel so honored that you've taken an interest in me."

"I haven't taken an interest in you. You said some things and I told you what I thought. I probably won't ever think about you again after you drop me off."

"You're brutal," Dolly said. "But I appreciate it."

They were in the half-circle driveway in front of the hotel.

"I can't tell you how much this has meant to me," Dolly said.

The simpering nature of her thanks was exhausting, but on the other hand, there was something touching about how bulletproof she was.

"Thank you," Florence said. "You've got a lot going for you. Don't sell yourself short."

She pulled on the door handle but nothing happened. She looked for the little knob on the windowsill that would unlock the door, but there was no little knob there. Little knobs on car windowsills had disappeared at some point, when Florence hadn't noticed.

"I really can't . . . I really can't express how great this conversation was," Dolly said. "I'm going to blog about it."

"Great."

"I really am. I'm not just going to tweet about it. I'm really going to go into it in depth."

"That's great. Could you . . . ?"

"Oh. I'm sorry. Sure."

She said this, but she didn't release the door lock. She just sat there basking in Florence's nearness.

"I just want to hug you," Dolly said. "Is that all right?"

Without waiting for an answer, she closed her eyes, and her face came forward, looking curiously disembodied in the darkness.

"That'll do," Florence said, and she twisted in her seat, trying to find the elusive button that controlled the lock. As Dolly's head floated toward her, Florence finally found the thing, unforgivably concealed beneath the armrest. She pushed the button, pulled the door handle, and jerked away from Dolly's attempted embrace.

"Okay," Florence said. "That'll be all. Thank you for the invitation. And if your biographers do rescue me from oblivion someday, I thank you for that too."

"Oh—I—" Dolly said.

"Good luck," Florence said. "Take care."

She was trying to move as quickly as she could, but somewhere between the car and the curb she lost her footing, and she landed on the sidewalk in a tangle much more complicated than she could have achieved if she'd been trying.

The pain was intense.

Dolly had sprung out of the car.

"Oh, my God, Florence. Wow. You have to take more care. That looks bad. Ouch."

She put out her hand but Florence ignored it. The pain was too intense for her to try to stand.

"Do you want me to take you to the emergency room?" Dolly said.

"Thank you, Dolly, but I'm fine."

"You're not fine. Look at you. I think you might have broken your leg."

"I just twisted my ankle. I'm fine. I assure you. I've had experiences much more painful than this. Childbirth, for example."

"Your children came out of your ankle?" Dolly said, a joke that made her strut back and forth for a moment.

"I'm fine," Florence said, lifting herself up, again declining Dolly's hand. "It's nothing."

The truth was that it wasn't nothing. The lobby was only about thirty feet away, but it felt much farther. Dolly accompanied her, perpetually asking her if she was all right, while Florence tried not to show how devilishly bad her ankle felt.

It might actually make sense, Florence thought, to get medical attention, but she had to get out of the clutches of her admirer. When she reached the elevators, she shook Dolly's hand — keeping her arm out stiffly — and said goodbye.

She'd been looking forward to the train ride back to New York as an opportunity to luxuriate in a book without distraction, but instead she spent those three hours in a sort of symphony of pain.

When she got back to the city, instead of going home, she went to a hospital, where they X-rayed her, wrapped her sprained ankle, and told her about a nearby place where she could buy a cane.

35

Daniel and Janine were walking up Broadway.

"You really know how to walk in the city," he said.

"Yes," she said. "I've mastered that art."

It *was* an art, and he'd been away from New York for so long that he'd forgotten how to practice it. When he wasn't getting in people's way, they were getting in his. During his time here so far, he'd managed to train himself out of stunned-tourist mode, where you stop to gawk at some startling urban apparition and people jostle you from behind, but he hadn't mastered the sudden webstop, where the person in front of you pauses without notice to check something on his iPhone.

"Do you think Emily's happy?" Janine said.

"She seems good to me."

"I keep thinking she should get out more. It would be nice if she met a nice boy."

"It's got to be hard to get over Broccoli Boy," Daniel said.

"Don't be mean," Janine said, but she was smiling.

Broccoli Boy was Emily's high school boyfriend, who'd been very nice, but droopy, and somehow moist. They'd given him the name after he came over for dinner one night—he had strong views about broccoli—but they'd never called him that in front of Emily.

Janine was going to the lab, and he was meeting an old . . . it was hard to know what to call her, really.

Caroline was standing in front of Columbia University's entrance gate at Broadway and 116th. She kissed Janine and then she kissed Daniel.

"Jesus," Janine said. "You got gorgeous. Isn't she gorgeous, Daniel?"

"Yup. She's gorgeous."

Caroline twirled in a circle, happy to display her gorgeousness.

He'd taken responsibility for her ten or twelve years ago, after her parents were killed in a street-corner mugging. It wasn't technically in his bailiwick, but he'd made her his concern. She had no other family, and he did his best to see her placed in a decent foster home, breathing down the social workers' necks to make sure she didn't get lost in the bureaucracy, and then he checked in on her from time to time, encouraging her to go to community college, to look into scholarships at four-year colleges after she did well there, and finally to go to New York, where she'd always dreamed of living.

"You're gorgeous too," she said to Janine. "Not you, old-timer. You're in decline."

Caroline had become a woman. Tall, glowing with health, with wild blond hair and eyes that were gray and green and yellow and somehow both friendly and ferocious.

"Make him take you someplace nice," Janine said. "Don't let him take you to Dunkin' Donuts." She turned and headed downtown.

Caroline took Daniel's arm.

"I do look pretty, don't I?" she said.

He took her to lunch and she told him the story of her life since he'd seen her last. She'd been trying out for parts. She was going to sneak up on Hollywood by way of Broadway—that seemed to be the plan. In the meantime she was doing commercials to pay the rent. She'd been in three so far: Stouffer's single-serve microwave dinners, Bose headphones, and Glade air freshener.

"You didn't see that one? I was taking a shower in an elevator."

"I've never seen anybody do that."

"You should see me do that."

"I'll look out for it," he said. "And what do you do when you get home? Do you cook?"

Daniel believed that people who cooked for themselves were stable. If she cooked, he could feel assured that she was taking care of herself nicely.

"Why would I cook?" she said. "I have a phone."

He asked her where she was living, who she was living with, what her friends were like, what she did in her free time.

"Do you carry all this in your head?" she said. "It's like you have a checklist."

But he could tell that she was happy he was asking all these questions and happy to be able to give him reassuring answers.

She told him about some of her auditions. So-and-so had thought she was great but not quite right for the part; so-and-so couldn't offer her anything right now, but she was sure he fell a little bit in love with her during the audition. Daniel found all of it interesting, but sometimes he wished people wouldn't go into so much detail.

"I really think I could be a star if I get a chance. I think I have greatness in me."

He looked at her to see if she was joking, but it didn't appear that she was.

"What does that mean?"

"What does what mean?"

"To be a star. What does it *mean*?"

"What are you, a Martian? You know what it means."

"What does it mean to *you*."

"Do you ever watch *In Treatment*? You'd make a really good shrink."

"That's Janine. So what does it mean?"

"It means you can choose your parts. You can have your pick. It means you don't have to worry about money. It means that you get to wear pretty dresses and go to premieres and walk down the red carpet. It's the closest you can come in this life to growing up and becoming a princess. That's what it means."

When he and Janine took the kids to Disneyland for the first time, Emily, who was five or six, after seeing Cinderella and Snow White, had turned to Janine and said, "So they *are* real!"

He remembered this and wished he were back at the apartment. He was glad to be seeing Caroline, but the only thing he wanted at this point in life was to be with his family.

"Anyway, you already know what it means," Caroline said. "Why are you asking me?"

"I don't know. I just . . . it's something I don't really understand."

The question of stardom. It had been eating at him for the past few weeks, ever since his mother told them about the review. Everyone was responding as if it were such big news. Janine was acting as if she were no longer worthy to spend time in the same room with her. Saul was acting as if it had somehow put an end to all his hopes. Florence was acting as if she'd been crowned. But what *was* it, really? It was a book review. It was a good review, but no better than a lot of reviews Florence had received in the past. The main thing that was special about it wasn't the what but the where. The main thing that was special about it was that it was on the cover of the *Times Book Review*.

But, really, why was *that* a big deal? It wasn't the *New York Times* that thought Florence was hot stuff; it was just one lady who'd happened to get the assignment. If she'd been busy that week and they'd given the book to somebody else, they would have gotten a different result. And yet everyone was acting as though the spirit of literary authority had descended from the heavens and wrapped around Florence's shoulders the mantle of never-dying greatness.

Yes, he had a fancy internal monologue for a policeman, but look at how he'd grown up.

He felt as if he lacked some gene or some organ of sense perception. He'd seen an article a while ago about sounds that adults can't hear; maybe there were concepts that a few of us can't understand, and being a star was one of them. What *was* it? Those who wanted to be stars seemed to believe that if enough people knew who you are, then you . . . what? Wouldn't be unhappy? Wouldn't die?

"Maybe it's just New York," he said. "Emily needed to find a dentist last month. One kid she knew from college gave her a rec-ommendation, and he told her, 'He's a good dentist. He isn't a star, but he's a good dentist.' Can you imagine? Is there anyplace else on earth where somebody'd apologize for sending you to a dentist who wasn't a star?"

"I'd never go to a dentist who wasn't a star," Caroline said.

Maybe the yearning for stardom wasn't like a sound he couldn't hear but a disease he was immune to. *I have greatness in me.* Jesus.

If it was a disease, there was no mystery about why he was im-mune to it. Both of his parents had spent their lives in its grip, and he'd witnessed its stupidity. He'd lived the effects of it. He was one of its effects.

"What if it doesn't work out?" he said. "What's your backup plan?"

"That's what I love about you, Daniel."

"What's that?"

"You're never afraid to be blunt."

"So what's your backup plan?"

"My backup plan is not to have a backup plan. If you're making plans about what to do if you fail, aren't you just planning to fail?"

"That's one way of looking at it."

"Do you think I'm being childish?"

Yes, he thought. But then again, what do I know? So he took the optimistic view.

"I think you're being brave. You know what you want and you're going after it. I think you're doing exactly what you should be do-ing. Put that away."

"Come on. You're my guest."

"You're a budding artist. I'm a member of the bourgeoisie. My only value in life is to buy lunch for the young."

He told himself that he shouldn't worry for her too much. She was smart and resourceful. And she was beautiful, which wouldn't hurt. Maybe she'd become what she wanted to become. It some-times happens, he supposed.

36

To get to her office, on the fifth floor of the lab, you took an elevator that had mirrored walls. As it rose slowly, Janine studied herself.
She looked critically at her—

Who the hell cares what I look like? I look good enough.

Lev had been away for the last week, doing one of his rounds of
cross-country fund-raising and conference-going. He was supposed
to be returning today, but he wasn't in the office when she got there.

Even when he wasn't there, it felt as if he were. She'd never known
a workplace that was as friendly as this one was, and she was sure it
was because of his influence.

She spent the morning talking to college students, most of whom
had been on Ritalin so long that she wondered whether it had subtly addled them, and then she reread an article she was writing. Actually, she was helping two other people write it. It was about the
brain chemistry of willpower; they knew the science and she knew
how to render it in clear language.

In the late afternoon she drifted out to the living room.

When the townhouse was converted into an academic building,

Lev had retained the living room, wanting to provide a comfortable space where people could talk at their leisure.

From where she sat, she could see him in the kitchen. He was back. She felt suddenly happier and more alert.

He was standing at the coffee machine. Hot water was dribbling out of the side of it, bypassing the carafe and pooling on the counter.

"This damned Mr. Coffee. When we had the old thing . . ."

She resisted the urge to do the traditional womanly thing and get it working for him.

"Good luck," she said, and went back to her office.

Lev's smell was a little bit mothball-y. She liked Daniel's smell, but it had never felt like home to her. This used to make her sad when they were younger. When she was first becoming troubled by her feelings for Lev, she was relieved to note that he didn't smell like home to her either.

When she was done for the day she went back to the kitchen, made herself a cup of coffee, and visited him in his office.

His office was always in a state of cheerful disorder. Papers piled up in his inbox and next to his inbox; books sitting on top of books—on the filing cabinet, on the desk, on the floor. It was as if they were spawning.

"How did you get it to work?"

"As well as being a top-flight psychologist," Janine said, "she makes a fine cup of coffee."

"Right," he said. "Oh, well. Listen—I read the last draft of your article. You're doing a marvelous job."

They talked about the marvelous job she was doing, and his comments made it clear to her that she had another few drafts to go. His criticisms were extensive and specific, but somehow none of them stung.

"And what about Pittsburgh?" he said. "Are you going to have time?"

"I think I am, but I'm still not sure. I might have some things I can't get out of that weekend."

"You've been saying that for the last two months, but never mind. Just let me know by Wednesday, okay?"

The lab was empty except for the two of them.

The peculiar intimacy of the workplace after everyone else is gone. His office door was open; his wide desk was between them; there was nothing untoward about the situation or the setting; but being here with him at five on a Friday evening was somehow more intimate than it would have been to be with him in the darkest bar.

"I have half an hour," she said. "What shall we discuss?"

"What shall we discuss. Let's see. Well, you can tell me how you got into this."

"Into . . . ?"

"How did you become a psychologist? We've been doing nothing but gabbing for months, but you've never really told me how you got started."

"How did I get into this. I got into this because I just love listening to people. I love listening to people tell their stories. I mean, I could tell you about my mother this and my father that, and my self-esteem, and my probably culturally conditioned desire to help people, but really that's pretty much it. I'm never that sure if I *am* helping anybody, though. Sometimes I feel like all I can do is accompany people through life's disasters."

"Maybe that's all anybody can do."

She knew he didn't mean this, since his whole approach was practical and quantitative, searching for measurable results to measurable problems. He was just being kind.

"What about you?" she said. "Why did you get into this?"

"Self-interest," Lev said. "I don't think I was in love with the idea of listening to people or helping people. Not like you. I think I got into it because I wanted to figure myself out."

"And how'd that go?"

She tried to make this sound hipsterishly arch and mocking, but she wanted to know.

"You know what Mao said when they asked him to sum up the consequences of the French Revolution? 'It's too soon to tell.'"

"No. Really."

"It helped. Thirty years thinking about how the brain works, how the mind works—it's taught me I'm not nearly as different from everyone else as I thought I was. And that's what I needed to learn. It gave me 'permission,' as they say, to accept myself. I think that was what I was after, even if I didn't know it at the time."

He absentmindedly brought his coffee cup to his lips, looked at it, put it down.

"Do you think less of me?" he said.

"Why should I think less of you?"

"Because I didn't go into it for noble reasons. Because I didn't go into it to help others."

"I do think less of you."

"That's too bad."

"It had to happen eventually," she said. "I couldn't go on idealizing you forever."

"And yet you're still here," he said.

"And yet I'm still here."

They were silent. They looked at each other until she had to look away.

If I were sitting on a park bench with him, she thought, we'd probably start to kiss now.

But there was a desk between them, and although it was starting to feel like a kissing situation, it wasn't a slithering-over-the-desk situation.

She stood and said goodnight.

His coffee cup was standing empty on his desktop. She picked up her cup, held it above his, and, slowly, poured.

Then she turned and left, without looking back.

37

Florence got to the coffee shop a few minutes early, but Saul was already there. He didn't comment on the fact that she was using a cane. When she sat down, he looked at his watch and shook his head, as if she were late.

It was the first of two meetings that she would have preferred to avoid. Saul had been bugging her about getting together, so she'd scheduled lunch with him on a day when she already had a doctor's appointment, in order to get both of them over with at once.

Saul looked unhealthy—but he always looked unhealthy these days. He was wearing a white shirt and a dark sport jacket—everything was clean and respectable—yet somehow he had the air of a man who was going to seed. He was the kind of person who doesn't smell bad, as far as you can tell, but who looks like he smells bad.

What *was* it? She could never quite put her finger on it. There was something shifty and evasive about him; he seemed like a man who was spending his discretionary income on some surly domina-trix in Brooklyn.

"Well, well, well," he said. "Hail the conquering hero."

It begins, she thought.

"If you were fifty years younger I would have wondered if you'd given somebody a blowjob for that review. But who would want a blowjob from you now?"

"Maybe I gave a blowjob to someone very old."

"*A Blowjob for Methuselah.* That should be the title of your next book. So is your life any different, now that you're the queen of bourgeois mediocrity?"

"Is that what I am?"

"Of course it is. When you were a young firebrand, or whatever the hell you were, you never would have gotten a review like that. They only give reviews like that to people the establishment considers totally safe. Life is pretty good for you now that you stopped being a radical."

"You obviously don't read my stuff anymore, if you ever did," she said. "Every word I've ever written has been in the service of human liberation, as best as I can imagine it. Every word I've ever written has been in the service of feminism, of antiracism, of anticapitalism, of a vision of a world in which people are both equal and free. Nothing I've written has ever deviated from that, Saul. Not one line."

In her own ears, this sounded stirring. She felt as if she were outside herself, near the ceiling, watching herself with admiration as she delivered this statement of her beliefs.

Saul scrunched up his face and in a high, mincing, baby-talking voice, said, "Every word I've ever written has been in the service of the cervix."

A waitress turned up, poker-faced about whether she'd heard this, and they ordered, and the waitress went away.

"Florence Gordon!" he said. "Everywhere I turn, it's Florence! Florence! Florence! People who haven't mentioned your name in years: 'Have you heard from Florence?' 'Aren't you happy for Florence?' 'Florence must not even have any time to talk to you.' All these people who're acting like you've accomplished something. Just because some lesbian took her clothes off for you in the *New York Times.*"

"I don't think she's a lesbian, Saul. Not that it matters. And I don't remember the thing about the clothes."

"The *New York Fucking Times*. These are the bozos who told us that Iraq had weapons of mass destruction. These are the pussies who stopped using the word 'torture' and started talking about 'enhanced interrogation' because they didn't want to say anything that would get Dick Fucking Cheney mad at them."

She had known that Saul would try to make her pay for her good fortune.

If a similar review had come Saul's way, he'd be crowing now about the greatness of the *Times;* he'd be saying that it was the one newspaper that even the most radical and daring thinkers had always had to take seriously.

She had known that Saul was going to try to make her pay, and she had known that she was going to take it. Not because she feared him, but because she pitied him. Saul had been growing sadder and more bitter and more desperate for the last twenty years, and on the infrequent occasions when they got together, he invariably started by attacking her, and she never had the heart to fight back.

After the coffee arrived he took out a vial and shook some pills onto the table. Pills of many different colors and sizes and shapes.

"I have to take fifteen of these goddamn things a day. Five in the morning, five in the . . . shit."

One of the pills had rolled off the table. He bent over in his chair and picked it up and wiped it with his napkin.

When you and your ex-husband are in your seventies, the advantage normally goes to the man. The man will look maybe not as good as he thinks he looks, but better than you do.

But with Florence and Saul, fortunately, the facts were otherwise. Bald except for shaggy remnants on the sides of his head, alarmingly red-faced, not fat but puffy and paunchy, Saul was a ruin.

She herself wasn't exactly turning heads, but she was presentable.

"How are things going?" she said. She sensed that the force of his anger was spent, and that they could move on to other things.

"Great. Things are going great. I'm finishing up two books, if you can believe it, and a couple of publishers are very interested."

"That's wonderful, Saul."

Small talk for a while, and then: "The reason I asked you to lunch, actually, is that I thought we could do each other a mutual favor. I heard about the job in the Cultural Criticism Department—the lectureship thing. I was thinking you could recommend me. It would be good for you, and it would be good for me."

It would be good for her, in Saul's reckoning, because his greatness would add luster to NYU. In this, as in many things, he was delusional. Most of the people who'd heard of him were dead.

It was remarkable, though, that he was presenting this as an occasion when they could do each other a favor. His normal way of talking about something like this would be to represent it purely as a favor that he wanted to do for you. His normal way of approaching this would be to say that it would be a painful bore for him to have a lectureship, but he'd be willing to take one, to help you out.

"Well, I'll have to look into it, Saul."

"Of course you'll have to look into it. I know you can't just slap a contract down on the table. But I'm a great teacher. I'd be perfect for this job. I wouldn't be bringing it up if I wasn't."

"I know that. But these aren't decisions I can make on my own. I can only make recommendations."

"Right. Of course. Like you recommended Tanya."

That had been a misstep on Florence's part. She'd gotten her friend Tanya a job at NYU a year earlier, pretty much steered her into it. Getting her the job hadn't been the mistake; the mistake had been telling Saul about it.

"You've been a fucking bureaucrat for so long that you don't even realize when you're lying anymore."

Control yourself, she thought.

Saul was one of the few people in the world on whom she didn't feel free to unleash her aggression. She felt permanently guilty toward Saul. Not because she'd divorced him, but because she'd married him in the first place.

When she was young, she'd had a future in mind for herself, a future as a scholar and writer. She hadn't yet conceived of herself as a feminist—this was the early 1960s, and she found her way to feminism only toward the end of the decade. But she'd already known that she didn't want to be a housewife. And sometimes she thought that she'd married Saul with a touch of bad faith.

It was hard to remember it now, but at the time Saul had seemed like a winner: ruddy, hardy, healthy, and alive. He'd seemed like someone you could make good children with. And he'd also seemed like someone who wouldn't detain her. It was as if she'd sensed from the beginning that the ties that bound them wouldn't be that confining. He seemed easy to marry and easy to leave.

He'd had affairs all through their courtship, and she knew that he'd continue to have affairs after they were married. In a display of frankness that in retrospect she sometimes counted as her first act of feminist self-assertion, she told him that she didn't give a damn about what he did in his free time as long as he didn't embarrass her and as long as the children didn't find out. (At first she'd planned on having more than one.)

That seemed like an unbelievably good deal to him.

What it came down to was that she'd wanted children, but she'd never really wanted to be a wife. And despite all his foolishness and running around, despite all the behavior that led everyone who knew them to consider her the injured party, she now believed that, in some not quite conscious way, she had used him all along.

She had divorced him in the mid-seventies, when Daniel was still a boy. It had seemed like a good time to leave him. Saul was thriving: he had a comfortable job at Adelphi University; he was writing regularly for *The Nation* and *Dissent* and the *New Leader* and the *New American Review*. And when she left him, he didn't seem to mind. Still an incorrigible philanderer, he'd been seeing someone, an editor named Camille, for more than a year.

But then Camille was diagnosed with pancreatic cancer and died with an astonishing quickness, and a few years later he lost his job at Adelphi because of a mess of his own making. (He had fallen in love with a student, who reciprocated his interest for a while and then drew back, and after she drew back he went a little nuts. Florence had viewed it with a kind of detached sympathy: true, he'd made a fool of himself, but he'd been crazy about the girl. And probably there was an element of delayed reaction to Camille's death.)

After that, it had been thirty years, no comebacks. He'd never gotten a comparable job—instead he taught for a year here, a semester there, and worked horribly long hours as a freelance copy editor. He'd moved to increasingly shabby neighborhoods as his income declined, finally moving all the way to Brooklyn, which was the ultimate insult to his ego. (For an intellectual of his generation, the great heroic journey was the journey out of Brooklyn into Manhattan; it was devastating to have to make the journey in reverse.) And although he claimed to be writing, and was forever telling her about publishing companies that were panting to see his work, he hadn't published anything in almost twenty years.

Even his name, his first name, was a burden. When he was a young man, he was proud to be named Saul: his name had been an inducement to greatness, because he had no doubt that he'd unseat Saul Bellow as the premier Jewish writer of the age. It hadn't quite happened that way, and now his name seemed to mock him. It was like being a mediocre ballplayer who happened to be named Michael Jordan.

Florence had been looking forward to a Saul-free middle age, but she found out that things don't work that way. When everything in his life fell apart, she felt she had to prop him up. She didn't respect him, didn't trust him, didn't even like him, but she was going to have to look out for him, as best she could, probably for the rest of her life.

"So how come you never showed up for the big family dinner that night?" she said.

"I had a cold."

"You couldn't call?"

"I thought I left you a message. How's Dan?"

"Daniel's good. They're all good. They're thinking about moving here, you know."

"Yes, I know. That would be heartwarming. I've always wanted to get to know my son better."

That was a joke. Saul seemed to have no interest in his son.

They chatted for another twenty minutes, but Saul seemed restless. He'd wanted to see her so he could ask her for the favor, and now that that was done he wanted to leave.

"Well, I'm going home to take a nap. I was thinking I'd give myself a treat tonight and jerk off, and I gotta rest up for it."

"Thanks for letting me know that, Saul."

"I'm not saying it's a sure thing. It's more a hope than a plan. You reach a certain age, you've got to pop a couple of Viagra even if all you want to do is jack off."

"That's also good to know."

He talked too much about his sex life, when he was having one, and his lack of one, when he wasn't.

A year ago, Saul had been seeing someone, and he was always laying down heavy hints about the alleged excellence of his sex life. Florence didn't believe him—when someone keeps telling you how good his sex life is, you can be sure that it isn't—but even if it was as dandy as he claimed, it didn't matter to her. There was no residual hurt here, and no jealousy, and no wish to have a physical life comparable to that which he claimed to be having.

Florence still experienced sexual desire, of course, but it had been a long time since she'd actually wanted to have sex. Sex was too messy, too unsettling, too inarticulate, too revealing, too disappointing. She didn't miss those faintly comic exertions. The thought of paunchy, boiled-faced Saul having sex—she couldn't imagine it as anything but comic.

He took a long drink of water, and then he had a coughing fit, which went on for so long that it worried her. When it was done, it seemed to have aged him. As she looked across the table at him, with his forever-affronted face, the face of a man who believed that life had played a trick on him, she had an image of his heart giving out while he was laboring atop some doughy sex worker, and she imagined the sex worker taking the bills from his wallet, slipping out of the hotel room (why was this fantasy taking place in a hotel room?), and leaving poor Saul there all alone.

She had the silly notion that she could see his fate. Someday Saul's corpse would lie abandoned in a cheap hotel. She could see it clearly. And despite everything, for a moment she felt an infinite tenderness toward him, and toward the sad failed project of his life.

38

Florence's doctor pressed a button on the sanitizer, spritzed some into his palm, and rubbed his hands together, gazing reverently at her all the while, as if he were in the presence of greatness.

She had called him to tell him about her sprained ankle, and during the course of the conversation she'd worked her way around to the things she really wanted to talk about — her frantic fingers and her flappy foot, which were starting to worry her a little — and he'd asked her to come in so he could have a look.

"Florence Gordon," he said. "My hero. My heroine."

"You always seem amused when you see me, Noah. Do all your patients amuse you?"

"My patients don't amuse me. You don't amuse me. What you're mistaking for a smile of amusement is a smile of admiration."

"And do you admire all your patients? Why do you admire me?"

"I admire your accomplishments."

"About which you know nothing. Have you read even one of my books? Even one essay?"

"I *have* read your work. I read that article of yours. The one we talked about. I liked it very much."

"That article. You read that article fifteen years ago."

"No. Has it been that long?"

While they were talking he was listening to her body with his stethoscope, testing her reflexes, pressing on her lymph nodes. He had a knack of making you feel as if you were spending twenty minutes doing nothing but joking with him, even while he was examining you scrupulously.

He obviously hadn't seen the review; if he had, he would have been talking about it.

The world, for her, was now divided into two groups: people who'd read the review and people who hadn't. She trusted that this state was temporary.

"But your accomplishments aren't the only thing about you that I admire," he said.

"What else?"

"I treat a lot of writers. You know that, right?"

"I didn't, really. I knew you treated some."

"A lot. A lot of very good, very established writers. And they're all very different, of course — they're all rugged individualists — but there's one thing they have in common. Every writer I've ever had as a patient, every one, has been a hypochondriac. Except you."

"I was going to say —"

"You're the only one. You're not cavalier about your health; when something is bothering you, you come in and see me. As you should. But you're not a hypochondriac. And I find that remarkable."

He was shining a light into her eyes as he spoke.

"And that's why, when you come to me with a concern, I know it's real. I know enough to take it seriously. You're not the Boy Who Cried Wolf."

"I think you mean Chicken Little."

"I mean the Boy Who Cried Wolf. But if you want me to say Chicken Little, I'll say Chicken Little. You're not Chicken Little either. You know what I'm trying to say. You're not somebody who comes in to see the doctor for no reason."

She mentioned her ankle again, as if it were the reason for her visit, and he said her ankle was healing perfectly. He said it almost dismissively, as if a mere sprained ankle wasn't distinguished enough for either of them to be concerned with.

He asked her for fuller descriptions of the other things she'd been experiencing. He made her walk in a straight line; he made her follow the beam of his flashlight with her eyes as he moved it back and forth a few inches from her face. Then he took a look at both hands and both feet, testing their range of motion very gently—her left ankle was the one she'd sprained, and he somehow manipulated her left foot without bringing any more pain to the ankle.

He took his stethoscope off. He always turned it into a dramatic act.

"Okay. Suit up and meet me in my office."

That was part of the ritual of seeing Noah. After he examined you, he asked you to put your street clothes back on and join him in his office, and you talked like two real people, not like a doctor and a poor, defenseless patient in a paper gown.

When she got to his office he was furiously emailing away, but he closed the lid of his computer when she sat down.

"These little complaints you have. They're interesting."

"I'm glad to be able to interest you, Noah. It's been a dream of mine."

"No, they are. When my star Stoic comes in to tell me she feels a little weird, it gets my attention." His phone started vibrating and he slapped it and it quieted down.

"Now, there are about a thousand things that this might be, and the huge majority are nothing. So the first piece of medical advice I have for you is this: don't go on the Internet. If you go on the Internet, you can make yourself crazy. You're free to spend your time that way, if that's your thing, but I have a feeling you have better ways to spend your time. All the bad things that it might be are very exotic and very unlikely. You may have heard this before, but if a good doctor hears hoofbeats, he thinks it's probably a horse. He doesn't think it's probably a zebra. We're going to have you do some tests—some blood tests, an MRI, maybe an EMG, maybe a nerve conduction test—and we're going to have you see a very good neurologist, and we'll find out what kind of a horse it is. Okay?"

He picked up his stethoscope and put it back around his neck and came out from behind his desk. He was ready for his next appointment.

"And listen," he said. "You live, what, ten blocks away? You shouldn't be a stranger."

He patted her on the knee.

"That's a reassuring nonsexual pat, by the way. Don't sue me."

"I won't sue you, Noah. My family'll sue you, though, if this turns out to be a zebra and you keep looking for horses and fuck this up."

"Well, let's not get ahead of ourselves. I haven't fucked anything up yet."

"That's what I like to hear from a doctor," Florence said.

39

During the two months that Emily had spent alone with her mother in New York, they'd seen Florence twice, at her birthday party and after the Town Hall event. Now that Daniel had joined them, they were seeing her almost every week.

Emily had the impression that Florence didn't enjoy these visits, but there was something about Daniel's commitment to family life that made it impossible to say no to him, even for Florence Gordon, the master of the art of saying no.

Whenever they got together, of course, Florence held center stage. Tonight, in the living room at West Ninety-fourth Street, she was complaining a lot—about her students, who, even in the summer, wouldn't let her alone; about her sprained ankle, which still hurt, and still left her dependent on her cane; about her success, which was preventing her from concentrating on her work.

"For the first time in my life, I can't take care of everything I need to take care of. I'm behind on my emails, my apartment is a mess, I have books overdue at the library. I have research I need to do but it's a hassle to get down there to do it. I need a wife."

"You don't need a wife," Emily said. "You just need a trusty assistant."

"Are you nominating yourself?" Janine said.

Emily expected Florence to quash the idea, but Florence didn't say anything.

Emily had time on her hands—she was taking a literature class at Barnard two evenings a week, but other than that she was free. And it would be nice to earn some money.

"I guess I am," she said.

Florence had been looking nowhere in particular; now she looked at Emily. The look lasted only an instant, but Emily felt as if she'd been scanned, searched, and sorted. She was sure that neither of her parents had registered anything at all, but Emily felt . . . it was absurd to think anything like this, but it was as if she'd been treated roughly.

"Excuse me a minute," she said, and left the room.

40

Florence's first thought: Thank God it was Emily who'd volunteered and not Janine. It would be just like Janine to thrust herself forward at a moment like that ("I have free time! I can help you!"), which would have meant that Florence would have had to say no, which would have been awkward all around.

Her next thought: Is there any way Emily might end up being a Trojan Horse for Janine? Not that Emily was intending anything like that, obviously. But if I let open the door to Emily, will her mother barge through?

Her next thought: Is Emily intelligent enough?

She took a look at the girl. She wasn't sure she'd ever looked at her closely before.

Over the years, Florence had had many assistants, and the main thing she'd learned was that people were stunningly inept. It wasn't just that they didn't know how to research anything competently; they couldn't even use a Xerox machine. It was amazing how few of them would fail to fuck up even that. They'd copy the pages out of order; they'd press the book down so weakly against the screen that the images ended up blurry and smudged; if they were students of hers at NYU, they'd be too lazy to go to the Duplicating Office to use the machines that were kept in good repair, instead using the crappy old machines in the library. Often enough Florence stopped asking her assistants to do anything more challenging than pick up her mail at the faculty mailbox. So she wasn't sure she could trust Emily to do the work. She seemed smart enough, but you could never be sure. If Emily fucked it up it would be painful. It would be painful to have to fire her, but damned if Florence was going to keep her on the payroll for the rest of the summer just to be nice.

Emily was leaving the room. Where the hell was she going?

When she came back, she was holding an iPhone or Black-Berry or some kind of smartphone—what a stupid term, Florence thought—and peering down at it. Infuriating.

"I can give you a week of work," Florence said. "After that, we'll see."

We'll see whether you're an idiot, she thought. If you're not, I'll keep you on. A week should be enough time to find out.

"Cool," Emily said, <u>making an effort to sound as unenthusiastic as possible</u>. "When do I start?"

She said this without looking up from her Android. There was nothing she needed it for; she just wanted to annoy the old battle-ax.

Idly she went to Google and typed into the search bar: *What have I gotten myself into?*

Emily spent the next few afternoons in the Tamiment Library's feminism and women's history collection, on the second floor of NYU's Bobst Library on Washington Square. A trove of material from the dawn of the contemporary women's movement was housed there, including documents and recordings that couldn't be found online. The idea that there *were* documents and recordings that couldn't be found online had never really occurred to her before.

Emily's first task was to read through a collection of periodicals and pamphlets from the late sixties and early seventies—*Redstockings*, *Off Our Backs*, the *Female State*—looking for references to a few key women and a few key events. Her second was to dive into the oral history collection, which included dozens of interviews with women activists. Some of them had been transcribed, but most of them were still available only on tape.

Emily liked going to Bobst. It was vast and quiet and humming with the thoughts of everyone who was studying there; and it had every book you could imagine wanting. She liked getting comfortable with obscure tools of research. Cassette tapes! Microfilm! She felt like a votary of ancient knowledge. She felt as if the experience were preparing her for going back to college, not that she'd be having any contact with microfilm and cassette tapes when she did.

She took more time in the archives than she needed to, because, in addition to doing the research Florence had asked her to do, she couldn't stop herself from doing research on Florence. If, next to an article that Florence had asked her to summarize, she found an article by Florence herself, she always took the time to read it. These were things that she was pretty sure had never been collected in Florence's books. Many of the articles were more personal than she would have expected. Sometimes she felt almost as if she were leafing through her grandmother's old diaries.

After she finished working for Florence, she would spend an hour just haunting the stacks and reading things at random. Then she'd take out a marbled composition book she carried with her everywhere, and spend some time writing her . . . whatever it was she wrote. Stories, or sketches, or snippets—she never knew what to call them. She liked to write in one of the glass-walled reading rooms over the square, from which you had a beautiful view of Manhattan, a city whose grandeur she was finally beginning to feel. She was coming to understand why her mother had been such a Manhattan-worshipper all her life.

At the end of the week, she went to Florence's and handed her a folder of material. Florence opened it and started looking through the notes and photocopies Emily had made.

"I was surprised about some of the positions you were taking back then," Emily said.

"What positions?" Florence said, not bothering to look up.

"If I understand what . . . during Vietnam, you were saying that protesting the war and stuff wasn't as important as fighting for gender equality."

"I never had any problem with protesting the war. And stuff." Florence was already leading her to the door. "I'm not sure if there's anything else I need from you. I'll call you."

Florence didn't say anything like "Nice job"—probably, Emily thought, because she considered herself too intellectually rigorous to say such a thing before she'd had a chance to go through Emily's notes and ascertain whether she actually had done a nice job. You couldn't expect Florence to engage in meaningless pleasantries.

You might, though, have expected her to say thank you, but she didn't do that either.

Fuck you too, Emily thought as she went to the elevator. Pardon me for being interested.

43

Emily got a call from Florence later that day. Florence wanted her to do more work. Evidently she had passed the test.

The more time Emily spent doing research for Florence, the more complicated her idea of Florence became.

It's just as difficult to imagine an old person's past as it is to imagine a young person's future. *True?* If you had asked Emily to imagine what Florence had been like in her twenties, she would have guessed that Florence had always been more or less the person she was now: a creature of rectitude and morality and sanity, though one who liked to demonstrate the virtues of sanity in attention-grabbing ways. The Florence of today was militantly sober. But it turned out that in her younger days, Florence had been a hothead. Among the articles Emily found were a silly thing about how wonderfully radical it is to stop wearing a bra (bralessness, Florence had believed, was a harbinger of the new, more liberated world to come), a diatribe against romantic relationships (it was so extreme that it made you think that maybe the author's true problem was that she couldn't get a date), and several semi-insane paeans to Cuba and Vietnam, each of which she'd visited in the early seventies, and each of which had struck her as a kind of a paradise (though not, curiously, a paradise in which she had any desire to live).

And the stuff about sex, drugs, and rock and roll! Some of it was enough to make you embarrassed on the writer's behalf; some of it was not so bad; but none of it reminded her of her grandmother at all. It made Emily wonder whether your identity has less to do with anything inside you than with the time in which you happen to be alive. The Florence of 1973 resembled other women of 1973 much more than she resembled the Florence of today.

All of this was stunning to Emily, because Florence, more than anyone else she'd ever known, had seemed to be a self-created being.

But maybe none of this was evidence that Florence was just a creature of her times. Maybe Florence *had* been a product of her times when she was young, but had gradually liberated herself from her influences. Maybe she'd only gradually come to be herself.

Emily would have liked to ask her about her transformation, but it was impossible to ask her about anything. You could ask, but you couldn't get an answer. One day Emily came across an essay about Doris Lessing's *The Golden Notebook* that Florence wrote in the late seventies. Florence made it sound like one of the greatest novels ever written. Emily promptly read it, and didn't find what Florence found. It struck her as one of those novels that hadn't outlived their moment. She told Florence that she'd read it and that she hadn't liked it that much.

"Read it again," Florence said. That was the end of the conversation.

44

She doesn't, Emily thought, understand how generous I'm being, in showing any interest at all in this stuff.

Emily wasn't particularly political, and she had no idea if she was a feminist. She knew she was a beneficiary of the women's movement—she'd read enough novels, she'd seen enough episodes of *Mad Men* to know what life before the women's movement was like—but at the same time, the word "feminism" didn't have great associations for her. The feminist girls she knew at Oberlin, her roommate among them, were the kind of people who made you feel bad for liking what you liked. Sometimes when Emily was tired or blue she liked to watch *When Harry Met Sally*, or *Love Actually*, or old episodes of *Friends*, and at Oberlin she'd had to wait until her roommate had gone out or fallen asleep.

45

"Are you discovering things about your grandmother?" Daniel said. "Getting to know her as only a granddaughter can?"

He had his ironic voice on, so that he seemed to be disavowing the question at the same time as he was asking it. But she knew him well enough to know that he was asking it.

"I'm discovering many things about her, Dad."

"Such as?"

"She's very clean. Which is something you like to see in an old person. We had a sandwich together and she snatched the plate out from under me before I was done."

"Maybe she just likes to take people's plates away. Anything else?"

"Have you been going through her medicine cabinet?" Janine said. "Snooping around?"

"Yeah, but there's nothing good there."

She had, in fact, gone through Florence's medicine cabinet. She was surprised by how little was there. From her babysitting days she had wide experience of the medicine cabinets of grown-ups, which were usually stocked with antidepressants, antianxiety drugs, and supplements that promised to keep you young. Florence took Lipitor, but nothing else: nothing to stave off sadness, nothing to stave off time.

"She's really getting to be the toast of the town," Daniel said.

"Yes. So she tells me."

"Did you get an invitation for that symposium thing?"

"I did."

The following month, NYU would be hosting a symposium on the women's movement, which was going to feature a tribute to Florence: Martha Nussbaum was going to talk about Florence's contribution to modern feminist thought.

"Did you see that thing of her on YouTube?" Daniel said. "That movie?"

"It's not a movie. And yes, I saw it."

Florence had sent—apparently to everyone she knew—a link to a YouTube video of a talk she gave at the "Modern Lives" series at the 92nd Street Y. First she talked about herself for almost an hour, and then, in the question-and-answer period, she talked about herself a little more. There was something off-putting about the way she talked about her life, her thoughts, her intellectual development. She sounded as if these were topics that every literate person should be familiar with, and she were merely presenting a little refresher course.

46

Emily would never criticize Florence in front of her father, but when she was alone with her mother, she felt free to gripe.

"She's just an old windbag," Emily said.

"Oh, come on. She may be an old windbag, but she's not *just* an old windbag. She's written a lot of good things."

"Also she's a hypocrite."

"How is she a hypocrite?"

"She's a feminist, but she took Grandpa's name."

"First of all, would it have been more feminist to keep her father's name? Second of all, everybody took their husband's name back then. Third of all, when you have a chance to trade in 'Silverblatt' for 'Gordon,' you make the trade first and worry about the politics later."

"And you know what I figured out about her?" Emily said. "You know what occurred to me? She's a *guy*."

"She's a guy?"

"When anybody talks with her, she's always got the conversational right-of-way. If she and somebody else start talking at the same time, Florence always keeps going. She expects *you* to stop. It's a total guy thing."

"Well, she's a grand old lady. She's earned the right to talk over people."

Emily didn't think it was a right you earn. She thought it was a habit you grow out of, and it was pathetic that Florence had never grown out of it. If Florence *had* been a guy, she would have been a guy who'd never outgrown the habit of leaving the toilet seat up after he peed.

47

The one enviable thing about Florence was that, as irritable as she was, she seemed, when all was said and done, to be enjoying her life.

"Was your mother always happier than your father?" Emily asked her father.

They were on Broadway. She was heading toward her class; he was meeting some old friend of his at . . . she actually didn't know where they were meeting.

"He used to seem pretty jolly when I was a kid," Daniel said.

"What happened?"

"Nothing happened."

"Something must have happened."

"I don't think it's a matter of anything that happened to either of them. It's a matter of who they are. My mother's always had a cause. She always had something to believe in. He only had himself."

"I don't really understand what that means."

"Yes you do."

"I don't! I'm not as wise as you think I am!"

"Saul just has his career. So when his career is going badly—like, for the past couple decades or so—as far as he's concerned, everything in the universe sucks. Florence has always thought of herself as participating in something that will outlast her."

"What?"

He knocked lightly on her head with his knuckles.

"Women's history. Feminism. Man-hating."

"Dad!"

"I'm joking."

"They say there's a grain of truth inside every joke," she said.

"How do they know that?"

"They take tiny little X-rays," she said. "So what about you? Do you have something larger than yourself? What do you believe in?"

"I don't know. Yoko and me."

She didn't get the reference, but it didn't matter. She had known as soon as she asked the question that he'd never give her a straight answer.

"And you?" he said. "What do you believe in?"

"I'll have to get back to you on that."

What she thought she believed in was something she'd been thinking about since she'd read *Middlemarch*: the idea that each person is the center of a world. She didn't know what to do with it; she didn't know where it led; but it kept coming back to her mind.

Emily

48

Emily had set a stack of books on Florence's kitchen table, and Florence was looking through them. Florence had asked Emily to find some good studies of politics in New York during the era when she, Florence, was growing up.

"Before my time," Florence said, pushing one of the books away. *A Hazard of New Fortunes*, William Dean Howells, 1890.

"Now I know what you think of me," Florence said. "You feel like you're doing research about the horse-and-buggy days."

"That's just something I'm reading," Emily said. "Not every thought I have is about you, believe it or not."

She felt bold as she said it—Florence's self-regard was so high that she might find the news a shock—but to her surprise, Florence laughed. It was the easiest laugh Emily had ever heard from her.

"You're supposed to think about nothing but me. That's why I'm paying you so handsomely."

Emily didn't bother responding.

"So what's he got that I haven't got? William Dean Howells?"

Emily thought she actually detected a trace of rivalry in her voice.

"He was more of a radical than you are, for one thing."

"William Dean Howells?"

It occurred to Emily that she might know more about the subject than Florence did. If so, it would be a first.

"Did you read him in some class?" Florence said.

"No, I didn't read him in some class. I found him on my own. He was a friend of Henry James."

"I know he was a friend of Henry James. He was a friend of Henry James and Mark Twain, and he was an editor of the *Atlantic Monthly*. That's the only reason anybody remembers him."

"Well, it shouldn't be. He was a better writer than either of them."

"Oh, please. Don't be ridiculous."

"Have you read him?"

"I probably read him in some survey class. I'm sure I must have read him at some point."

"You're sure you must have, but you don't remember. So you're *not* really sure if you've ever read him. But you're telling me that he can't possibly be as good as some other people you *have* read. I'm disappointed in you, Florence Gordon."

"You're right. I don't know anything about him. There's no way I can pass judgment on him."

This was dizzying. Florence was paying attention to her. Florence was enjoying being teased by her. Florence had admitted being wrong.

"That's one good thing about you," Emily said. "You're old but you're still learning. That's what I tell your detractors."

49

A change. Florence wasn't kicking her out as soon as she got there. And rather than simply accepting the notes Emily made about what she was reading, she was asking Emily questions about what she'd read.

They started having coffee together. Coffee for Florence, herbal tea for Emily, which she provided for herself. "I have no intention of going out and buying special tea for you," Florence had said. "But if you want to, you can leave something in the cabinet, and I'll supply the hot water."

And she was obviously trusting Emily more. She'd asked Emily to put aside the research for the memoir and do some work that would help Florence with her talk at the NYU symposium. Her talk was going to be about feminism before the First World War, and she wanted to draw on Tamiment's collection of letters and diaries from turn-of-the-century suffragists. These were things that hadn't been published and that couldn't be checked out. "I don't have the time to go through it all myself," Florence said. "But you'll be able to get me everything I need."

It wasn't as if everything had changed between them. Sometimes it felt as if nothing had changed at all. Occasionally Emily wondered if Florence was giving her more time only because she liked to insult her. When Florence mentioned a book or a historical event, she would ask Emily if she'd heard of it, and if Emily hadn't, a look of irritation would pass over Florence's face. Emily was tempted to pretend she knew about books and events she didn't actually know about—but it was a good thing she never did, since she soon found out that if she said she knew about a subject, Florence would start quizzing her.

Why was she like this? Florence was a teacher, but this wasn't very teacherly. Emily's best teachers, at least, had never been like this. They didn't expect you to have been born with a particular set of facts in your head. But Florence, when she found out that Emily didn't exactly know what the Seneca Falls Convention or the Port Huron Statement was, would go silent for ten seconds or so, as if holding herself back from giving Emily the tongue-lashing she deserved. And then she would content herself with saying something like, "Sometimes I think you young people believe that all the rights you enjoy every day just sprouted up by themselves."

But Emily was comfortable enough with Florence now to give it back. One day, after Florence asked her to take a look at her computer, Emily said she was going to clean the cache and get rid of some of the cookies, and when Florence said that she didn't know what that meant, Emily put her head in her hands.

"Sometimes I think you people just expect your cookies to get rid of themselves," Emily said.

When Emily looked up at her, although she couldn't be sure, she thought for a moment that Florence almost smiled.

50

Sometimes Emily felt as if she were engaging in a summerlong research project about how to be a human being, or, rather, about what kind of human being to be.

The two models of humanity that were the most vivid to her at the moment were her grandmother and her ex-boyfriend. If that's what he was. Maybe he was her former ex-boyfriend. It was hard to tell.

Justin might have been the dearest person she had ever known. The kindest, the most considerate, the most thoughtful. He was a wry, quiet, funny boy whose ambition in life was to design toys and parks and playgrounds.

Emily had met Justin during her junior year in high school. She'd first noticed him in the public library. An old woman was trying to get onto the Internet, and the librarian was nowhere to be seen, so this elflike, curly-headed boy took it upon himself to help. The woman was trying to read her email, but didn't know what email provider she used, and he had sat there with her patiently, without sighing, without wincing, without rolling his eyes. Witnessing such kindness put Emily in a good mood, and when she found out he went to her school — she saw him in the lunchroom a few days later — she knew they were going to be friends.

Justin had gone to Emerson when she went to Oberlin, and for a while it had seemed as if they were growing in different directions. It didn't feel like a bad thing; it felt a little sad, but mostly it felt natural.

But now he'd begun to show up again, Facebooking her, Gchatting her, sending thirty-second videos of toys he'd made for a design class, toys that marched for a few steps and then fell down. She didn't know what she wanted with him, ultimately, but she found this very endearing.

When a teacher in high school once asked the class about people they admired, he chose not a real person but the Tom Hanks character from *Big*, who gets a job at a toy company and dreams up toys that no grown-up could ever have imagined. Justin's aim in life was to make things that would bring people joy.

51

Florence offered a rather different model of how to be human. Much had changed, over the years, about Florence's beliefs and the manner in which she expressed them, but Emily was coming to think that in the most important ways, she hadn't changed at all. Florence had always been a feminist, and she'd always been a fighter.

In an essay that Florence had written about a historian named Gerda Lerner, Emily had come across the phrase "a militant ethic of overcoming." The phrase, Emily thought, could have described Florence herself. She was always outraged, always indignant about something she'd read or heard or seen, yet there was something about her that was forever hopeful. She seemed truly to believe that she was taking part in a struggle that might yet end with the power of universal sisterhood and brotherhood winning out against the forces of sexism, exploitation, greed. In another essay she'd quoted a passage from Chekhov in which he'd imagined writing a story about someone who "squeezes the slave out of himself, drop by drop." Florence had said that such an effort could be a lifelong project, and Emily had the sense that she'd described her own.

And she was always *thinking*. Even her habit of interrogating you was starting to feel not so obnoxious, because often she seemed to be thinking out loud, asking questions of you that she was also asking of herself. Florence seemed voracious for argument because she was voracious for learning.

Florence's old friends were sometimes there when Emily visited. One day Emily left Florence's apartment along with Vanessa—Vanessa, who had arranged Florence's surprise party, and who had gushed so embarrassingly about her during the three minutes in which the party had lasted. Emily and Vanessa walked to the subway together, and, unsolicited, Vanessa began to talk about Florence.

"She gave me my life," Vanessa said. "When we met, I was on track to being nothing more than a helpmate. I had my daydreams, but they all seemed out of reach for someone like me. Florence encouraged me—not just encouraged me: she wouldn't leave me alone. I don't think I would have gone to graduate school if she hadn't badgered me so. I'm a shrink—I'm not sure you know that—and I wouldn't be a shrink if not for Florence. I'd be seeing a shrink, maybe, but I wouldn't be one."

Emily was aware that she was beginning to idealize her grandmother, but she didn't think idealizing someone was a bad thing, as long as you knew what you were doing. She couldn't imagine an experience that could daunt the old woman. You could imagine a force that would defeat her—no one is unconquerable—but it was hard to imagine a challenge that she couldn't somehow find a way to face on her own terms.

52

Sometimes Emily helped Florence with her errands. Venturing out in the world with her could be an adventure. She would stop to berate people who littered. One day she told a beggar to stand up straight and look people in the eye as he begged.

At a Duane Reade one afternoon, ten or fifteen people were waiting to pay for their purchases. Two cashiers were working, and there was one line. A man in a business suit took a look at the situation and evidently decided that there were actually two lines—a line for each cashier—one extending all the way into the distant reaches of the dental care section, the other magically unpeopled. Going to the head of the magic line, he started unloading his basket in front of a cashier.

The woman at the front of the actual line, a worn-out-looking woman in her thirties, stared at him with cartoonish outrage—her mouth was open—but didn't say anything.

Florence wasn't even in the line—she and Emily had just entered the store—but what she'd seen had incensed her.

"Can't you see the line here?" Florence said to him, pointing with her cane.

"There's two lines," he said, without even looking at her.

"Take another look."

"What's it to you?"

"You don't throw your trash on the street, you don't serve yourself first, and you don't cut in line. It's called civilization."

The girl at the cash register called out to the bedraggled woman: "Next customer," and said to the man, "End of the line, please."

"Fuck you, you crazy old bitch," the man said to Florence. He dropped the basket and left the store.

The tired-looking woman came forward with her shampoo.

"Thank you," she said to Florence.

"You should stand up for yourself," Florence said.

53

"Were you talking to somebody?" Janine said.

"You scared the hell out of me, Mom."

It was two in the morning. Emily had thought her mother had gone to bed hours ago.

"I'm sorry. I thought I heard you talking with Mark."

"I was Skyping with Miranda."

"I know you were Skyping. I thought it was Mark."

"Yes, Miranda does sound a lot like Mark, now that you mention it. Except she has a deeper voice. What are you doing up?"

"I don't know. Looking for snacks."

"Well, go to bed."

"Okay, Mom," Janine said, in a little-girl voice, and closed the door.

Close call.

Emily was Skyping with Justin most nights now, but she always waited until her parents were asleep.

It was weird to want to hide him, since he was the sweetest boy she'd ever known. But she wasn't ready to tell her parents that he was back in her life.

Her parents seemed to have complicated feelings about Justin. When she first used to bring him around, they'd liked him a lot. They'd liked him a little *too* much. Her only previous boyfriend had been moody, self-absorbed, leather-jacketed — basically, he'd been James Dean — and her parents' mistrust of him had pleased her. But Justin they loved. Or rather, they loved Justin at first.

After a while, they began to have questions. He used to leave her little notes, in tiny handwriting, and one day, after she'd left one of them lying around, her father said, "Why's his handwriting so small?"

It was the most innocuous question in the world, but somehow it bothered her.

Justin was vegan, as she was, but he took it further. He got skinnier and skinnier during their senior year, and one night when he was over for dinner he turned down the broccoli her mother had made, explaining that he was now trying to eat only the simplest forms of plant life. He was feeling increasingly bad about killing vegetables. She still remembered the look her parents exchanged. They thought she hadn't caught it, but she had.

"Justin's getting awfully skinny, dear," her mother said a few days later. "Is everything okay?"

Emily replied that he was fine. She was indignant about it, and later she wondered why she'd gotten so bothered. At first she blamed her mother, for finding problems where there weren't any, but later she started to think that she herself had been noticing problems for a while, and had been trying not to notice them.

One night that summer, a few weeks before they left for college, she slapped a mosquito on her arm — she had a feeling of accomplishment when she saw the smushed blood — and Justin got so upset that he jumped up and walked off and disappeared for the rest of the night.

And then there was the question of sex. She and Justin had never actually had sex. In fact, she'd never actually had sex with anyone. With James Dean, as much as she had a crush on him, she'd held back, because she wanted her first time to be with someone she truly loved. With Justin, she'd spent a few months doing everything short of having sex, and it had seemed right: they were enjoying each other; they were getting to know each other slowly. But then there came a time when she wanted to have sex, and Justin didn't. He said he didn't feel enough like a grown-up.

She'd cared about him more than she'd ever cared about a guy, but she hadn't been able to rid herself of the thought that it might be good for her not to be near him anymore. She knew herself well enough to know that she tended to take on other people's troubles as her own, and she wasn't sure she was strong enough to take on whatever he was going through.

But sometimes she'd despised herself for thinking like this. It was selfish to be so concerned about protecting herself when this gentle, generous, childlike boy needed her help.

When Justin had gotten back in touch with her a few weeks ago, she'd felt so happy to hear from him that she'd tried to push all her little question marks out of her mind. But she wasn't sure what she wanted with him. And until she was sure, she'd just as soon that her parents not know he was back in her life.

54

Florence was planning to go to a meeting at NYU, not far from the library. She asked Emily to find her there that day and give her the next packet of research.

"Faculty meetings in the summer?" Emily said.

"It isn't a faculty meeting," Florence said. "It's a protest."

She put her fist in the air, signifying protest.

"What are you protesting?"

"A group of teachers and students want to keep the bloodmobile off the campus, and I want to put my two cents in."

"What've they got against the bloodmobile?"

"The blood-donation laws discriminate against gay men. If you're a man who's had sex with another man, you're not allowed to donate."

"That's crazy," Emily said.

"It's not so much crazy as cowardly. In the early days of the AIDS epidemic, they didn't know how to test for HIV in the blood supply. So a law like that, as repulsive as it was—well, maybe it was the best they could do. But now? Now they can do the test, but they still haven't lifted the ban. They're cowards, they're homophobes, they're ignorant, or they're some combination of the above."

When the day came, Emily found Florence without any difficulty, but instead of just handing her the packet and leaving, she stuck around. She was curious about observing Florence in her natural habitat, the protest meeting.

The meeting, held in an auditorium in a building on Washington Square, was much more crowded than Emily would have expected.

When Emily got there, the meeting hadn't yet started, but already there was an atmosphere of anger in the room. Emily felt both innocent and ignorant—a shameful combination. She felt innocent because she didn't think she'd been in a room with quite the same feeling in it before. She felt ignorant because she had nothing to compare it to. She ran her mind through the novels she loved, trying to remember whether any of them had featured big meetings. There were parts of *Anna Karenina* where Levin was engaging in all these arguments about land reform, but she couldn't remember them that well. She'd sort of skimmed those parts.

When the discussion got started, the issues seemed simple. A few people wanted the bloodmobile to continue to pay its monthly visits, because blood donation was important. Most of the speakers wanted to ban it, because the laws restricting blood donations were intolerable.

As she listened to the arguments, she didn't know how she felt. On the one hand . . . But on the other hand . . .

When some of the speakers were making their points, other people were snapping their fingers. At first it struck Emily as inexplicable, but then she realized it must be some political-meeting version of applause. The finger snappers looked serenely approving of what was being said.

She wondered how this custom had come to be. What was wrong with clapping? The finger snapping made it seem as if a group of beatniks had beamed in from a 1950s jazz club.

After many people had spoken—students, teachers, other people who worked for the university—Florence walked slowly to the microphone. She looked uncharacteristically fragile, and she was leaning on her cane, but her voice was strong.

"Some of you might remember Larry Ackerman. He used to teach sociology here. About ten years ago, he had the bad fortune to get hit by a car. He was hurt pretty badly, and he needed transfusions on a daily basis. Everyone who loved him was lining up to help. But Larry was a gay man, and many of his friends weren't allowed to donate. I remember Larry's partner talking about going to the blood bank and being turned away. He felt humiliated—and he felt angry, because he knew that his blood was clean. He'd been tested; Larry had been tested; and they'd been a monogamous couple for years.

"I'm no scientist, but even a glance at what the experts are saying is enough to make it clear that we need to do everything we can to take that stupid and offensive law off the books."

People were snapping their fingers like crazy. The beatniks were liking what they heard.

"At the same time as we're defending our sons and our brothers from being stigmatized and excluded, we need to make sure that we're not victimizing another group—people who can't survive without blood transfusions. We've got two vulnerable groups here, and we have to look out for both of them. We need to educate, we need to organize, we need to speak out, we need to exert all the pressure we can muster to get the law changed. And at the same time, we need to encourage those who *can* give blood to give it."

The fingers had stopped snapping.

"I know this is complicated," Florence said. "But social change usually is. So I'm saying that we need to respect the complexity, and to do justice to both vulnerable parts of our communities. We need to welcome the blood drive, and encourage people to give blood; and we need to use the blood drive as an opportunity to educate people so we can change this disgusting law."

When Florence finished, she turned away from the microphone and walked back to her seat. The room was silent.

55

The meeting went on for another hour. Most of the people there wanted to ban the bloodmobile, and finally someone made a resolution to stop it from entering Washington Square Park. It was due to arrive in less than twenty minutes. The resolution passed; the meeting was over.

Emily took the elevator with Florence. When they emerged from the building, about twenty or thirty students had already formed a line at the north entrance of the park. There was a light drizzle; Emily and Florence stood not far off, under the arch.

"I can't see any of the teachers here," Emily said.

"They must have gone off to Starbucks."

"Should we go off to Starbucks too?"

"I'd like to stick around," Florence said.

A short time later, the bloodmobile came down Fifth Avenue and crossed into the park. It was met by a line of students, chanting . . . something. Emily couldn't make out what they were saying.

The nose of the bloodmobile was in the park but the body was still on the street.

More quickly than Emily would have thought possible, police

cars appeared—three of them—and then two police vans. From each of the cars, two cops emerged. From the van came more intimidating figures—four, five, six officers in riot gear. They were clad in black from head to toe, with thick vests and helmets with tinted visors.

"Starbucks now?" Emily said.

"This is why we're here," Florence said. "To make sure the cops don't get out of hand."

"Are you sure that's possible?"

"Of course not. But sometimes it's amazing what a sobering effect an old lady can have. Particularly an old lady with a cane."

She looked at Emily as if she'd just remembered something. "You should probably go home, though. It wouldn't do for you to get arrested. Your papa wouldn't be proud of that, I assume."

"Why should I get arrested? We're just standing around."

Florence laughed and shook her head.

It was true that her father wouldn't be happy if she got arrested. It wasn't like he defended everything the police ever did . . . but he *was* a cop, after all. Emily had noticed that when a subject like police brutality came up, he was never as open-minded as you'd expect him to be.

"If I have an arrest record will I still be enjoyable?"

She'd meant to say "employable," but she was so nervous that she got mixed up.

"I don't know how to answer that one, my dear."

The cops had taken their nightsticks out.

"That's my cue," Florence said. "You stay here. So you can remain enjoyable."

She smiled at Emily—suddenly Florence looked distinctly young—and moved toward the heart of the trouble.

56

Emily hadn't moved. She wanted to follow her grandmother, but she was afraid to.

Another van had arrived, and more black-padded men stepped out. There were more police than students now.

The riot police—there was something inherently terrifying about them, something intended to terrify. With their thick black uniforms and their dark visors, behind which you could see nothing, they seemed to represent violence and nothing else. Emily remembered something she'd read somewhere about how a man won't kill you if you can look him in the eye. Your humanity will find his humanity and he will stay his hand. But these were people who could not be looked in the eye.

The terror shook loose something inside her, and she felt overwhelmed by love and respect for her grandmother. Florence had dragged herself down here, bad ankle and all, to take part in a debate she must have known she would lose. And now, having lost it, instead of going home, she was standing in the rain to try to make sure that no harm came to the people who had disregarded what she'd had to say.

The riot police started moving toward the line—toward the students and the one old lady.

It was like seeing the police advancing on a softball team. It was like seeing a boxing match between the heavyweight champ and a blogger.

Florence was standing between a boy and a girl, and Emily felt strangely jealous of the girl. She was a slight, pixieish figure, and she and Florence had their arms entwined, and after the demonstration, Florence was going to take her home and adopt her.

Something happened—a kid jumped forward? Somebody pushed somebody? A cop hit somebody?—and instead of two lines there was one surging blob. Emily couldn't tell what was happening. All she knew was that people were pushing and people were falling to the ground, and that she'd lost sight of her grandmother.

57

Emily ran forward and started pushing. She forgot to be afraid—well, almost. She was struggling through the crowd and trying to cover up at the same time, because she didn't want to get hit on the head.

If it was a bigger crowd, she didn't know what she would have done, but she was able to push and swivel and crawl her way to Florence, who was on the ground, holding up her cane to try to protect herself from people's boots and knees and elbows.

The crowd was a writhing thing. Emily couldn't tell what was happening. All she could see were people's legs. Someone stepped on her hand. Someone kicked her on the chin. Someone stumbled over Florence.

"Get away," Emily said. "That's my grandma."

She was embarrassed as soon as she said it. Florence surely would have preferred "That's my grandmother" or, better, "That's Florence Gordon." But the word had just popped out of her mouth.

Emily thought it was strange to be embarrassed in a moment like this—aren't there any situations in which you can just lose your self-consciousness?

All this passed through her mind in an instant.

Emily helped Florence up, and kept an arm around her, and they found their way out of the tangle.

Even from the outside, it was hard for Emily to tell what was happening. Too much was going on at once. Police were pushing people down. Some of the students, including the pixieish girl, had moved away and were chanting "Shame on you!" Some of the students were being arrested; others were sitting with their arms behind their backs as police tried to get them to stand up.

She was reminded of the chapter in *The Charterhouse of Parma* where Fabrice takes part in the Battle of Waterloo, but he doesn't know it—all he knows is that he's scared and confused.

"I failed to exercise a calming effect," Florence said, or something like that—Emily couldn't hear her well in all the noise.

Emily was about to say, "At least you tried," but she stopped herself. She didn't know if it was the wrong thing to say. Or the wrong thing for *her* to say. She could imagine one of Florence's friends saying it, but if *she* said it, Florence might be annoyed.

They stayed until the scene was cleared. Some of the protesters had been arrested; others had gone away. The bloodmobile too was gone.

They walked to Sixth Avenue and took a bus uptown. Emily was sore all over, and Florence had scrapes on her arms and legs.

"What did you make of it all?" Florence said.

"It was like *The Charterhouse of Parma*," Emily said.

"I have no idea what you're talking about," Florence said. "You're a strange girl."

This, oddly, made Emily feel proud of herself.

58

If I leave Daniel, what will become of him?

This was the question on Janine's mind.

She had decided to go to the conference with Lev, and she was nervous about it.

Caroline, Daniel's old protégée or whatever she was, had turned into a fetching young woman—sophisticated, charming, poised. Surely Daniel found her attractive. How could he not? So if Janine left him, maybe he'd end up with her. Maybe a happy ending was possible here. Even though Caroline was, like, twelve years old.

What *would* Daniel do? Take up with a new woman, or live by himself for the rest of his life? Both of these possibilities were hard to imagine.

One of the things Janine had always loved about Daniel was that he never looked at other women. When a typical guy is out and about with his wife, his eyes will rove around insanely, checking out this woman's breasts and that woman's legs and that other woman's who-the-hell-knows-what-else-men-look-at, and you, the wife, will wish you had a little flag that you could pull out and wave in front of him to get his attention, or a little club that you could whack him with. Daniel, alone among men, was never like that. When he was with Janine, she was the only person he seemed to see. It made you feel secure.

She imagined Daniel with his other woman, ten years from now. Not Caroline—someone older and more seasoned. They're in a restaurant, and he's gazing at her, this new woman, with his patented "There's no one in the universe but you" look. And then the door opens and Janine comes in—maybe with Lev, although the reverie didn't require it. And then—and then, nothing. Daniel continues to gaze upon his age-appropriate, wrinkled-but-still-attractive mystery woman, and he doesn't notice Janine at all.

And then what?

Then I stride across the room and slap that little hussy silly, and take Daniel home with me.

This fantasy didn't make a lot of sense, if she was planning to leave him. She was aware of that.

59

"Why did you become a cop?" Janine said.

After Lev had told her about why he'd become a psychologist, she'd thought that Daniel would never give her a comparably straight answer about why he became a cop. But maybe she was selling him short.

"Why did I become a cop?" he said.

"Yes."

"Why did I become a cop? That's what you're asking?"

"That's what I'm asking."

"Haven't we already talked about this?"

"We probably have, but I can't remember."

He looked as if he were thinking, and then he said, "Are you sure we haven't talked about this? You were *there*."

"I'm sure we talked about it at the time, but I can't remember."

He'd applied for the job just after they got married. All she could remember, really, was being happy about the salary and the benefits. It meant they'd be able to start a family.

"I know why you went into CI," she said, "but I'm not sure I know why you became a cop in the first place."

There was no reason for him not to want to talk about this. It was as if he belonged to some cult that held that it's immoral to talk about anything important.

"Okay," he said. "I'll tell you. You know, on the news, you'll see some guy who's been arrested, and he's getting into the back of the squad car? And the cop always puts his hand on the guy's head? Like criminals are this breed of people who don't know how to get into a car without bumping their heads?"

"Yeah. I have noticed that."

"That's the secret to why people become cops. We like to put our hands on people's heads."

Janine got up and started making herself a cup of coffee.

"We just like to do it," he said.

"I thought that was it," she said.

60

Janine was leaving for her weekend in Pittsburgh.

She had thought that Emily would be with Daniel, but it turned out that Emily was going away too. She was going to Boston to visit one of her college housemates.

Daniel would be alone all weekend. How would he take care of himself? What would he do?

Janine knew it was silly to worry about this. He was a grown man. He was a grown man who had just spent months alone in their house in Seattle. He seemed to have survived the ordeal, and he'd survive the weekend.

But she couldn't stop worrying.

"Sweetheart," Daniel said. "Do you think you could remember to buy me those socks?"

He liked a kind of sock that was hard to find in stores, and for some reason he could never find them on the Internet.

"Of course. I can do it as soon as I get back."

It wasn't until she said this that she realized she was truly going.

She pictured Daniel, in some sad future, without her, helpless, no longer able to find the socks he liked.

"You should get packed," Daniel said.

And then, to make things worse, he started quizzing her about whether she'd remembered to pack everything.

This was something he did for her every time she took a trip. He went through a mental checklist for her: cell phone, computer, chargers, reading glasses, book, pen, extra pen, notepad, tissues, hand sanitizer, gum to keep her ears from popping on the plane.

Normally she found this touching, but today it was breaking her heart.

Janine took her suitcase to the lab and spent the morning working. At around noon she looked for Lev. His secretary told her that he'd gone to lunch.

When he went to lunch by himself, he liked to go to an old-fashioned ice cream parlor on Broadway. Janine left the lab and found him there. He was sitting at a table near the window.

She went inside and stood over him at his table.

He was eating an ice cream sundae and reading a book by George Vaillant. He brought his spoon to his lips, and as he was bringing it back toward the ice cream, he looked up.

For a moment he must have thought she was the waitress: there was no sign of recognition in his eyes. Then he did a double take.

He looked delighted to see her, but then again, he looked delighted when he saw everyone—

No. It was time to stop telling herself that she didn't make him any happier than anyone else did. She made him happy. She knew this.

"Would you like to hear the specials?" she said.

To her own ears, she sounded throatily seductive, but he might have just thought she was struggling with a glob of midsummer phlegm.

First the provocative coffee-pouring moment, and now this. She was flirting. She had become a flirt. But she didn't know if she was doing it right.

When was the last time she'd flirted with anyone but Daniel? It was way back in the Chips Ahoy era. That was ages ago, back in a time when Whoopi Goldberg was considered edgy.

She sat across from him.

"I have a question," she said. Still throatily seductive, or maybe still sounding like Andy Devine.

"Yes?"

"I was wondering. If I hadn't said yes, and you'd taken somebody else to the conference, would you have missed me?"

"I wouldn't have taken anyone else. It was always you. Only you."

This sounded off to her. It sounded too ardent. She'd wanted him to reply in an understated fashion, because feeling shows itself most vividly in restraint. It occurred to her that she'd been hoping that he'd give the kind of answer that Daniel would have given. She told herself not to dwell on this.

The waitress showed up. There was something in her manner that struck Janine as subtly reprimanding. The waitress was about twenty, yet it was as if she were an authority figure. Janine ordered a dish of ice cream, because it seemed like the thing to do.

She'd once heard someone say that each man is either a husband or a lover, and that it takes only a glance to tell which category any man belongs to. Daniel was a husband: she had known it from the moment she looked at him, or at least that was the way she remembered it now. The funny thing was that Lev was a husband too. Everything might have been simpler if he weren't.

"I should tell you that I'm afraid of plane rides," she said.

"I'll be right next to you."

"If I get scared, will you hold my hand?"

"I think I can manage that," he said.

He extended his arm, with his hand palm-up on the table. She reached out and took his hand.

This isn't so big. This isn't adultery. We're just holding hands.

63

"You're going to be all alone, Dad," Emily said. "It's so sad."

"Nonsense."

"What are you going to do without us?"

"I'll go to the ball game. I'll eat Sugar Smacks for dinner. Guy things."

It was ten in the morning. Emily's train was leaving a little before eleven.

Daniel said he'd accompany her to Penn Station, because he was going downtown himself.

"Where are you going, actually?" she said.

"I'm seeing an old friend. In the Village."

"Who?"

"You don't know him."

"Does he have a name?"

"You couldn't pronounce it."

This was a *Star Trek* reference, one of the jokes they shared.

They took the subway and got off at Thirty-fourth Street.

"You really have someplace to go?" she said.

"Of course. You think I'd say I had somewhere to go if I didn't?"

"I think you wanted to come to Penn Station with me."

"Why would I want to do that?"

She didn't know why. Because he was overprotective? Because he was going to miss her, even though she'd be gone for only two days? The one thing she felt sure of was that he wasn't meeting anybody downtown.

Normally this might have made her annoyed with him, but she couldn't be annoyed with him now. She felt too guilty. She had told her parents that she was going to Boston to see her friend Miranda, and that was true. She would make sure to see Miranda while she was there. But what she hadn't told them was that she'd be staying with Justin, or that she and Justin had a plan to take Ecstasy and have sex.

She hadn't had either of these experiences before—having sex or taking Ecstasy. It was time for both. She felt terribly behind in life: all of her friends had had sex, and most of them had done every drug there was.

She didn't want to do every drug there was—drugs didn't interest her—but she wanted to try Ecstasy. And she wasn't sure she wanted to be with Justin, but she didn't want to be a virgin anymore. It was embarrassing to be a virgin at nineteen.

But at the same time as she wanted to do these things, she couldn't stop herself from feeling that it might not be a good idea to do them with a boy she wasn't sure she wanted to get back together with.

She still didn't know if she wanted to see Justin at all, let alone have sex with him, but he'd kept asking her to visit, and finally he'd just worn her down.

She had made her plans for the weekend rationally and calmly; she'd talked herself out of her second thoughts; but still, there was something horrible about this moment. She wished her father wasn't taking her to the train.

She felt safe around him. She always had. She had always loved walking in the city with him—the city, up till now, meaning Seattle—because there was something delicious in experiencing the energy of the city while still feeling utterly protected at her father's side. But now his nearness made her feel almost ill.

She felt as if she were lying to him—well, she didn't *feel* that way: she *was* lying to him. What would he have thought if he knew what she was planning? She didn't think he would have tried to stop her. That wasn't his way. He would have asked her why she was set on doing these things, and he would have listened to her answers, carefully and respectfully, and then he would have told her what he thought ("This is my advice, not that you asked for it"), and then he would have let her make her own choice.

Her certainty that he wouldn't have tried to stop her made everything feel worse. He trusted her—trusted her to be responsible, trusted her to take good care of herself—and here she was, heading off to have sex with a boy whom she knew to be unstable and to take a drug that, for all she knew, might be strong enough to put her own stability at risk.

Her father thought she was one thing and she was really another thing.

"Have you ever seen pictures of the old Penn Station?" he said.

"I didn't know there was an old Penn Station."

"It was beautiful. It might have been even more beautiful than Grand Central."

"So what happened?"

"They tore it down in the name of progress."

"Did you used to love it?"

"I've only seen pictures. They tore it down before I was born. In the sixties, or the fifties. I'm not sure."

The fact that her father didn't know this struck her as very sad, somehow.

When you're young and strong and coming into your own, your parents can seem terribly vulnerable.

Maybe I shouldn't go, she thought. Maybe I should stay here and take care of him.

He would have smiled at the idea that he needed taking care of, but she believed he did.

Walking through Penn Station by his side, she felt as if she were heading toward someone's doom. Hers or his.

"I could stay if you wanted me to."

"Why would I want you to stay?"

He was looking at her with an expression of amused dry distance.

"I don't know. I thought maybe you had more valuable life lessons to teach me."

They were at a ticket machine, and before she could get her wallet out, he was feeding it his credit card.

"I don't think I have any life lessons I need to teach you this weekend. I think you've earned the right to relax and have fun."

"All you have to do is say the word, Big Guy."

He stopped and looked at her quizzically. Maybe it was occurring to him that she was upset about something.

"Why should I?"

She felt like a fool, suddenly.

"I don't know. I'm just joking. You shouldn't."

The machine printed out her ticket, she removed it, and they walked on. She was going to have sex and she was going to do drugs. When she came back she'd be someone different from who she was now.

And he would be someone different too. He wouldn't be the father of the same girl he was the father of now. He would be the father of a girl who was older and more worldly and sneakier and more cynical, and he wouldn't even know.

How does this happen? How do you betray someone you love? Of the two of them, she thought, he was the more innocent, because he trusted her.

I'm sorry, Dad, she thought. I'm so sorry.

"Stay safe, kid," he said, and he embraced her, and she felt something going on in her backpack. He was probably putting some money in, knowing that if he tried to hand it to her, she'd refuse it.

She watched him walking off alone through Penn Station. He seemed so small. He seemed so old. She needed to do what she was doing; she needed to grow; but she felt as if, by growing in this way, by taking up a different kind of space in the world, she was inching her father toward his death.

She could still stay home. She didn't have to do drugs and get naked with a boy who was probably a little unstable. She could still stay home. She could go back uptown with her father—they could walk all the way, just for fun—and tonight they could make popcorn and watch *Star Trek*, just like they used to do when she was twelve.

He was still in sight. She wanted to call out to him; she wanted to run to him. She watched him until he disappeared.

64

After he said goodbye to Emily, he didn't know what to do with himself. He took a bus to escape the ugliness of midtown, and got out at Seventy-second Street, a few blocks from where Janine worked.

He wasn't sure what time her flight was leaving. Maybe he could catch her and they could meet for lunch.

It felt like a childish impulse — they'd already said goodbye — but he missed her.

Part of the reason he missed her was that they'd barely had sex since he got here. In the past, whenever they'd drifted away from each other, the intensity of their mutual attraction had brought them back together, but now, for some reason, this wasn't happening. Instead they seemed to have settled into a disconcerting routine: an old married couple's parody of romantic attraction. This morning, when he was taking a shower, she had come into the bathroom to brush her teeth, and she'd pulled the shower curtain aside and waggled her eyebrows at him Groucho Marxishly, and then she'd passed her hand over him, slowly, and then gone back to brushing her teeth. The implication seemed to be that if only they'd been free—if Emily weren't in the apartment and if she, Janine, didn't need to leave—she would have wanted to have sex with him. But every time they actually were free, they didn't have sex. There was always a book or a paper that Janine needed to read or an email she needed to write. It was bad, and he didn't want it to stay this way.

He called her office, and the friendly young woman who worked at the front desk told him that she wasn't there.

He tried to figure out whether there was anything he needed to do in the neighborhood. A high-end toy store had just opened up on Seventy-ninth Street; he fleetingly thought it would be nice to get something for the kids, and then remembered that his kids didn't play with toys anymore. He was ten years late on that one.

He couldn't think of anything he wanted to do. There was a Richard Thompson concert at Town Hall that night. Maybe he could still get a ticket. But it wouldn't be fun without Janine.

At the corner of Broadway and Seventy-fourth he was waiting for the light to change when something made him turn his head, and he found himself looking at a couple sitting near the window of a restaurant. The woman was familiar. The woman was Janine.

He got that feeling he always got when he saw her, that little lift. She and the guy were holding hands.

He crossed the street against the traffic—away from them—scuttling awkwardly to avoid a taxi or two. At a newsstand he bought a copy of the *Daily News*, and then he turned around and held it up and tried to look around it, like some hapless detective in a movie. It was the first time, in all his years of copdom, that he'd tried to observe anybody without being seen.

When he was in retreat mode, trying not to get hit by a car, he'd allowed himself to doubt that it was really Janine. From his observation post behind the *Daily News*, he couldn't deny it. She even had her hair in a ponytail, the better to display her glowingly beautiful face.

And who was the guy?

The guy had to be Lev, of course. Had to be.

They were holding hands.

They were sitting behind big cups—those tall silver fluted cups they have in ice cream parlors.

They were having ice cream sundaes. Or maybe one was having ice cream and the other was having a nice fruit cup.

They were laughing. They were still holding hands. This seemed important, as though, if they'd held hands for only a minute, there might have been an innocent explanation.

He felt disoriented. He was afraid he was going to fall down.

He didn't feel angry, which surprised him.

Maybe it was the ice cream sundaes. Somehow the ice cream made the two of them seem less tawdry. It made them seem less like adults having an affair than like high school students out on their first date.

How could she be doing this?

Daniel had met Janine when they were barely out of their teens. Both of them pretended to great sophistication, of course, but they were children. Everything they'd gone on to discover about life, they'd discovered together.

That was the deal, wasn't it?—that they would go through *everything* together. Their children's marriages, grandparenthood, old age . . .

Wasn't that the deal?

He could trail them. It would be a piece of cake, since he was a cop, except that he'd never actually trailed anybody in his life, and had no idea of how to do so, apart from what he could remember from old episodes of *The Rockford Files*. And anyway, what would be the point? He knew where they were going: to the airport, and then to Pittsburgh, where they'd spend the weekend talking about the multiple nature of the self and fucking their brains out.

Maybe he should go into the restaurant and beat the guy up.

He was supposed to be someone who would do that sort of thing. He'd taken boxing lessons. He was an off-duty cop. Off-duty cops were always getting involved in street hassles, embarrassing the badge.

But he had no desire to.

When Mark was in first grade, some other boy in the class kept hitting him, and when Daniel suggested that Mark hit him back, Mark said, "I don't *want* to hit him." Not in a voice that suggested he was afraid, but in a voice that suggested that hitting someone was an absurd thing to do. Now he felt the same way.

They were still laughing, still holding hands.

He'd seen enough. He walked north, and after ten blocks, still feeling dizzy, he stopped at a coffee shop. He didn't want coffee, though. He wanted to have something that he'd never normally have, as if to set this afternoon apart from his life. So he ordered a slice of cherry pie. Only after it arrived did he think about how close it was to an ice cream sundae, and he wondered why he'd ordered it. It felt as if he were trying to horn in on their happiness.

What do I do now?

He didn't know what to do, with the afternoon or with his life.

I should ask Janine, he thought, and then remembered that he couldn't.

He imagined trying to tell the children that he and Janine were separating. Which of them would be affected more? Emily usually seemed so poised, so imperturbable, but in her quiet way she felt everything. Mark, the explorer, never coming home for more than a few minutes, it seemed, would be the obvious candidate to be less affected, but you couldn't be sure.

He wondered what Janine would say about how the children would react to a divorce.

Every thought led back to the family.

How could she be walking away from this?

He paid for his order without having touched it and left the coffee shop.

What kind of person, when he discovers that his wife is cheating on him, decides to get himself a slice of pie?

What kind of person sees his wife holding hands with some joker and just slinks off? Why hadn't he walked in and punched the guy?

Why the fuck am I thinking about myself now, anyway?

He was thinking about himself because he had such trust in Janine that he thought that if she were turning away from him, then he must deserve to be turned away from.

He felt revolted by his self, his identity, his history. His act. It seemed to him that he was a fraud, and not even a successful fraud at that. He was a fraud whose fraudulence was obvious. Over the decades he had worked to transform himself into something that it was not his nature to be, but the transformation had never been effected. He'd tried to turn himself into a strong and silent cop; he'd tried to turn himself into some archetypal figure of calm, benevolent male authority—he'd tried to turn himself into Henry Fonda—but inside he was still a quiveringly oversensitive boy, and anyone who looked at him hard enough could see that. That was why the other cops called him "the professor."

Of course she was leaving him. Of course she was running off with the grit investigator. She was leaving him because he'd never really become himself. The grit enthusiast—that's who it was, of course: it had to be Lev—as pudgy and unimpressive as he'd seemed at a glance, was at least *himself*, thoroughly and unapologetically himself, and though Daniel could undoubtedly knock his teeth out if he wanted to, the plump psychologist's comfort in his own skin made him the better man.

He wanted to feel good old-fashioned fury. He wanted to be the kind of guy who might be tempted to kill the ice-cream-eating sage, and kill Janine in the bargain, maybe. But that wasn't, it turned out, who he was.

He was crossing into Riverside Park. He saw each stranger with a kind of double vision. He wanted to stop them all and cry on their shoulders, but at the same time he was scanning them all for suspicious behavior. Apparently he *was* a cop.

If you cultivate a set of habits long enough, they become second nature, and then they remake you. Maybe he was no more a fraud than anyone else.

Life was confusing.

His cell phone vibrated. It was Janine, calling to say that she'd almost made a terrible mistake, but had suddenly come to her senses, and wanted him to know that what the two of them had together was the most important thing in her life.

No. It wasn't Janine. It was his mother. He let it go to voice mail.

Thank God Emily was away for the weekend. He could just go back to the apartment and collapse.

What was Janine *doing*? Why was she doing this?

He realized that he hadn't yet wondered what was on her mind. This gave him another reason to feel bad: the thought of how selfish he was. He'd been thinking only about himself and the question of whether he was a fraud and the question of whether he was unlovable. But what was it like for *her*? What was she going through? What did she need that he hadn't given her?

It shouldn't have been that surprising that his wife was having an affair. She'd been restless. She'd been dissatisfied. Wasn't that what all the Internet crap was about? All the Facebook bullshit, all the time spent friending people and bookmarking people's tweets, or whatever the hell she was doing online all the time. If you're in love with your life, you're not spending time worrying about how many "friends" you have on Facebook.

He was feeling sick to his stomach. He wanted to vomit. The only thing that kept him from vomiting was the fact that he'd always hated it in movies when people vomited in reaction to upsetting news. It always seemed so phony. So he was damned if he was going to vomit now.

But he was feeling worse and worse. A pain that went from his stomach all the way up to his jaw.

He started to wonder if he was having a heart attack.

You're not having a heart attack. You're just freaking out.

But how could he be sure he wasn't having a heart attack?

He'd had a friend who'd just dropped dead one day, with no warning, at the age of forty-five. Maybe that was happening to him, here, now. And maybe it wouldn't be so bad.

No, he thought. I'm not ready. I don't want to miss everything. I'm not ready to go.

You're not having a heart attack. Don't be fucking silly. You're not having a heart attack.

With a clownish fastidiousness, with a degree of considerateness that even he found absurd, he felt as if he were exhibiting bad manners: having a heart attack and upstaging Janine, on what might—who knows?—have been the happiest day of her life.

He had no reason to think that it was the happiest day of her life, happier than any of the days she'd spent with him, but jealousy tends toward self-debasement.

He tried to focus. If I *am* having a heart attack, what should I do?

It was a warm, calm day. The park was filled with gorgeous people—beautiful long-legged girls, hunky boys with their shirts off—and none of them would ever die, and none of them would help him.

I should call someone, he thought, but who? He couldn't call Janine. He didn't want to call Emily. He knew that if he needed her, she'd rush back to help him, but he didn't want to lay that kind of burden on her. His son—ach. Forget it. Even if Mark had been nearby, the thought of Mark's being any use was laughable.

He didn't want to call his mother, because he knew she was working hard on her memoir, and he didn't want to ask her to take time off from her work.

His father? If he called Saul for help and Saul met him in the hospital, the first thing Saul would do would be to ask for reimbursement for the subway ride.

He had a few old friends left in the city, but no one he would want to trouble with this.

He was burning from his stomach to his chin. He kept thinking that this faux heart attack would pass, but with every minute it seemed a little less faux.

He should go to a hospital. He had no idea which.

I finally found a decent reason to have a fucking iPhone, he thought. If I had a fucking iPhone, I could just search for "best emergency rooms NYC."

He thought of finding a cop and asking him where to go, because there was a fraternity among cops, a brotherhood of the blue, but on the other hand, there wasn't a cop anywhere in New York who would regard a cop from Seattle as a real cop. There was no brotherhood of the blue.

He left the park and took a cab to Roosevelt Hospital. During the ride he tried to reach Janine with a psychic message. Call me. Stop whatever you're doing and call me. Don't go away this weekend. Stay.

As the cab was crossing over to Tenth Avenue his phone went off again, and again it was Florence, and again he let it go to voice mail.

In the emergency room, after he told them he was having chest pains, they went to work fast. A male nurse took him to a little makeshift room, where he was separated by dull gray curtains from a coughing old man on one side and a retching kid on the other. He couldn't see either of them but it was as if he could. It struck him as strange that you could tell how old people were without seeing them, and then he wondered whether the fact that this struck him as strange meant that his mind wasn't right. Would this seem strange to me on a normal day? He didn't know.

Everybody was speaking Spanish. Daniel couldn't understand much. He was given an EKG, and then he was hooked up to a blood-pressure monitor and a blood-oxygen monitor, and then they ran an IV tube into his arm.

He was trying to stay calm, by means of paying an almost detached attention to the details of his treatment. He noted with approval that the team that was treating him was adhering in a methodical way to a checklist. It was good to know that he was in the hands of competent professionals.

Then he was alone. His emotions were repeating in a tight little loop. For a minute he was nothing but embarrassed. This wasn't a heart attack; it was fear confusion grief panic bewilderment rage. His mind was going crazy so his body was going crazy too. In the next minute he admitted to himself that this pain was like nothing he had felt before.

He had a pen in his jacket, which was draped over a chair near the bed. He asked an aide if she could find some paper, and she came back with two bright-blue sheets. He began a letter to his wife.

My darling. I don't know what's going to happen but I have a spooky feeling. I don't want to go without telling you what I hope you already know: you're the love of my life, and you've always been the love of my life. I've always loved you and I've always been in love with you. Loving you has been my life's great adventure.

Do you remember that night when we were kids and we went up to the top of the Empire State Building and all the lights of the city were around us, and you said that no matter how big and fantastic it all was, what we had with each other was even bigger and more fantastic? I felt that, and I feel that, and I feel that, and I feel that, and I always, my darling, will.

On the second sheet he wrote, *To my dear children*, and then realized that he didn't want to write to them both at once, but before he could write anything more, the curtains parted and a doctor, frizzy-haired, fortyish, walked in. She looked schlumpy, in a friendly, human way.

"I'm Dr. Sam," she said. "What's the trouble with this one?"

She was looking at her clipboard, talking to herself.

"Seattle Police. Far from home." She looked at him for the first time. She put the clipboard down and put her stethoscope against his chest. "What are you doing in the Big Apple, fella? Chasing down a fugitive?"

"Right," Daniel said. "Tracking down a fugitive. Visiting my mother too."

"It's always good to visit your mother," the doctor said. "On the other hand, not if it sends you to the emergency room. Maybe you should have stayed in Seattle."

"Maybe so. But this is probably indigestion. Don't you think?"

He was feeling suddenly better. He was feeling rather mellow, in fact.

They must have given him something when they'd hooked him up to the IV—Valium, maybe?—because he was feeling much more mellow than he had any right to feel, under the circumstances.

"Well, could be," said the doctor, scribbling something on the paper on the clipboard. "Could be a lot of things. That's what we're going to find out."

She was still writing. It went on for a while.

"What the hell are you writing?" he said.

"I'm writing my memoirs. Don't worry. Nothing about you."

On a TV somewhere nearby, Bill O'Reilly was doing his blowhard thing, shouting at one of his guests.

"Can somebody turn that bullshit off?" Daniel said.

"What?"

"Fox News. Right-wing bastards."

"A white male officer of the law who doesn't like Fox News. This gets stranger and stranger. Well, I agree with you about their politics, but we've got to give the people what they want. When we tried putting it on CNN—hello!"

Evidently she'd noticed something on one of his monitors, and then he felt a spike in his chest that was stronger and sharper than anything he'd felt so far. It was like a feeling that *wanted* something, if that made sense.

The doctor and some nurses were in action around him; he didn't know where the nurses had come from, but one of them was pretty, so that was something, that was something he could use to take his mind off whatever it was that was killing him. Was something killing him? Was he dying? Am I dying? He wanted to ask somebody—the frizzy doctor, the pretty nurse—to tell Janine that he loved her, Janine and Emily and Mark, but talking would be too much of a strain. Maybe they'd given him too much pacifier—pacifier? Was that the word?—and maybe he was dying; all he knew was that he was shutting down. He knew he was going under, and he didn't know whether he'd come back up again. He put his wife and daughter and son at the center of his mind, and as the wave of something sweet and soft came up, he tried to hold fast to the thought of them. He wanted his last thought to be love.

65

Janine was in her bathroom in the Wyndham Grand Pittsburgh Downtown, shaving her legs.

The situation was too complicated to be borne. She was going to the conference center next door to attend a panel discussion about the psychology of impulse control in adolescents, and then she was going to sleep with a man she shouldn't sleep with.

I should write a paper, she thought. The role of the impulsive self versus the rational self in the planning of extramarital affairs.

She couldn't remember the last time she'd shaved her legs for Daniel. Yet here she was, shaving her legs for Santa.

Damn it, Emily, get out of my head!

She wasn't thinking about Daniel that much, but she couldn't stop thinking about her children. What would Emily think? What would Mark think?

What would it *matter* what they'd think? They were her *children*. There was nothing relevant about what they'd think about her having illicit sex with Santa. The thought of her having lawful wedded sex with *Daniel* would gross them out.

If she'd been trying to have an affair ten years ago, it would have been impossible, because, while slipping illicitly into bed, she would have been worrying about whether there was enough peanut butter left to make lunch for the kids the next day. You can't have an affair in that condition. You have to wait till the kids are grown.

But one of the reasons it had always been so glorious to make love with Daniel was that everyday concerns didn't deflate the experience, because the experience of making love with him included everything. From her highest erotic and spiritual longings to the question of whether she'd remembered to buy peanut butter, everything in the world was in that bed.

Why had it ended? Why hadn't it remained?

She went to the window. Her room looked out on Greater Pittsburgh, if there was such a thing.

Pittsburgh, however wimpy it was, however terribly it had been laid to waste by an uncaring capitalism, was a city, and she could never fail to be thrilled by the lights of a city in the evening.

It would have been nice to share this with Daniel.

If only Daniel would *talk*! If only he would dance! If only he would willingly *do* things with her — go to museums or shows or karaoke bars, go hiking or bicycling or swimming or ice-skating. He would do these things, but never willingly. He didn't do anything willingly except read and have sex and go to the movies. Anything else and it was a smiling "Believe me, darling, I won't do that." It was funny, but sometimes it made her want to brain him.

She didn't know what she wanted. Here she was, in the heart of Pittsburgh, that hotbed of sexual transgression, and she didn't know what she wanted. The thought made her so disconsolate that she forgot to finish shaving her legs.

66

In the morning he discovered that he wasn't dead. He couldn't remember being transferred, but he was in a regular room now. He
was still hooked up to an IV pole; he still had a blood-pressure cuff
on his arm and a blood-oxygen clip on his index finger.

A nurse came into the room to check his machines.

"Did they operate?" he said.

"Excuse me, hon?"

"Did they operate on me?"

"Not that I know of. You want them to?"

"No, I—" he started to answer, until he realized that she was
joking.

He had the sense that he'd had an important dream, a dream that
would help him understand his life, and when the nurse left he tried
hard to remember it. But the only thing he could dredge up from it
was that Emily had written a book called *The Internet in Winter*.

Later a doctor came in—a calm, slim, elegant man named Chatterjee. He told Daniel that he didn't appear to have suffered a heart
attack, but that they couldn't be sure.

"Coronary events can be chameleons. We'd like to keep you here another day or two, so we can get more acquainted with the idio-syncrasies of your cardiological system. We don't think there's any damage, but we want to be certain."

After the doctor left, Daniel once again began to think that he should let somebody know he was here. Florence seemed the ob-vious choice, only because she was around. But he couldn't bring himself to call her.

He'd once read that when soldiers are dying, most of them cry out for their mothers, if they cry out for anyone at all.

But most soldiers don't have Florence Gordon for a mother.

Maybe he wasn't giving her enough credit. She was, after all, the only person who'd called him while he was going through whatever he'd gone through yesterday. She didn't know that it was happening, but maybe, on some psychic level, she did know. She, and no one else.

He got his phone out of the bedside table. He started to press the numbers in, but before he was finished, the keypad lit up. It was her.

"Hi, Mom. I was just about to call you."

"That's funny, because I've been calling you nonstop since yes-terday afternoon."

"Yes, I'm sorry about that—"

"Where have you been? I don't understand the point of carrying a cell phone around if you're not going to be available."

"Sorry."

"Is this the way you are on the *job*? If one of your irredeemables calls you, needing to be bailed out or whatever you do, is this what you do with them? Let it go to voice mail?"

"No. That's probably not what I'd do."

"Then why do you let *my* calls go straight to voice mail?"

He closed his eyes. Why indeed?

"I actually didn't hear it ring."

"But why do you have a cell phone with you if you keep it in a place where you can't hear it ring?"

He glanced over at his monitors, expecting to see that his blood pressure was climbing out of control, but it didn't seem to be changing.

"I wasn't calling for a frivolous reason. I can't find some research material Emily was supposed to have given me, and I have no idea whether she actually did the research or not. I've got a huge amount of work to do, and I really need it."

"Why don't you call Emily?"

"Of course I called Emily. She didn't answer either. I called her and I *texted* her, and she hasn't responded, and that's why I called you. So I'd appreciate it if you'd speak to her and get her to help me straighten this out."

It was true that Emily never answered her damned phone, at least not for adults. He and Janine had been hassling her about this for years.

"She's away for a couple of days. She's up in Boston."

"Boston? What's she doing in Boston?"

"She's giving a lecture at the Kennedy School. What do you think she's doing? She's visiting some friends."

"When is she getting back?"

"I'm thinking she'll be back tomorrow night."

"What are those noises? Where are you?"

It was the hospital public address system—not voices, but mysterious boopings and beepings.

"So can you wait until Monday?" he said.

"Forget about it. I'll go down to Bobst myself."

A nurse came into the room and started emitting pleasantries.

Can you tell your nurse to keep it down because you don't want your mother to know you're in the hospital? Is that done?

"But next time I call you people, can one of you pick up your phone?"

After they got off, he wondered if there'd been an exact moment during the conversation when he'd decided not to tell her where he was and what was happening.

After another day's worth of tests, Dr. Chatterjee told Daniel, once again, that he didn't seem to have had a heart attack, but he strongly advised that Daniel see a cardiologist. "Your cholesterol's too high, your triglycerides are too high, your blood pressure's too high. You'll consider this a wake-up call, if you know what's good for you. Time to start exercising. Time to eat right—you should look into the Mediterranean diet. Time to learn some simple relaxation techniques—meditation or tai chi. Statins, definitely; maybe a beta blocker too."

The doctor kept going. He had a lot to say. Daniel listened glumly to this recitation of all the different ways in which he had to change his life.

Florence was working when the phone rang, but she felt she had to answer. There were not many people whose calls she had to take right away, but Peggy Greer, the social worker at the Mount Kisco Jewish Senior Center, was one of them.

It was a Thursday afternoon, the day after the bloodmobile protest. She was still aching. Being stepped on can do that to you.

Florence picked up the receiver and said, "What happened? Is she okay?"

Peggy was silent for a moment, apparently having expected a more conventional greeting.

"Florence?" she said.

"Yes, it's Florence. Is Yetta okay?"

"Yes, she's fine. It's not an emergency. It's not a crisis."

"Well then why are you calling me? Isn't it Ruby's turn?"

"It is Ruby's turn. But she's out of town, and she asked me to find out if you were available."

"All right. What do we need?"

"We respect Yetta. We respect her a great deal. She's a remarkable woman."

"Yes yes yes, we all know that. What do you need?"

"We need you to talk to her. We need you to talk to her about personal hygiene."

During her youth, Yetta Berman had been known as the Rosa Luxemburg of the Bronx. She'd been active in the labor movement, the civil rights movement, the antiwar movement, and, when the women's movement was being born, Yetta had been one of the first to sense its possibilities. She'd been an inspiration to Florence and to most of Florence's old friends. Five years ago, Yetta had endured a series of strokes, and now she was like a vague allusion to the woman she used to be. Her children were on the other side of the continent, so everyone in Florence's circle—all of Yetta's daughters, as Vanessa once said—undertook to take care of her when she needed it. They'd worked out a rotation, with one of them on call every month.

"What's the problem?" Florence said.

"Yetta's been giving off powerful odors. Our staff started to notice it a few months ago. Even some of the other seniors have started to complain, and if they complain, you know it's serious, since most of them can barely smell anything anymore. She wears the same clothes day after day. She may even be sleeping in them. And we're sure she hasn't been bathing herself."

"So what's the odor? Body odor? Piss? Shit? All three?"

There was a long pause. When Peggy discussed difficult subjects, she liked to speak in a roundabout way, thinking that this softened the impact of the hard facts she was forced to deliver. Florence's bluntness made her uncomfortable.

"The staff and I believe—we're relatively sure of this, actually—that it's primarily urine," she finally said. "It's a powerful odor of urine."

"Thank God for small favors," Florence said. "So what do you want me to do?"

"It would be wonderful if you'd come up here and speak to her. She simply won't listen to any of us here, and we're hoping that she'll listen to her old friends."

"And what do you want me to say?"

"Ultimately we want her to understand the importance of bathing regularly and changing her clothes. But as a first step, it would be fabulous if you could help her see that she needs to start wearing adult briefs."

"Adult briefs? You mean diapers?"

"We prefer to call them adult briefs."

"She actually needs diapers?"

"She can't control herself anymore. She's had several accidents. Some gerontologists believe that when a woman reaches a certain age—"

"That's all right. I don't need the theory. Diapers it is."

None of this was a surprise. Yetta hadn't been taking care of herself for years. It was a wonder that Florence hadn't received a call like this before.

On Friday morning, Florence took the train to Mount Kisco. She was refreshed by the simple clarity of her mission: she had to get Yetta to agree to start wearing diapers.

Despite the state she was in, Yetta still lived alone. Ever since her strokes, her friends had been advising, and her children pleading, that she move into an "adult community." But she insisted that she was perfectly capable of caring for herself, and although she was addled and forgetful, she wasn't far gone enough to be declared incompetent, so no one had the power to force her to leave her home.

Sometimes Florence thought that what kept Yetta at home wasn't independence but rage. She was angry at her children for living on the other side of the country; she was angry at her friends for not visiting more often; she was angry at her husband for having died. Sometimes Florence thought that Yetta's militant neglect of herself was like an obscene gesture toward everyone she believed had abandoned her.

The senior center was her main connection to the world. At nine in the morning, Monday through Thursday, a jitney picked her up at her door and took her there, and for five hours she sat there in the most uncomfortable chair she could find, refusing to take part in any activities. She took a grim satisfaction in rejecting anything that might make her life more pleasant.

From the train station, Florence took a taxi to Yetta's house, a Victorian so broken-down and with a yard so weedy that it looked as if it had been abandoned long ago.

"What are you doing here?" Yetta said when she opened the door.

"I told you I was coming. We talked on the phone."

"Oh. Right," Yetta said. Florence was sure she didn't remember.

"Well, you might as well come in," Yetta said. "Too bad you missed Simon."

"Was Simon here?"

"He just left. I'm surprised you didn't see him."

Shortly after her stroke, Yetta had started to speak of an imaginary friend named Simon, who seemed to be an amalgam of her long-dead husband, Oscar, and some more dashing figure—perhaps someone Yetta had known in her youth, perhaps someone from the movies.

Florence took a long breath before she stepped inside. Yetta hadn't opened her windows in years, and the smell inside her house was indescribable. The deep breath was mostly symbolic—you couldn't hold your breath throughout the visit—but Florence needed to take it even so.

"What happened to you?" Yetta said, nodding toward Florence's cane. Florence told her the story, and Yetta seemed a little disappointed that it was only a sprained ankle.

Pushing aside a pile of junk mail and newspapers, Florence took a seat on the living-room couch. There was a shriveled, blackened banana on the coffee table, with fruit flies circling it in the air.

"Where can I throw this out?" Florence said.

"What? Are you crazy? What do you want to throw it out for?"

"Yetta, it's inedible."

"It's edible. I'll do something with it. I'll make banana bread."

Florence put the banana down.

"Save me a piece," she said.

Yetta picked it up and put it down on top of the TV, where it would probably remain for months.

"How are things going?" Florence said.

"How are things supposed to go?"

"How's the senior center? Are you still enjoying it there?"

"Oh, sure. Watching old idiots play bingo all day. I'm having a ball."

"Is the food still decent? You used to say they served a decent lunch."

"Of course. Better than ever. It's a five-star restaurant."

"Have you been getting any exercise?"

"Very much so. I'm studying for the Olympics."

"What else have you been doing?" Florence said.

"Nothing. What am I supposed to do? Watching TV."

"What have you been watching?"

"My station—what's it called?"

"MSNBC?"

"MSNBC. I like that one . . . what's her name? The lesbian girl."

"Rachel Maddow?"

"Rachel Maddow. I doubt *she* would be leaving her mother alone."

Yetta ticked off a list of complaints about her children: they didn't visit enough, they didn't call her enough, they didn't include her in their vacation plans.

"Yetta," Florence finally said, "I'm here for a reason. I got a call from the social worker at the center."

"Who—Penny?"

"Peggy."

"Penny, Peggy, Piggy. What did she have to say? Does she want to ban me?"

"No. She doesn't want to ban you, Yetta. But she does have concerns."

"She has concerns? She has concerns about me?"

"Yes, she does."

"Well you can tell her that I have concerns about her. Tell her to put that in her pipe and smoke it."

"What are your concerns about her?"

"She's a yenta, and a wimp, and a bitch."

"She's a wimp *and* a bitch?"

"That's right. She's a bitch on wheels."

"That's a combination you don't see that often. A wimp and a bitch."

"Well, she breaks the mold."

Yetta was smiling now but she was still angry.

"That must make her at least somewhat interesting," Florence said.

"There's nothing interesting about her. She's boring. She's bored people to death. It's been known to happen."

"Yetta, what she told me was—"

"Don't call me Yetta all the time!"

"What are you talking about?"

"That's the third or fourth time you've Yettaed me. People only call people by their names like that when they're treating them like a child. I'm not a child, so don't treat me like one."

"All right. I'll stop calling you Yetta, but I'm not going to stop treating you like a child until you stop behaving like one."

"How am I behaving like a child?"

"The bitch on wheels told me that you've been refusing to wear adult undergarments."

"I have not been—what do you mean adult undergarments? What are adult undergarments?"

"Diapers. It's a polite term for diapers."

"That bitch thinks I should be wearing diapers?"

"She says you've been soiling yourself, Yetta."

"If you call me Yetta one more time I'm going to jump out the window and then you'll have a lawsuit on your hands. My son likes to go around suing people right and left."

"Calm down," Florence said.

"Soiling myself? She said I've been soiling myself? That's ridiculous."

"How is it ridiculous? You've told me there are plenty of times when you can't make it to the bathroom on time."

"That's only when I'm coming home. I'll put the key in the door and—"

"So how is it ridiculous? That's what she's saying. That there are times when you're not continent, and that you need to have something to protect you—"

"It's their fault. If they let Simon pick me up at the end of the day he could take me home in no time, and I wouldn't have any trouble holding anything in. But instead they make me go on that bus, which takes about an hour to get me home. If you want to help me you can tell them to be nicer to Simon."

"I will tell them to be nicer to Simon. But—"

"You say his name like you don't think much of him."

"I think the world of Simon," Florence said.

"And you say *that* like you don't think much of him."

Yetta's bullshit detector was intact; her sense of humor was intact; her pride was intact. But gone was the faculty that makes you want to take care of yourself, and gone was the faculty that enables you to distinguish between what is real and what is not. It reminded Florence of the dreaming mind, which retains all the qualities that make you you, except for the capacity to know when you're awake and when you're dreaming.

"Diapers?" Yetta said. "No siree. I'd sooner you just go to Plan B and lock me up."

"No one's thinking about locking you up."

"The way you say that makes me sure that someone *is* thinking about it. Maybe you."

"Nobody wants to lock you up, and nobody wants to 'ban' you."

"If they don't want me there, that's fine. I'll stay home. I'll eat cat food for all I care. It's better than the stupid meat loaf they're so proud of."

"Yetta—"

"Don't—"

"I'm going to. I'm going to Yetta you as long as you keep behaving like an idiot. It so happens I brought a couple. I'll show you. They don't look bad at all."

Florence had bought a sample pack of diapers at a drugstore in Grand Central before getting on the train. She took it out of her purse and broke the seal.

"You've brought some, have you? How kind. How very kind."

Yetta snatched a diaper out of Florence's hand.

"How wonderful! How marvelous! You've completely changed my mind! Do you think I could get them in pink?"

"I'm sure you could get them in any color you like."

"Do you think I can get them in red? To show the world I was a red-diaper baby?"

"We can look into it," Florence said.

"Let me check it out. Let me figure out how to put one of these things on."

"You want me to help?"

"I don't think I need any help. I think I'll be a natural. See? There!"

Yetta had put the diaper on her head. It fit snugly, like a cap.

"Perfect. Now I never have to worry about blowing my top, if that bitch on wheels annoys me again."

"I'm glad," Florence said. She stood up. "I'm glad we had this little chat."

"Me too. Come again soon!"

Florence decided to walk to the train station rather than calling a cab, but although her ankle was feeling better, she felt stiff and sore from Wednesday's exploits, and she finally had to sit on someone's stoop and call a cab. As she waited, she thought of Yetta with something like admiration. Florence had to admire the spirit that made her refuse to do anything in any way other than her own.

She couldn't admire it unreservedly, though, because Yetta stank and her house was appalling. Florence thought that after an hour there, she probably stank too. She made a mental note to wash her clothes as soon as she got home, but the stench in Yetta's house had been so thick that Florence wasn't at all sure that her clothes were salvageable.

68

As wretched as Yetta was, she'd probably live long enough to get much worse. Medical science was working tirelessly to extend the life span, but it would be more humane to find new ways to shorten it.

On the train Florence remembered a piece of research that Emily had evidently failed to do. It concerned a meeting held in the early days of the Redstockings. It was only a little piece of the puzzle, but it was the piece that Florence needed now.

She called Emily and got her voice mail.

"Have you done the research on the meeting? Please call me back."

By the time she got to Grand Central, Emily still hadn't called back.

Florence left another message, and then another.

It was incredibly rude of the girl to be out of reach. She said she'd be my "trusty assistant." She wasn't looking so trusty now.

She tried her son, and got no answer there either. She tried her daughter-in-law. No answer.

My son and his family have all been wiped out in a car crash, she thought idly.

How could they be so rude? That Daniel and Janine were snubbing her was bad enough, but it irked her no end that the girl, who was supposed to be working for her, was snubbing her too.

What had become of responsibility? What had become of loyalty? What had become of simple human courtesy?

She was so angry that she dialed the wrong number, not once but twice, and ended up quarreling with the person at the other end of the line.

When she got home, she heard workmen in the apartment next to hers. She needed to escape the banging, and although she hated to write in public, after showering and changing her clothes, she took her laptop and went down to a quiet café she knew on West Sixty-seventh.

In the café she scrolled through her memoir, what there was of it, and began to type. What with everything else that had been going on recently, she'd sometimes found it hard to concentrate on her project, but now she worked on it in a fury. She'd learned over the years that her writing went best when she could find material to match her mood. Now she decided to write about men and women who'd betrayed their ideals over the years. In the span of an hour she wrote a chapter about the different forms that failure of nerve had taken among people she'd known, and she felt sure it was the best thing she'd written in a long time.

A dapper little man in his eighties approached her table, with a coffee in one hand and a plate of little muffins in the other.

"Are you a writer?"

"Get away from me," Florence said.

69

Daniel thought he'd have the apartment to himself for a few hours, but when he got in, Emily was at the kitchen table, reading a book. It was some enormous tome. He couldn't see the title.

"Wanna fight?" he said as he passed her, which was one of their usual greetings. She didn't look up—thank God, because he could only imagine what he must've looked like.

He went straight to the bedroom he shared with Janine, and closed the door. The bedroom had acquired a new personality since he'd been there last. He felt as if he were visiting the room of some-one who'd died.

I don't know her anymore, he thought, but he wasn't even sure if that was true. In one moment, what she'd done seemed inconceiv-able; in the next, it felt like something he'd expected all along.

But that might be the way it always is when you learn something surprising. If a friend dies unexpectedly, much too young, at first it's impossible to believe, but in time you come to feel as if you knew he was going to die young the first time you met him.

He couldn't even feel very angry anymore. Maybe it was the

right move for her to have an affair. If she'd told her friends about it, maybe the ones who truly loved her and truly understood what she needed—maybe those friends had told her she was doing the right thing.

He pulled off his clothes and got in the shower and made it as hot as it could go, and stayed in for a long time.

70

Emily had been back for two or three hours when her father came in.

"Wanna fight?" he said, and then he vanished into his bedroom, and then she heard the shower.

She hadn't been able to look at him. She was vibrating with guilt. She had done everything she knew she would do, but more so. She'd spent the weekend having sex—which had turned into unprotected sex—and doing drugs. Not just Ecstasy. Drugs she'd never planned to take. Major drugs. Weird drugs. Drugs that hadn't even been invented yet.

She'd come back a different person from the person who'd left, but she didn't know exactly how. It would take a while, she thought, to understand how.

She was sitting in the kitchen reading *Little Women*. She reread it sometimes, parts of it, when she was feeling low.

After half an hour he emerged from the bedroom. She didn't look up at him; she kept reading, or at least she kept her head down. If she looked at him, she might cry.

Her parents had always trusted her completely. Not completely, but they'd always trusted her. And now she was brain-damaged from all the drugs she'd taken in the last two days, and she was pregnant, and she had AIDS, and the baby had AIDS too.

And Justin, at the end, had been so strange. Just before she left, he'd taken both of her hands in his and said, "This is forever, you know. This is forever."

And then he'd asked her to say it with him, and she hadn't known what to do. She'd tried to make a joke of it, but that didn't go well, and when she escaped from his dorm room, her head felt like a malfunctioning music box.

Her father opened the refrigerator. He still hadn't spoken to her, which was weird.

Or maybe not so weird. Obviously he sensed that something was going on with her, and he was being tactful.

She heard him taking things out of the fridge, and then she heard the rattling of pots and pans. He was making so much noise that it was almost as if he wanted to get her attention. But that was so unlike him that she instantly dismissed the idea.

She heard a knife slicing through things; she caught the scent of onions frying.

Although he claimed to be baffled by her veganism, and liked to make dumb Dad jokes about slipping bacon bits into her meals, he in fact had always treated her choice respectfully, to the point of learning how to cook for her. When she was in high school, he used to make tofu scrambles for her on the weekends, and he was making one now.

She wished he weren't so attentive. Even if he was silent, you felt like you could never be alone with your thoughts when he was near. She wished she could make him realize—without actually telling him—that if he ever lost her, it would be because of this. Some parents lose their children because they don't pay enough attention, some because they pay too much.

She wasn't sure she knew what she was talking about, but it sounded right.

The tofu scramble was ready in a few minutes. He put a plate in front of her, and another plate with two pieces of whole wheat toast, and a glass of orange juice, and a napkin.

"Take it away, Angelo," he said, which was what he always did when he served anybody. She didn't know what it meant.

She nodded, vaguely, in his general direction, still unable to meet his eyes.

She had no idea why he was doing this: cooking for her, not making her speak. It was uncanny. How could he understand what she was going through? Of course he didn't know the details of it, but somehow he understood—he understood *something*—and somehow, she was beginning to think, he forgave her.

71

His daughter couldn't look at him. It was as if she were embarrassed for him. Could it possibly be that she knew about the affair? Could it possibly be that she knew that he'd been humiliated, and felt that he deserved it?

He forced himself to concentrate on the scramble thing so as not to think about anything else. But he couldn't stop himself from thinking about the possible scenarios. Maybe Emily too had come upon Janine nuzzling up to the Great Man, and had been shocked at first, but had come to sympathize once Janine explained her motives.

"I still love your father, but he doesn't . . . he isn't . . ."

I don't *what*? I'm not *what*?

It was obvious what he didn't; it was obvious what he wasn't. He wasn't the man she thought she'd married; he hadn't given her the life she'd hoped for. He had trapped her in the Great Northwest, and she'd put up with it for the sake of the children, but she'd always been a big-city girl at heart, and these months of intellectual excitement in New York had made her finally realize that she just couldn't bear the smallness of her life with him anymore.

But did she really have to tell Emily? Before she told *him*?

But maybe she hadn't told Emily.

But if she hadn't told Emily, why was Emily averting her eyes?

Maybe Emily was averting her eyes not because she knew, but because she knew *something*, even if she didn't know what. Maybe he was giving off a smell that animals give off when they've been defeated. A smell that animals give off when they've been — what was the word? There was some word for when your wife is sleeping with somebody else, but he couldn't remember what it was. He remembered first hearing it in a Shakespeare class he took in college — all those stupid jokes about men wearing horns. Shakespeare thought that getting cuckolded — that's the word — was the funniest thing in the world.

Shakespeare was a fucking idiot.

What did Emily know, and when did she know it?

He made the scramble and put it in front of her, with toast and orange juice. All she could do was nod at him. He thought the chances were slim that she actually knew about the affair, and yet she couldn't look him in the eye. She was ashamed of him, even if she didn't know why.

72

Daniel had planned to be out when Janine came home that night, but she got back earlier than expected.

"It was great," she said, in answer to his question. "I don't know. It was and it wasn't."

She was pulling things out of her pockets—pens, coins, ticket stubs—and dropping them on the kitchen counter. Slob.

Receipts, tissues, condom wrappers.

No, she wasn't pulling condom wrappers out of her pockets. But he expected her to.

He had been thinking of little else than what he wanted to do, but he still had no idea.

He was standing in the kitchen with a spatula, in the middle of making dinner. All he did, in the family's new dispensation, was stand around and cook. He should have been wearing a fucking apron.

It enraged him that he was fucking cooking at the moment she walked in the door.

"So what have you guys been talking about?" Janine said. "What did I miss?"

"Not very much," Emily said, from the living room.

"What? Your dad hasn't been his usual chatty self?"

"Dad's been Calvin Coolidge."

"I like a girl who makes Calvin Coolidge jokes," Daniel said. "Too few teenagers have the moxie to do that these days."

"What's the trouble?" Janine said. "Cat got your tongue?"

She dropped a few more coins on the counter. Why the hell was she doing that? It was as if she were tipping him, for years of service. Fifty-two cents.

When he went to the shelf for some garlic, he took a good long look at Janine, for the first time since she'd walked in the door.

She looked radiant. She looked aglow.

He was hoping that she'd learned over the course of the weekend that whatever she'd thought was missing from their marriage wasn't missing at all. But this wasn't a happy-to-be-back radiance; it was a still-in-the-glow-of-the-weekend radiance.

He wasn't sure how he could tell, but he was sure he could tell.

"That sauce smells good," Janine said.

Why the hell is she talking to me? he thought. Why is she bothering? Why doesn't she just collect her things and go?

"You don't have to wait here. I'll bring it to you when I'm done."

"Why would you bring it to me when you're done?"

"Because it's dinner."

"Where am I supposed to go? Why shouldn't I wait here?"

"I don't know. You just got home. Don't you need to freshen up or something?"

"What if I want to wait here? What if I feel fresh enough already?"

"Suit yourself."

He cut up the onions, the carrots, the mushrooms, the red peppers, the green peppers. She got herself a glass of wine.

"You want hot peppers?" he said.

"You know I don't like hot peppers."

"I thought your tastes might have changed."

He knew he was acting strangely. If he'd acted like this on any other day—any day before this past Friday—she would have asked him what was going on. He knew that she wouldn't ask him now, though.

Why not just tell her? Why not just tell her he knew?

If he told her, what would he say?

I saw you holding hands with a boy down at the ice cream parlor.

What would he say after that?

Are you going to the sock hop with him?

He continued to prepare the dinner. Janine drank her wine and looked through the mail. He was thinking of attacking her with the spatula.

He started making some bruschetta for Emily. Janine didn't like bruschetta, but fuck her.

Emily showed up in the kitchen.

"Why are *you* being so quiet now?"

"I'm not," Janine said.

"Yes you are. I've been right outside. It's like you caught his disease."

"We've been talking a mile a minute," Daniel said.

"You people haven't seen each other in days. I expect you to be exchanging nuggets of information. I expect repartee."

Emily sounded, to his ear, a little desperate. Her lips were peeled, as if she'd been chewing them. A habit she'd had since childhood but only when she was stressed.

He'd decided that she probably didn't know that her mother was having an affair. But it was clear that she sensed that something was wrong.

He would have liked to say something reassuring to her, but he had nothing reassuring to say. He finished making the bruschetta and held the plate out to her, and she took a piece.

"So how was your conference?" Emily said.

"Well, it was a mixed bag."

He couldn't get it up? Daniel wanted to say. He disappointed you in some way? He weirded you out? He wanted you to spank him and tell him he was a bad boy?

"Why?" Emily said.

"There's a lot of exciting work going on in the field. But the more I look at it, the less I feel I fit in. They're interested in doing quantitative studies. I just like listening to people talk."

He was trying to figure out if this was a coded way of saying that her affair had been a dud.

"On the other hand, they're asking the questions I've been asking for years, and they're asking it in a systematic way. So . . . I don't know."

"Sounds like you should stay here for a while past December," Daniel said. "Give yourself time to figure it out."

"What?" Emily said. "She can't stay here."

"What's it to you?" Daniel said. "It's not like you'll be at home."

"That doesn't matter. I need both of you to be where I expect you to be."

73

Over the next few days, Daniel found ways not to say anything more consequential to his wife than "Could you pass the milk?" He wasn't sure why he was being like this. It wasn't as if he were afraid to talk to her. It wasn't even as if he were afraid she was going to leave him. He'd already put himself into a state in which, if she told him she was moving out, he would be able to respond stoically.

He wasn't sure why he was being like this, and then he figured out that he was just being himself. He was waiting for her to make a move. When he used to box, he'd been a counterpuncher; when he used to play chess he'd always been more comfortable playing black. He was in counterpuncher mode now.

But he couldn't stay in counterpuncher mode forever.

Can I live with it? If she wants to be with him and be with me at the same time, can I live with it?

No.

And could I live without her?

Yes. Of course.

When he first knew her, back when he still had a lot of poetry in his head, he'd once told her that he loved the "pilgrim soul" in her.

He still loved her pilgrim soul—and in the distant seat of the mind that looks upon all things with a serene detachment, he respected her even now for being so responsive to life as to allow herself to feel new things for a new person. But that didn't mean he could live with it. If she insisted on following the promptings of her soul wherever they led her, then she'd pilgrimmed herself out of his life.

74

Janine found her homecoming eerie. It was almost as if Daniel knew. But how could he know? He couldn't know.

But it felt as if he knew.

One evening a few days after she got back, Emily looked up from her laptop and said, "Van Morrison is at the Beacon next week. You guys should get tickets."

Janine loved Van Morrison, but she wasn't sure she felt like going to a concert.

"Can we wait on it a little?" she said to Daniel. "Is that okay?"

"Sure . . ." he said. Then he paused. He held the pause. He held the pause. Then he said, "But it would be good if you figured out what you wanted to do." And then he left the room.

He was angry with her. That much was obvious. But maybe he was angry at her for some other reason. That would be wonderful—if he thought she'd done something terrible, but he knew nothing about what she'd really done.

She tried to think of what it might be, but came up with nothing. And obviously she couldn't ask him. "Excuse me, are you angry at me for some bad thing I've done, on a scale of seriousness up to but not including having an affair?"

Lev was traveling. He was visiting his mother in Arizona, and then he was going to see his oldest daughter at the spiritual community in California where she'd been living for the past ten years. Janine hadn't heard from him since Pittsburgh, except for a skimpy text message or two.

Daniel had the television on. He was watching *Doctor Who*. A woman was being strangled by a mannequin. Daniel was nodding—nodding with approval, she thought.

75

One morning, just after dawn, she went for a run that took her up above Grant's Tomb and back down to the Soldiers' and Sailors' Monument in Riverside Park. It was still early; she didn't feel like going home and showering yet; so she walked through the park, slowly following its mazy paths to the water.

North of her was the George Washington Bridge, long and unadorned, beautiful in its strength and its simplicity.

On one of their first dates, back in college—did they think in terms of "dates" back then? It was hard for her to remember—she and Daniel had gone to a jazz brunch at the West End, and then they'd taken a long walk in the park and ended up near the river, close to the spot where she was now standing.

It had been a chilly afternoon at the end of the fall. They were wearing gloves, but that didn't diminish the intimacy she felt holding hands with him.

They sat on a bench near the river.

She remembered turning to face him and drawing her scarf off slowly.

"Nobody's ever paid attention to my throat before," she said. "You could be the first."

He smiled at her, a quizzical smile, and brought his lips to a point where her throat met her jawline.

She remembered that it felt as if the city were disappearing—the skyscrapers receding, the bridge floating off like smoke.

76

Florence received a call from her doctor's office. His secretary said that he'd be on in a moment, and then she put Florence on hold. Florence promptly hung up.

When the phone rang again a few minutes later, it was Noah himself.

"We must have gotten cut off there."

"I cut us off. I hung up."

"Why? You've got a thing about telephones?"

"Phones are fine. I've got a thing about power trips. If you want to call me, you can call me yourself."

"Pardon me. I forgot it was you. I forgot who I was power-tripping."

"You forgot who you were trying to power-trip."

"Exactly. Anyway, I've looked over your tests, and there's not much of interest. I mean, everything about you is of interest, Florence, but it's all perfectly normal. How was the nerve conduction, by the way?"

One of the tests had been a nerve-conduction study, in which she'd received bursts of electricity from many tiny needles.

"One part science, one part acupuncture, one part voodoo. It was divine."

"I'm glad you enjoyed it," he said. "Anyway, I've gone ahead and ordered a few more tests."

"So we aren't any closer to knowing what's going on?"

"Well, we've ruled out a few things. But we've still got a way to go."

"So are you saying that we need to start thinking about zebras?"

"That depends on how we define zebras," he said.

"What does that mean?"

"I'm just kidding. A little medical humor. It's not zebra time yet. This could still be something extremely ordinary, extremely trivial. In fact it's more likely to be something trivial than not. It could be stress. It could be arthritis. It could still be any one of those horses. And even if it is a zebra, not all zebras are bad. A zebra is just something unusual. Not all zebras are trouble. I just think we should get ahead of this thing, in case it's anything we need to get ahead of."

"So what are the tests?" she said.

"Well, first I'd like us to get that MRI, which somehow seems to have slipped off your to-do list. What's so funny?"

"Us? Are you going to be there? Planning to climb in?"

"I'd like to, but I'll only be able to climb in with you in spirit."

"That'll be quite enough, thanks. But why an MRI? You want them to do an MRI of my hand or something?"

"Well, not so much. I think we've seen just about everything there is to be seen in your hands and feet. So now it's time to look at other parts of you."

He made this sound very reasonable. She felt like a distinguished piece of statuary. Parts of her had been thoroughly studied by the scholars, but other parts had been neglected so far.

She wondered whether she should be nervous, but she didn't feel nervous. She went back to her work.

77

Saturday was evidently a good day for them to peer into your brain. Florence went up to Columbia Presbyterian that afternoon for her MRI.

At the medical center, after she filled out a form confirming that she contained no metal—no pacemakers, no artificial hips or knees, no shrapnel, no ball bearings, no bullets—a very tall young man led her to a tiny locker room where she was to store her valuables and change into a gown.

The gown had two sets of laces, at the waist and at the neck, but they were hard to tie. None of the laces was long enough to comfortably reach its mate.

Why were hospital gowns always like this? Why did they never fit? They seemed to have been designed for a different species. Maybe they were made this way because if they were too nice, people would steal them. Or maybe they were made this way to leave you feeling vulnerable and humiliated, thus making it easier for doctors and nurses and technicians to order you around.

The young man returned. She supposed he was a technician, but she wasn't sure. Maybe he was a nurse. Whatever he was, he seemed unusual. He was kindly, gentle, apple-cheeked, but in his eyes there was something shrewd and ironic. He had the look of someone who was taking mental notes.

Outside the MRI room was a sign: POWERFUL MAGNETS! DO NOT REMAIN IN ROOM WHILE IMAGING IS IN PROGRESS!

She tried to imagine a magnet powerful enough to call for exclamation points.

You were told that they posed a danger to you only if you were partly made of metal—so why was there a need for this general warning?

She decided that if you thought about it, it made sense. Each drop of hemoglobin contains a core of iron. Wouldn't this mean that when the magnets go on, they reorganize your internal architecture, sucking the iron to the periphery of each cell?

The magnets, in her case, would be trained on the brain. Maybe when she came out of this thing she'd be a neoconservative.

Finally the gentle technician—his name tag said HUDSON—showed her into the room, directed her to lie down on a sort of table covered by the usual paper sheet, and asked her what she'd like to listen to. "Classical? Light jazz? Elton John?"

"Do you have any hip-hop?" she said, just to mess with him, and when he hesitated, she said, "Classical will be fine."

He left the room and, shortly afterward, her table went sliding into the narrow tube of the MRI machine. She felt like a corpse on a TV show, lying on a shelf in a morgue. They slide you out, because the detectives have some hunch they want to check, and then they slide you back in again.

She was inside the drawer. It was a very tight space.

She could see that this would be distressing if you were claustrophobic, but she wasn't.

A tremendous banging started up, as if insane people with hammers had taken over the hospital. Florence began to see that if you had even a slight touch of claustrophobia, this could be very uncomfortable.

The banging kept up mercilessly, and after a while she started to get used to it, and then it stopped, and then another noise took its place, even louder and more noxious—it sounded like the grinding noise of an airplane that was about to crash.

She thought of an old friend of hers, Joanna, who hated elevators. If Joanna ever had to have an MRI, how would she get through it?

She could see how this could get to you if you even knew someone who was claustrophobic.

She was confined so tightly in this small space that, rather than a corpse, she began to think of herself as a mummy.

That's probably a bad idea. Don't think of yourself as a mummy, tightly bound—

Several of her friends had become serious meditators over the years, and had become proselytizers for the practice, claiming that it could cure high blood pressure, insomnia, problems of concentration, and more or less everything else. Florence's attitude toward it had always been a mix of curiosity and scorn, but now she wished that she had taken it up.

How on earth had they figured out they could use jumbo-size magnets to peer into your brain? Magnets that enabled doctors to see what was going on inside your head—it didn't even make sense. On the other hand, how had they figured anything out? How had they invented the telephone? How had they invented the camera?

Finally the banging stopped, and the table moved out again. Hudson took her arm and helped her off the pad, and she felt a childish wish for approval. She wanted him to say something like, "We monitor your vital signs in there, and I've never seen anybody remain so calm." She was a seventy-five-year-old woman, and she wanted a word of approval from this child.

But one of the fine things about life is the difference between what goes on inside you and what you show to the world. After he took her arm, she withdrew it, putting on an air of irritation that she didn't actually feel. She valued his kindness, but she was damned if she was going to let anybody treat her like an invalid.

She went to the locker room and put her clothes back on. Young

Hudson was waiting for her in the hall. He reached out to take her arm again and then stopped himself, which made her like him all the more.

"That thing can shake a person up."

"I'm fine," she said.

"Do you have anybody with you?"

"No. Just me."

"Anybody you can call? Anybody who can take you home?"

She thought about it. Any one of a number of her old friends would have been happy to pick her up.

There was Vanessa, of course—but no. Vanessa was too tuned in to Florence's feelings. Vanessa would feel all of Florence's anxieties, but without Florence's ability to suppress them, and Florence didn't want to put her friend through that. There was Cassie—but Cassie had written two books about the American health-care system, and she'd want to know the details of what Florence was going through, and Florence didn't want to talk about the details now. There was Ruby, but Ruby had been throwing herself into solidarity work with women in Egypt, and although Florence admired the headlong way in which Ruby had pursued her political passions, she didn't want to listen to news about Egypt this afternoon.

The problem with Florence's friends was that they were all as intense as she was, and she couldn't deal with that kind of intensity right now. She needed someone who would just let her be.

The only person she seriously considered calling was her granddaughter. She had no idea why. It wasn't as if Emily were that impressive. She was all too obviously a member of her generation, with one eye on the world and one eye on her fucking smartphone. Emily had a lot going for her, but she also had a lot going against her, and there was no reason to think that her promise would win out over the impairments she'd suffered as a result of having been born in a certain time and place.

"Nope," Florence said. "I can get home on my own. There's no reason to dramatize things."

He wouldn't let it go, though.

"What'll it cost you if you ask somebody to help you out?"

"Mind your own business, young man," she said, in a tone that she hoped sounded at least somewhat playful.

"Lone wolf, are you?" he said. "Well, all right. Your life."

"Indeed it is," she said, and instantly regretted the fusty "indeed."

The young man turned back to the unit, smiling and shaking his head.

On Friday, Florence's doctor called. This time it wasn't his secretary, calling on his behalf; this time it was Noah himself.

"So what's up?" she said.

She tried to make her voice steely and ready for anything, in the hope that this would help her feel steely and ready for anything.

"Got your test results. Still nothing definitive. But you should come in, so we can talk about our next few moves."

"Can't we just talk on the phone, Noah?"

"I want to see you. I want to get your blood pressure, take some blood, maybe tweak your meds a little bit."

She didn't believe this. He'd taken blood a few months ago, and the only medication she took hadn't needed "tweaking" in years. She knew that he had bad news to give her and that he didn't want to give it over the phone. But finally she acquiesced to the fiction that he wanted to see her for reasons that were more routine.

She walked to Noah's office. It was an unseasonably chilly day in the middle of August; a thin, ungenerous rain kept spritzing from the sky. It was a perfect day to stay home and read and write. But here she was.

Now that her ankle was better, she was more aware than ever that there was something wrong with her left foot. She wasn't sure it was anything that anyone would notice, but when she was walking, it was as if her left foot didn't want to come along.

When she got to his office, she wasn't asked to wait in an examining room. This was a first. She was shown into his office, where he was sitting behind his desk.

"I've been looking over your results," he said.

He seemed as matter-of-fact as ever, and she had a little flare of hope. Maybe he asked me here because he likes to give good news in person.

"There are a lot of things we can eliminate at this point," he said.

"Hangnails?" she said. "Hangovers?"

"Yes. That's right. It's not a hangover. We can rule that out."

"I'm so relieved."

"Seriously. It isn't a nerve problem. We can be pretty sure of that. And it isn't MS. MS can be pretty bad. And I don't see anything that makes me wonder if you had a stroke."

She imagined him patiently, matter-of-factly eliminating a thousand things, and finally, at midnight, telling her she had a brain tumor and would be dead by dawn.

"So what are the possibilities?"

"There are still a lot of possibilities, Florence."

"What are the probabilities."

"Even there, I'm not sure I'd put it that way. When you're a doctor, you don't want to shotgun it; you want to ballpark it, so to speak."

"Noah."

"I just don't want you to think—"

Her dignity had always been her most effective tool. She drew herself up in her chair and, with what she hoped was a tone of starchy imperiousness, said, "Noah. I'm a busy woman. I don't have time for all this beating around the bush. You have to be direct with me."

She consciously rejected the phrase "I need you to be direct with me," a phrase that, to her mind, would have been both groveling and manipulative. Better to demand than to plead.

"We still can't be sure of anything," Noah said. "We'll need to do a lot more tests. And it still might turn out to be something entirely transitory and benign. But right now the most likely thing we're looking at is ALS."

She took a moment to try to absorb this.

She was struck by how odd it was that she hadn't thought of the possibility before. But then again, she hadn't thought of anything before. She'd assumed that whatever she had was trivial. It was as if she thought she'd been taking these tests as a sort of masquerade. It was as if she'd retained her twelve-year-old's belief that she and she alone would never die.

"What are you thinking?" he said.

"I'm thinking about a writer named Tony Judt. He was diagnosed a year ago and he's still going strong."

Tony Judt: the historian who, universally considered an arrogant pain in the ass during his healthy years, had become an inspiration to everyone who knew of him after he was diagnosed with ALS. Unable during recent years to press his fingers down on a keyboard or hold a pen, he was said to be dictating two books, the first a polemic in favor of social democracy, the second a collection of autobiographical sketches. By dint of sheer willpower and unstinting hard work he'd turned himself into a symbol, a reminder that if you have enough courage you can find a way to triumph, spiritually speaking, over anything.

"I'm almost looking forward to it," she said. "Wasn't it Lenin who said that a spell in prison is indispensable to an intellectual career? A little bout of ALS is probably the best thing that could happen to me."

"That's the spirit. But don't get your hopes too high. It may turn out not to be ALS after all."

They talked about the further tests she'd have to take, and then he stood up.

"You all right to get home? Anybody you want to call?"

What the hell was this? All of a sudden everybody was acting as if she couldn't make her way home without *calling* someone. She lived six blocks away.

"Oh, please, Noah. Who do you think you're talking to?"

He led her toward the door, and they awkwardly paused there. Then she reached for the knob and turned it.

She could feel how relieved he was—at least she thought she could feel it: how relieved he was to be getting rid of her without having to hug her.

If she had seemed to need comforting, he would have tried to comfort her, but he must have been glad that she didn't.

After she left the office, she reflected that if she did have ALS, her life from here on in was going to consist of one performance after another. She was determined to play the role of the brave woman. However terrified she might feel, she was determined not to let anyone see it. I'll make them forget Tony Judt, those fuckers, she thought, though she wasn't sure who she was referring to.

If she did turn out to have the disease, the conversation in Noah's office would turn out to have been the first such performance, and she concluded with satisfaction that she could give herself a passing grade.

79

At home she went online, went to feministing.com, logged in to the Comments section, and started vigorously correcting the errors of the young. For a while she felt alive—not just alive, but unconquerable.

But after half an hour or so, she felt tired. She lay on her couch and fell asleep, woke at midnight, and couldn't get to sleep again.

She tried hard not to think about ALS. There would be time to think about it later, if this was what her affliction turned out to be. She had a conference to attend the next day—the symposium at NYU on the women's movement, which was going to include a tribute to her from Martha Nussbaum—and she wanted to make a good showing. She wanted to sail through it with the same aplomb that she had summoned in her doctor's office. She wanted to comport herself in such a way that no one would suspect that anything was wrong. But it would have been easier if she could have gotten back to sleep.

At two in the morning she'd felt jittery and overstimulated, but by daybreak she felt benumbed. Not the best frame of mind in which to attend an event at which she needed to have her wits about her.

Her buzzer sounded and she wondered what fresh nuisance this could be. She pressed her intercom and asked who was there. It was her granddaughter.

She buzzed her in. As she waited, she was surprised by how happy it made her to know that Emily was here. But she was damned if she was going to let Emily see that.

80

One of the things that Emily had discovered about herself in the last year was that she might not be as stable as she'd thought she was. In high school she had watched friends and acquaintances go through theatrical breakdowns—because of drugs, because of homesickness, because of heartbreak—and she had always "been there" for them. She was the person you called if your drug experience went bad. She was the person you went to for advice, because she was the only person who didn't give any: she would listen and ask questions, and from your answers you'd discover what you wanted to do. She was the rock in other people's lives, and she'd always enjoyed being the rock in other people's lives.

At Oberlin last fall, once she'd started to feel sure that it wasn't the right place for her, she was surprised by how quickly she went from unhappiness to misery. She knew her parents would have been happier if she'd stuck it out for the full year and then switched schools in an orderly fashion, without falling a semester behind, but she'd seen two girls in her hall come apart completely during her first year, and she had no reason to believe that she was any stronger than they were.

Lately Justin had been pressuring her to visit him again, and when she tried to put him off, he'd started to sound like he was disintegrating.

He was still sending her little videos of toys he'd made, robots and Jedi and goblins. But now the videos were sadder. The robots were frightened of the goblins; the Jedi were wandering lost in the dark.

He'd also started sending videos of himself. One of them was funny: Justin accompanying himself on the dulcimer, singing about how he missed her. One of them made her uncomfortable: Justin singing about how he couldn't live without her. And one of them scared her: toy robots carrying razor blades, which were almost as big as they were, and advancing toward a sleeping Justin. She didn't know anything about making videos, so she didn't know how he managed to make it look so real.

At the end of the video, a robot pushed the tip of his blade against Justin's neck, and a spot of blood emerged. Then the robot's head swiveled toward the camera, and, in a deep, creepy, mechanical voice, he said, "If you don't visit us soon, the kid gets it."

Since when did boys cut themselves? She hadn't thought that that was something boys *do*.

When she talked to him that night, he said it was just a joke, but it didn't feel like a joke.

She knew she was in over her head, and she didn't know what to do.

And on top of all this, her parents had gotten strange. It was the worst possible time for that to happen. She needed them to be solid right now.

She couldn't figure out what was going on with them, and she didn't want to try. She just wanted them to go back to normal.

So when she went to her grandmother's on Saturday morning, she went there in a needy frame of mind. But all she really needed was for her grandmother to be herself. She didn't want her grandmother to offer her any particular kindness. She didn't want her grandmother to listen to her talk about her problems. All she

wanted was her normal presence—acerbic, impatient, semi-an-
noyed.

When she got to Florence's apartment, Florence was standing at
the open door.

"What are you doing here?" Florence said, which made Emily
happy.

"I'm going to the conference with you."

"Since when?"

"Since forever. Since last week. We talked about this."

"We did? Well, all right. Come in."

Florence was moving slowly. She didn't seem like herself.

Not you too.

"I need to get myself together," Florence said, and went into her bedroom, and closed the door. When she emerged, she was Florence again, brittle and curt.

"Make yourself some of that weak tea you like," Florence said. "I'll be ready to go in a few minutes."

"Don't insult my tea," Emily said, smiling.

Florence was a rock star. When they got to the Skirball Center, women kept coming up to her to tell her how much her work had meant to them. Florence responded graciously to all of them, which Emily found surprising. It was easier to imagine her grandmother barking at them all, telling them they were praising her for the wrong reasons.

The conference was a daylong event on the topic "The Women's Movement: Then and Now." There were many panels, half of which had titles Emily didn't understand. "Different Shades of *Différence:* French Feminism(s) in the Era(s) of Post-Subalternity," for example, was one she thought she could skip.

Florence was scheduled to give a lecture in the early afternoon. The last talk of the day was to be given by Martha Nussbaum, the philosopher who'd feted Florence in the *Times;* it was going to be about Florence's contribution to feminist thought.

One of the organizers of the conference, a woman named Elba, came lumbering up and gave Florence a hug; Emily could see Florence backing away while Elba's arms were still around her. Elba even hugged Emily, who wondered if someone watching them might find her to be backing away too. The three of them proceeded toward the part of the building where the morning panels were taking place, and Elba kept stopping to make introductions. At first it seemed as if everyone was equally excited to meet Florence, but little by little, Emily could see that it wasn't so. The oldest and the youngest women seemed to regard Florence with something like awe, but Emily noticed one or two women in the middle generation who seemed blasé, even rude, when they were introduced to her.

Emily started to try to construct a theory out of this, but then, remembering a statistics class she'd had to take in high school, she reasoned that this was too small a sample size to justify a theory.

Emily heard Florence saying, "That's too bad."

"What's too bad?" Emily said, after Florence rejoined her.

"Martha Nussbaum isn't coming. Supposedly she has the flu."

"Supposedly?"

"Well, you know. Martha Nussbaum. She must've had an idea for a new book while she was brushing her teeth. She's putting the finishing touches on it now."

Emily spaced out through the morning session. She attended two panels and didn't take in a word. Instead, she was thinking about Justin. She was worried about him, and she was worried about herself.

There was a luncheon, during which many women competed for Florence's attention.

At lunch, Elba leaned over toward Florence and said, "We're in luck! You'll never guess who we got to step in for Nussbaum."

"Who?"

"Willa Ruth Stone."

"Really?" Emily said.

"Who?" Florence said.

"She's a famous blogger," Emily said.

Florence raised an eyebrow at this, but didn't say anything.

Emily had read Willa Ruth Stone all through high school, in places like *Jezebel* and *The Awl*. In the last year or two she'd gone on to other venues, and Emily had stopped following her work. She didn't seem like the obvious person to give a talk here—she was sort of a snark artist—but if someone as hip as that was a fan of Florence's, Florence was even more of a rock star than Emily had realized.

"She said she's really excited," Elba said. "She said she's always wanted to get the chance to honor you."

After lunch, Florence gave her talk: "Mary Datchet at Ninety," a meditation on the state of feminism today in the light of its early-twentieth-century aspirations.

Florence read from her notes without looking up. Emily had seen her grandmother speak in public several times now, and this was the only performance she would have described as uninspired.

Emily recognized traces of some of the research she'd done: Florence quoted from the letters of Mary Gawthorpe to Edward Carpenter and Havelock Ellis—letters that Emily had copied out by hand, because the paper they'd been written on was now too fragile to be pressed against a photocopier. Emily kept wondering if Florence was going to mention her by name, and then kept telling herself that her wish to be acknowledged showed how childish she was. But that didn't stop her from feeling disappointed when Florence finished without acknowledging her.

After the talk, there was more milling around, more sitting through panel discussions, more worrying about Justin, and then there was the last event of the day.

The auditorium was packed—entirely with women; Emily hadn't seen more than a couple of men all day. Looking over the audience, Emily guessed that a lot of the women there had come just to hear Willa Ruth Stone. They looked stylish and fresh, not like people who'd been listening to lectures all day.

Amazing how fast word gets around. Emily had grown up in the age of social media, but it still felt amazing to her.

Elba reminded everyone that they'd rented a room in the Kronstadt Bar on Thompson Street, that it would be open as soon as the symposium ended, and that drinks would be half price. Then she made way for the keynote speaker.

Willa Ruth Stone was lithe, blond, beautiful—not movie-star beautiful, but beautiful for a writer. Everyone else who'd spoken that day had sat behind a microphone, but she had a wireless mike clipped to her shirt, so she could glide around the stage.

Florence was seated behind her. The lighting on the stage made her look ghostly.

The first twenty minutes of Willa's talk was a sort of tour of the cultural landscape. After this part was finished, she turned and bowed to Florence, and then she turned back to the audience.

"It's an honor to be here today to celebrate Florence Gordon, a woman I respect deeply," Willa said. "Who could fail to respect Florence Gordon? Our lives would be inconceivable without her. She's as indispensable as the Pill. She's as indispensable as Tampax."

Emily was shocked by this. It was disrespectful. It was vulgar. But no one else seemed shocked. It got a laugh.

She tried to read her grandmother's reaction, but from this distance Florence was unreadable.

"When the women of the New Left were being exploited by their boyfriends, Florence Gordon was there, to blow the whistle on it. When the media was ignoring sex discrimination in the workplace, Florence Gordon was there, with eloquence and statistics, to prove that it was a national disgrace. When women's studies and women's history departments were being strangled in their cradles during the Reagan years, Florence Gordon was there to press our claims. Florence Gordon and her sisters created the world we're living in today, and we thank them."

Everyone applauded, and Florence nodded regally.

"But I know that Florence Gordon would want me to speak frankly today. To do anything less would be to fail to honor her. And, speaking frankly, we have to admit that for most of us here, Florence Gordon's world is the world of our grandmothers. We love our grandmothers, and we're thankful to them, but we don't want to be them. When I look around this room, at the faces of the women of my generation, I see women who want to express all the different sides of themselves. There are times when we want to speak out against the injustices of the world. And there are times when we want to put on stilettos and a little black dress and find a party.

"When we do want to stage a protest, our grandmothers are right by our side. They're proud of us. But when we go out to party, our grandmothers get very upset. They call to us from the doorway: 'What are you partying for! Men are still oppressing us! Capitalism is still evil! The Republicans still want to repeal *Roe versus Wade*! You can't go out and party! There's work to be done!'

"And when we hear our grandmothers calling to us like this, we have to respond honestly. We have to say: Yes, and yes—but no. Yes, women are often still victimized. Yes, capitalism still leaves us in a world of risk and constant change. But no. We don't identify this world as evil. Unlike you, we embrace the risk. Unlike you, we see this imperfect world not as a world of wall-to-wall oppression, but a world of opportunity. In today's world, women are in the boardroom, asserting themselves; and women are in the bedroom, enjoying themselves. It's not the black-and-white world that you saw. It's a world with many colors, and some of them are amazing.

"Sometimes I think this intergenerational argument comes down to pleasure. Our grandmothers seemed to believe that pleasure is a sin. We believe we need pleasure, just like we need fresh air and clean water and light. They believed you can't do good in the world if you keep stopping to refresh yourself; we believe you can't do good in the world if you don't.

"We honor you, Florence Gordon. We honor you and your generation. We wouldn't be here if not for you. To you and your sisters, I say thank you. We've learned so much from you. And one of the things we've learned is strength of mind, the strength of mind that now gives us the courage to say that your way is not our way.

"And now, at the end of this glorious day of conferring and confabbing, I turn to my sisters, and I say (cover your ears, Florence): Bitches, let's party!"

Willa Ruth Stone left the stage without so much as a glance at Florence. The applause didn't diminish until she'd left the auditorium, surrounded by friends and admirers. Florence was left by herself on the back of the stage.

Florence looked unhappy, but above all she looked tired.

Almost everyone was leaving, but several older women were

striding toward a microphone near the foot of the stage. One of them was Vanessa. She looked furious. She planted her feet in front of the microphone and started to speak, but the sound had already been cut. She kept speaking into it, for some reason, as if she didn't realize that no one could hear.

The talk made Emily angry, not just because it was unkind, but because it was untrue. From all those weeks in the archives she knew that although many women in her movement had been puritanical, Florence and her friends had never been. They'd been cheerleaders for sex and drugs and rock 'n' roll; above all else, they'd been cheerleaders for freedom. Every kind of freedom, from radical democratic politics to radically unconventional living arrangements.

And none of this was a secret. All of it could be found in the pages of Florence's first two books — essay collections from the seventies that were on sale in the lobby. "Against Propriety"; "Notes on What Just Happened"; "A Few Late Thoughts on Oscar Wilde"; "Opportunities for Heroism in Everyday Life": in her best-known early essays she'd spelled out a vision of personal liberation that might look cheesy today but was nothing like the caricature that Willa Ruth Stone had sketched.

A published writer who'd given a talk without checking her facts. Who'd based her talk on ideas she thought clever, not ideas she knew to be true. Emily was young enough to be stunned by this.

Florence's friends were surrounding her, making a lot of noise, as if to drown out the memory of what had just happened.

They all went to a restaurant across the street and commandeered a long table. Emily came with. Six of Florence's friends were there, including Vanessa and Alexandra. All of them seemed to have known one another for many, many years.

They kept up a steady flow of talk. For a while they talked about the idiocy of Willa Ruth Stone and everything she stood for, and then they moved on to other things. They were outraged about some new threat to second-trimester abortion rights in New York; they were outraged about some new threat to affirmative action. They were outraged about the Tea Party; they were outraged about the Supreme Court. They were outraged about Obama's lassitude in pushing his health-care agenda; they were outraged about Obama's zealousness in prosecuting whistleblowers.

"What do you think?" Vanessa said.

"What do I think about what?" Emily said.

"About whatever you're thinking about. You look like you're thinking furiously."

"I was thinking I'm amazed by the energy you all have. I was thinking I admire the way you can still get so indignant."

"It keeps us young," Vanessa said.

An article that Florence had written about the early days of the women's movement came to Emily's mind. Florence had described it as a "festival of talk." She said that it was impossible to describe what it had felt like to be part of an entire generation of women who were suddenly speaking to one another without fear.

Emily was still trying to figure out what had happened back there at the conference. The truly shocking thing wasn't that Florence had been insulted at an occasion where she was supposed to have been honored. It was that she hadn't fought back.

While Emily was listening to Willa Ruth Stone give her talk, at the same time as she'd been horrified, she'd also been excited, because she'd felt sure that Florence would destroy her. And then it hadn't happened. It was true that she hadn't been offered the opportunity to reply, but, knowing Florence, Emily had expected her to grab the microphone right off Willa Ruth Stone's shirt.

Florence's friends were being so raucously supportive that it took Emily a few minutes to realize that Florence wasn't really acting like one of the gang. Florence's normal manner was so peremptory that if she was sitting there without speaking, as she was now, she could easily be seen to be nothing more than her usual imperious self. But if you looked at her closely you could see that her withdrawn manner didn't have anything to do with being above it all. She had tipped her head back and was resting it against the wall behind her, as if she didn't have the strength to sit up straight. She looked, though it was a word that Emily could hardly have imagined applying to Florence before, defeated.

Loss of control

85

Florence and Emily took a cab together to the Upper West Side.

Emily noticed that Florence was clutching and unclutching her left hand.

"Are you all right?" Emily said.

"Why wouldn't I be?"

"No reason. I just wanted to make sure you're feeling okay."

"Why do you keep asking me that?"

"I just get the impression—"

"You try getting old, and tell me how well you feel."

"You're not that old."

"You're right. Of course. I forgot. I forgot we're living in the era of eternal youth. You're right. I'm young. I'm seventy-five years young."

This is too much responsibility for me, Emily thought.

Florence asked the cabbie to stop when they were still a few blocks from her apartment. She opened her wallet and passed him a twenty-dollar bill. Everything seemed to be taking her a long time—looking through her purse for the wallet, opening the wallet, passing the bill.

The driver gave Florence the change, and Florence gave him back a dollar. Taking a cab with Florence was always an embarrassment, because she was such a poor tipper.

They made their way back toward the apartment, Florence walking in a slow, foot-dragging way. Something was wrong—something more than the disappointment of the day. She'd had a stroke. She had Parkinson's disease. Emily didn't know enough about grown-up diseases, which is to say that she didn't know enough about diseases, to be able to hazard many guesses about what was wrong. But something was wrong.

Why can't I put my arm around her? Why can't I just demand to know what's wrong?

What are we made of? What is this passing moment made of?

With a young person's curious hyperawareness of the fleeting nature of life, Emily wished that she could stop everything, freeze everything, right now, so that whatever Florence's problem was, it wouldn't get any worse. She wanted to extend a sort of bubble of protection around her grandmother, an image she found beautiful, until she realized that she'd taken it from *The Incredibles*.

They stopped at a Rite Aid so Florence could buy paper towels, after which they proceeded to her block.

They were in front of her building.

"Just for the record," Emily said, "I thought that talk was awful."

"Hers or mine?"

"Hers, of course," Emily said.

"Duly noted," Florence said. "You can go home now."

"You didn't really eat anything back there. Do you want to get something to eat?"

"You can go, Emily."

She wanted to say, What's going on with you? Something is wrong and I want to know what it is.

But do people ever actually do this? Just flat-out ask each other what's wrong?

"Okeydokey," Emily said, and she left.

86

She walked back home, brooding about the way she had failed her grandmother.

If Emily had asked her to talk, Florence might have refused. But she might not have. Why didn't I even ask?

If there's anything I've learned from her over these past weeks, it's that you should always be bold. Take the chance. Take the risk that you'll end up regretting your speech, because it's better than regretting your silence.

She thought about this for another block, and then she went back to worrying about Justin. She had turned off her Android during the conference, and when she turned it on again, there was a new video. It was of a robot named Oscar. Oscar asked her to visit, saying that if she stayed away, he wouldn't have the strength to keep all his parts together. As the video went on, little pieces of Oscar disappeared, until he was just a tiny, fading voice.

Lone wolf, huh?

Florence was still haunted by what that technician had said.

Wouldn't it be nice if she were to tell Emily what was truly bothering her, and Emily were to . . . who the hell knows? Devote herself to finding a cure for ALS? Give her a nice big hug? Vow to keep Florence's ideas alive, by starting a Florence Gordon Appreciation Society?

Florence didn't even know why she was intent on keeping her illness a secret for as long as she could, but a deep-seated instinct told her it was the right thing to do.

So now, Janine thought, you kind of sort of have to choose.

Some people, when they leave a spouse for someone else, can tell themselves that only now, with the new person, have they found real love. That must make things easy.

She couldn't tell herself that. She had known real love with Daniel.

And some people, when they leave a spouse for someone else, can tell themselves that only now have they found real sex.

She couldn't tell herself that either.

When she and Daniel had had their first kiss—though she'd been a wised-up college student, conversant with Foucault and Derrida and Deleuze and Lacan and Kristeva, defended by a solid wall of critical theory against all sentimental illusions—it had felt like a kiss from a fairy tale. If you have a first kiss like that, you never really want to kiss anyone else. You know where your home is.

But she felt alert with Lev, intellectually excited, in a way she hadn't felt with Daniel in a long time. If she'd ever felt it with Daniel. Daniel was just as intelligent as Lev, but he used his intelligence for settling and not for searching. Daniel wanted to live a life in which everything, day after day after day after day, was exactly the same.

Would it be possible to have both? To live with Daniel in Seattle and Lev in New York?

She thought of a slogan she'd once read in a book about the May 1968 uprisings in France: "Be realistic! Demand the impossible!" Maybe she'd read about it in one of Florence's essays, actually. Perhaps she should be demanding the impossible.

Maybe it is possible.

But probably not.

When she was in high school, she did her junior year abroad, living with a family just outside Paris. For most of the year she dated a French boy, Denis. He was planning on becoming a philosopher. He already had a girlfriend, a fellow *philosophe*, and he wouldn't give her up. He'd explained it to Janine one night: "When I'm with her, I'm with her. When I'm with you, I'm with you"—as if nothing could possibly be simpler. If another girl interested him, he made it clear, he wouldn't hesitate to be with her too.

At first Janine had thought this was very advanced and very Sartre-and-de-Beauvoirish, and she'd tried hard to become French enough to find it appealing. Finally she'd decided that the boy was perhaps just a tad selfish, and that the arrangements he favored, impeccably avant-garde though they were, were notable chiefly in that they gave people new ways to hurt one another.

So living two lives wasn't an option.

She had friends at home with whom she could have talked about this, if she were with them. She couldn't see talking about it over the phone. She couldn't see talking about it over Gchat. This whole situation sometimes made her feel idiotically like a teenager, but not that much like a teenager—not enough like a teenager to Gchat about it.

She wished she could talk about it with Daniel. But of course she couldn't.

What will life be like if I stay with Daniel?

What will life be like if I leave?

If I do stay with him, she thought, I refuse to see myself as a woman who settled. Or someone who decided not to put her bourgeois existence at risk. I refuse to tell that story about myself. And I refuse to tell that story about Daniel.

89

At work it had become hard to think.

Lev, as always, was away half the time, speaking at conferences or chatting up donors. She hadn't been alone with him since their trip.

On a Monday afternoon, after she'd seen the last of her college students for the day, he knocked on her door and came in.

"Are we not talking?" he said.

"I don't know if we're talking."

"If we *are* not talking . . . why are we not talking?"

"You're the award-winning psychologist," she said. "You tell me."

"I suppose we're not talking because . . . you feel guilty? You've realized you don't want to be with me? You don't know what you want?"

"All of the above," she said. "Except for the middle one."

"Do you want to talk about it?"

"I don't think so, Lev. Thank you for asking, but I don't want to get into a conversation about our relationship before we even know if we have one."

"Fair enough. If you don't want to talk about it, do you want to go bowling about it?"

"Yes. Yes, I do. I thought you'd never ask."

A new bowling alley had opened up on Amsterdam Avenue. As they walked there, she felt uneasy, as if bowling were the new infidelity.

She was trying to walk with a stately beauty, unaware that her physical awkwardness was one of her charms.

She felt embarrassed, but she wasn't sure why. Maybe it was about the night they'd spent together.

It was a night that might have felt perfect if her life had been less complicated.

It was fumbling, not wholly satisfying, friendly, not without its moments of humor. Clothes had not fully been removed. It was a kind of pleased-to-meet-you experience that would have been delightful if she'd felt sure that this night together was the first of many such nights. But in the nervous and uncertain state that she'd actually been in, every moment of awkwardness had felt like a sign.

"I could make you happy," Lev said now. "We could be happy together."

"Happiness? Isn't that . . ."

She had intended to make some allusion to Freud's famous remark that the best one can expect of life is ordinary unhappiness, but she decided that there would be no point.

He began to talk about a project he'd been working on. He'd been in touch with Walter Mischel, his old mentor, the genius behind the Marshmallow Test. They were planning to work together on another series of studies, using neuroimaging to map the effects of music, multitasking, and other stimuli on the decision-making capacities of adolescents.

They were still a block from the bowling alley, but he stopped.

"Do you get what I'm saying?"

"You're talking about neuroimaging."

"That's not what I'm talking about. I'm talking about us. You're interested in the same things I am. But you see it all differently. You go at it all differently."

"I'm still not . . ."

"We could help each other think," Lev said.

The bowling alley was bright and modern; it had Wi-Fi and waitress service and a bar. She missed the shabby bowling alleys of her youth. They got their shoes—she remembered how exciting it was to rent bowling shoes when she was a kid—and found their lane.

Amazing how the personality doesn't change. She bowled the way she always had, as far back as she could remember. She would draw a line with her gaze to the center pin, only to discover that the ball had a mind of its own. It would start off as if carrying out her wishes, but by the time it reached the middle of the lane it would have second thoughts, and it would wander off, sometimes this way, sometimes that, obeying not the laws of physics, but its own whims.

Lev was lumpily graceful as he bowled. She thought of him as someone with only the most accidental relationship to his body. That's how he'd seemed during the months in which she'd gotten to know him, and their night together had not dispelled that impression, having been filled with warmth and hugging but few traces of what might conventionally be described as sex. But now he seemed to have a body. He glided down toward the lane and released the ball with a sort of loving reluctance, as if it were a child, a small, round child, whom he had birthed and whelped and cared for and whom he was now granting its freedom. There was something tender even about the way he bowled.

90

"Well, this isn't what I was hoping for," Noah said.

"I don't imagine it was. I'm going to try hard not to blame you."

"You can blame me if you have to. Not in the legal sense. Don't sue me or anything. But in the spiritual sense you can blame me all you want. I'm your doctor. I'm supposed to keep you well. That's what I'm here for."

It *was* what he was there for. He was her doctor, and she had trusted him, and his role was to stand between her and disease. His role was to make sure she never got sick. He had failed.

It was remarkable how, in a part of one's mind, one can actually believe this.

"Have you talked to your family?"

She didn't want to lie, but neither did she want to tell the truth. If she told the truth he might feel the need to intervene.

"Yes. They're all being very kind."

"Kind is nice, but what we need is helpful. It's good to have family to take care of you."

"I'm sure they will."

She let the conversation wander for a while, and then she said, "I was wondering if you could prescribe some antianxiety medication."

"Florence Gordon? Antianxiety medication? Now I *am* shocked."

"I'm glad to know that I'm still capable of surprising you."

He had his prescription pad out.

"Xanax'll do? You don't need anything stronger?"

For a moment she thought he knew. But he didn't know. He wouldn't be willing to prescribe something stronger if he knew.

"Well, a few years ago, when I had shingles, you had me on Vicodin. That was helpful."

The truth was that she'd never filled the prescription. She'd thrown it out. Shingles had been the most painful thing she'd experienced since giving birth, but she had preferred to endure it without cushioning.

"Vicodin's for pain. You don't need Vicodin. If you want something to calm you down, I can write you a prescription for Ativan. But take it only if the Xanax doesn't do the job. And don't mix 'em, all right?"

So she left the office with prescriptions for Xanax and Ativan. Those would do. In a month she would ask him to refill them, and in another month after that. By the time her situation became dire, she'd be well armed.

How many people claim that if they feel the onset of dementia or any kind of radically debilitating disease, they will make their own exit? And how many of them actually do? She'd be one of the few who actually did. She wanted to live—she wanted desperately to live. But she wanted to live on her own terms.

91

Saul was waiting for her in Bryant Park, walking back and forth. He was wearing a suit—from a distance, he looked almost elegant—but when she got closer she saw that it hadn't been cleaned or pressed in a while.

"Have you heard anything about the job yet?" was the first thing he said.

"We're beyond the formalities, are we?"

"What? What are you talking about?"

"Most people like to start with 'Hello.'"

"Oh. Hello. How are you. You look divine."

"Thanks. So do you."

They sat at a table in an outdoor café near the public library.

"Have you heard anything about the job yet?"

"Saul, I haven't heard anything about the job. As you know, it's not even certain that there's going to *be* a job."

"Well, aren't you in a position to make it happen now?"

"Why?"

"You're famous now. You're a star."

"Saul. You're overestimating the effect of one review. It's not that big a deal."

"It's not that big a deal? Are you crazy? This put you on the map. You can get things done now. You're not the same person you were a month ago. You might feel like the same person, but in everybody else's eyes you're different. Which is what matters. And if you want something to happen at your school, you can make it happen now."

She thought of asking him why it mattered so much, since, as he'd told her a few months ago, Brooklyn and Stony Brook and Purchase were "begging" him to work for them again. But that would have been too cruel.

If she told him she had ALS, would he stop nagging her? She almost wanted to tell him, just to see his response. It would be a fascinating experiment. Would he actually give a shit? He was so locked into his own egotism, so locked into his own bitterness, so locked into his obsessive recounting of the one story he had—the world never gave me a break; the world never gave me a break; the world never gave me a break—that she found it hard to imagine that he'd be capable of putting his needs aside and responding with a mature concern.

"I just don't understand why you can do favors for Tanya, who's never published anything, and for Murray Gold, who's someone you barely know, and Denise, who screwed you over not once but twice—"

"Denise didn't screw me over."

"You hired her twice and she screwed you over twice."

"She didn't screw me. Her mother was in a car accident and ended up with *brain* damage—"

"Her mother ended up with brain damage. Right. So she quit her job because her mother, who was senile in the first place—"

"And the second time she had to withdraw—"

"Because she had a better offer."

"She didn't have a better offer. The poor woman—"

"The poor woman! She *used* you and you respond by—"

"She never used me. How did she use me?"

"How did she use you? Do you remember the whole thing with the credit card?"

"That was a mix-up, Saul. That didn't even have anything to do with her."

"That didn't have anything to do with her, the thing with the library didn't have anything to do with her, nothing had anything to do with her, and yet you still—"

"Jesus Christ, Saul. What are we even *talking* about?"

"What we're talking about is very simple. We're talking about the fact that you've never seen fit to help me find a job."

"I've tried, Saul, and you know I've tried."

"Have you? Have you? Then why hasn't anything ever happened to turn up? You've made your inquiries, and you've told me to sit tight, but somehow nothing's ever come of anything."

"I *have* made inquiries—"

"Have you ever *told* them, really? Have you ever told them who I am? Have you ever told them that I was once named one of the top ten 'writers to watch' in a national magazine? Have you ever mentioned my column in the *Village Voice*, which Norman Mailer said was better than the column he was writing at the time? Norman fucking Mailer *admitted* it! Have you ever mentioned that I'm one of the few people around who could teach basically anything that needed to be taught, in the English Department or in the Writing Department, or the Politics Department or the History Department? Who else do you know who could teach the Bible and Milton and the Lake Poets and *Moby-Dick* and the Russian Revolution—has anybody ever heard of Martov anymore? Have Denise and Tanya and what's-her-face ever heard of Martov? And I could teach the history of the little magazine, from the whaddaya-callit, the *Westminster Review*—that was a great course. I taught it at Brandeis once and they had to move it to a bigger room it was so popular."

"I know, Saul. I know how great you are."

"Fuck off. I'm serious. You hire scholars, and I have more genuine knowledge than any of these phony little Ph.D.s. You hire writers, and I'm a better writer than any of the people you've ever hired.

So how do you explain that? How do you explain that, Florence? You hired some little pisher from *n+1* last year. I can write stuff that'll knock those little fuckers on their ass."

"You're dreaming, Saul."

She said it softly and almost involuntarily. She was almost surprised when it came out of her mouth.

"Excuse me?"

"If you're so talented, do something to show it. Don't just sit around talking about the amazing things you did forty years ago. If you're so talented, write something that gets people talking. If you can write things that'll knock those little pishers from *n+1* on their ass, then write them already. So when I mention your name to potential employers they won't say things like, 'Saul? Is he still alive?'"

He wasn't prepared for her to speak this way. She'd been protecting him for so many years, bending over backward to minimize her successes and his failures, to make every sliver of good news that came his way seem better than it was, that he was unprepared to encounter the other side of her. He must have remembered that she had this other side, but it was almost as if he'd forgotten.

"That's really all I can say, Saul."

And in another move that surprised her as much as it doubtless surprised him, she stood up, opened her wallet, put twenty dollars on the table, and walked away.

92

The trouble with making a spontaneous dramatic gesture is that five minutes later, you're likely to feel like an ass. Florence didn't normally regret her spontaneous dramatic gestures—she was proud of them; she was vain about them. But she regretted this one. The poor bastard was down already, and she had pointlessly pushed him down further.

She walked through midtown in the crowded lunch hour, wondering if there was any way to muffle the blow. But there wasn't, was there? The blow had already been dealt and suffered.

Her next destination was the West Village, where she was meeting her granddaughter at a café. Waiting at a bus stop near Times Square, watching people pass, she was struck by the general unloveliness. You can often forget. On the Upper West Side, where people are well off and you see a lot of students, you can think that beauty is the norm. But in other parts of the city you're reminded that it isn't true. Most of the faces of the people you pass are marked by hard living or ignorance or indolence or cowardice or exhaustion or smugness or intolerance or the simple causeless ugliness that can blight a life that might otherwise be reasonably pleasant.

She thought of calling Saul and apologizing. But she was afraid—not of him, but of herself. He was unlikely to take the apology well—he was almost certain to snap at her—and she was afraid she'd respond badly and insult him a second time.

But why should what she'd said be considered an insult, really? He was a writer. *Let* him write something good. Why was it an insult?

It was an insult because they both knew he couldn't. It was an insult because they both knew he was finished, and she had agreed not to acknowledge it until now.

93

Emily was delivering another folder to her grandmother: transcriptions that Emily had painstakingly made of tapes she'd listened to at Bobst, oral-history interviews with women whose lives had been touched by the new feminist thinking in the late 1960s and early 1970s. Although some of the stories were fun to hear—she particularly enjoyed learning about the street theater escapades of WITCH, the Women's International Terrorist Conspiracy from Hell—transcribing interviews was the most plodding, time-consuming work that Emily had ever done, and she was glad to be finished with it.

Florence had suggested they meet at a café in the West Village. Emily was a block or two away when Justin called back.

Last night, she'd finally decided what she had to do. She wished she could tell him in a text or an email. But she didn't want to be a coward, so she'd called and left a message. She hadn't told him anything, just asked him to call back.

"Hey, Auntie Em," he said. "When you coming up?"

"That's what I was calling about," she said. "I can't come up."

"You have to come up. You said."

"I didn't say I was gonna come up. You said I was gonna come up."

"But you have to."

There was a courtyard at the NYU law school, set back from the street, that provided a quiet place to talk.

It wasn't that it was any quieter than the street, actually; it was that it seemed wrong to try to break up with someone while you were walking. Justin wouldn't know the difference, but it seemed wrong.

"I'm sorry," she said.

"Can you come up next weekend?"

"No . . . no."

"I can't hear you."

"No," she said, but she said it as softly as before.

"No?"

"No," she said, a little louder.

"You don't understand. If you don't come up, I don't know what I'm going to do. I don't know how to live, Emily."

"I'm really sorry."

"Emily. Don't you get it? I'm *scared*."

She closed her eyes. If she let herself, she could put herself all the way inside him, and feel exactly what he was feeling. But she didn't want to. If she allowed herself to feel it, she'd need to go up and stay with him again. She wouldn't be able to stop herself.

"Please. You have to come up. Just one more time. Just once."

The impulse to say yes was so strong. What would it cost her to say yes? What would it cost her to go up there for one more weekend? What would it cost her to help him?

A clock on a church somewhere started bonging the hour. She was going to be late to see Florence.

Florence came powerfully into her mind—Florence, hurrying forward through life, sure of herself, intolerant of distractions. When Florence decided to do something, she did it. There was no corridor of uncertainty between the decision and the act.

She told herself to borrow her grandmother's decisiveness, and bluntness, and coldness. She told herself that for the next few minutes, she should pretend to *be* her grandmother.

"I'm sorry, Justin. I'm not coming up. We need to stop seeing each other. It'll be better for both of us."

"You don't know that. You're not the one who's going crazy."

"You're right. I don't know, actually. All I know is that it needs to be this way."

"You can't just be with a person and then leave them when they're drowning. That's not like you, Emily. That's not *like* you."

"You can get help. You can call your mother. You can call Steve. You can call the school psychologist."

"That's it? That's what you've got? The school psychologist? You get there two minutes late and instead of talking about your problems, they make you spend the whole session talking about why you were two minutes late. The school psychologist. You're just going to leave me? Is that really what you want to do?"

"I'm sorry. I have to go."

"I can't believe you," he said.

"I'm sorry."

She ended the call and put the phone in her pocket, and she resumed her walk.

She felt dizzy; she felt ill. She felt like curling up in a trash can and resting for a while.

She kept seeing two different Justins: Justin as he'd been on her visit, a boy who needed a kind of help she didn't know how to give; and Justin as he'd been on the first day she saw him, helping the old woman in the library, with tolerance and generosity and patience.

Her phone was vibrating. She stopped on the street to read the text.

Not just one text, it turned out. In the two minutes since they'd gotten off the phone, he'd sent her five.

The burden of each one was the same. *You can't do this. You're killing me. I'm going to die.*

Again the thought of Florence helped her. A few weeks ago she'd read an article that Florence had written about Virginia Woolf. Woolf had said that the task of a woman writer was to kill off the

"Angel in the House": the part of oneself that was trained to put the needs of others, in every situation, before one's own.

Emily couldn't be the Angel in the House for Justin. She couldn't save him. She didn't know whether he'd be able to save himself. All she knew was that she couldn't save him.

94

When Emily looked up, she saw that she was right outside La Lanterna, the place Florence had picked. She was excited to be seeing her—excited and a bit repulsed. She felt as if she'd learned something from Florence, but something she wasn't sure she'd wanted to learn.

She wasn't, of course, intending to tell Florence about how she'd channeled her spirit in order to find the strength and the bluntness and the coldness to do what she needed to do. Florence, who had never asked her a personal question, not a single one, wouldn't care. And yet Emily thought it was possible that her debt to Florence might be visible on her face, and that Florence, somehow, might understand, and might, without even knowing why, feel a little closer to her now.

95

Sitting at a table near the window, Florence could see Emily on the street, pulling out her phone, looking sad—stricken, really—and then looking . . . Florence couldn't tell. Resigned? Determined? In any case, something other than stricken.

If Emily had been reading a book, or a letter, and Florence had seen her facial expression change like that, the sight would have been intriguing—you'd want to know what could have affected her so strongly. But her phone? She'd probably gotten news about a party, and then realized she wouldn't be able to go, and then decided it didn't matter.

At another time, Florence might have found this a fit occasion to lecture Emily about the importance of resisting the brain-corroding allure of the new technologies. But her encounter with Saul was still weighing her down: the pathetic failure of his life and her own cruelty in exposing it. She didn't have the strength to lecture Emily about anything.

She'd been hoping that seeing her granddaughter would cheer her, but as she watched her climb the steps outside the café, the hope disappeared. There had been times when she'd felt close to the girl, but not now. The little scene on the street, the phone pantomime, had reminded her of how far apart they were, in terms of how they lived and what they valued.

96

When Emily got her first sight of Florence, she was shocked.

Actually, that's not true. When Emily got her first sight of Florence, she didn't register it at all, because she didn't realize it *was* Florence. Entering the dimness of the café from the bright mid-afternoon street, Emily had vaguely seen some decrepit old lady in the corner, and it was only when she passed her eyes over the place a second time that she recognized her.

After Emily sat down, looking at Florence closely, she couldn't be sure why she'd mistaken her for someone else. She looked the same as she always did. Her hair was still carefully set; her clothes were still severe; her posture was still uncompromising. What was different? Nothing.

Florence asked for the papers, and Emily gave them to her. They talked for about ten minutes, but not about anything that mattered. Every time Emily tried to say something half meaningful, her grandmother rebuffed her.

Emily's research over the past week had involved the life of Shulamith Firestone, a radical feminist writer and activist who'd been dragged down by mental illness and had retreated into private life.

When one of her books was reissued a year earlier, Florence had written a moving tribute, which Emily had read just the other day. She mentioned it now, and Florence brushed her hand through the air dismissively. "If you want to talk to me about Shulie," she said, "come back to me after you've read her books."

Emily tried a few other conversational openings, but Florence didn't respond. It reminded her of the way things had been when she'd first started working for Florence, and Florence wouldn't even let her in the door.

Emily's idea that Florence would somehow sense what she'd just been through with Justin, somehow sense that she'd drawn upon what she'd learned from Florence to do what she needed to do—she saw now that that had been pure fantasy.

She could deal with that. She didn't need her grandmother to mystically intuit what she was going through. But something else was happening here, something harder to deal with. Something was going on with Florence. The only way Emily could put it to herself was that it felt as if Florence was breaking up with *her*.

Emily excused herself and went to the bathroom, where she sat in the stall and tried not to cry. She wasn't even sure why she was feeling this way. Why am I so needy? When did I start to need *her*?

She put her head in her hands and thought. As she thought, she came to a realization.

Her grandmother was looking spiritless and wan and remote, but she'd been looking that way before Emily even sat down with her.

Think about it. Put it together. The way she'd sat onstage, immobile, while Willa Ruth Stone attacked her; the way she'd tipped her head back, exhausted, in the restaurant afterward; the way she'd looked in the corner here in this café, shrunken, when Emily came in. It wasn't that Florence was rejecting her. Florence was dying.

97

When Emily got back to the table, she asked Florence if she was all right.

"Of course I'm all right. Are you all right?"

"Are you sure there isn't anything I can help you with?"

"You have helped me." She held up the sheaf of papers.

"I've just had the feeling . . ." Emily said.

"Enough of these feelings," Florence said.

They'd started to mean more to each other over these past weeks. Emily knew that it wasn't an illusion. But she kept wishing they could reach a point where Florence would let her guard down once and for all.

Florence put her hand on Emily's.

"You're not the worst granddaughter a woman could hope for," she said. Then she called for the bill.

98

At home she rested, and then she worked on her book. She tried to pick up where she'd left off, with an account of a debate she'd had with the historian E. P. Thompson, a debate in which Florence had tried to open a genuine exchange of ideas about women and history, but without success, her efforts perpetually checked by Thompson's pseudo-poetic bluster about the ghosts of utopia and the serpent of empire. But after a few paragraphs she found herself drifting further into the past, finally writing about a few childhood memories of her mother. They had no connection to anything she'd written about so far—she'd always intended to leave her childhood out of the story—but now she was filled with the desire to record things that no one else alive would know.

Normally, when she was working on a book, she didn't ask herself to stick too closely to the plan. She liked to leave room to surprise herself; she liked to let herself wander off course. Today, she thought that if she let herself wander off course with this memoir, she might not live long enough to complete it. The thought left her shaken for a minute or two, but then she told herself that this is always the case: you never know if you'll live long enough to complete anything.

She returned to what she was writing, a memory from the age of five or six, watching her mother fold laundry in their apartment in the Bronx.

99

Janine was going to a convention at a conference center in Tarry-town. It was something she'd been looking forward to for weeks. The keynote speaker was Angela Duckworth, a young star in the field, who was studying persistence and perseverance in children and adolescents. She too was a guru of grit.

Lev had gone up early. He was staying there for the weekend, but Janine was just going up for the day. She didn't want to have to consider whether or not to sleep with him within the tristate area.

She'd floated through the early morning. It was a strange, self-defeating habit she had: sometimes when she absolutely needed to be punctual, she'd start to get ready long before she had to, but then fritter away the time, checking her email, trying on clothes, check-ing her email again.

"I'm going to be late for this thing."

"How do you get there?" Emily said.

"I'm not even sure if it's Penn Station or Grand Central. I think it's the Metro-North train. I don't know which—"

"Why doesn't Dad drive you? He's got the Zippy car."

Daniel had rented a Zipcar to take Emily to look at some colleges in the area.

"Dad's got better things to do."

"Look at him. It's not like he's figuring out a cure for anything. He's just sitting there reading the sports page."

Janine had had no intention of asking Daniel, and it had been clear that Daniel hadn't expected to be asked. You don't ask your husband to give you a ride to a conference where you'll be spending time with the man you might be leaving him for. That was one of the rules of marriage.

But she was so anxious about getting there on time to see Angela Duckworth that it just came out.

"Could you?" she said to Daniel.

He sprang up instantly. He had a strange grin on his face. He looked like a demented jack-in-the-box.

"Yes," he said. "Yes. That's a great idea. I'll just drive you right up there."

He had an air of jumpy intensity, as if he wanted to grab her by the neck before she changed her mind.

On the spot Janine invented a theory that there isn't a wife in the world who doesn't, in some tiny spot of her consciousness, carry the fear that her husband might murder her someday; and the face that Daniel was showing her now—this face of eager tense elation—was what she would see in the last moment of her life if her fear were ever to come true.

"Let's go. Or you can freshen up or something, and I'll bring the car around."

Bad idea. Don't go with him.

But this was Daniel. You couldn't be afraid of Daniel.

"Can I come?" Emily said.

"Why?" Daniel said.

"I love to take a turn in the afternoon."

"What?" Daniel said.

"That was something some French girl said in a short story."

"Don't talk like a French girl. And no, you can't come. Mom and I need some alone time."

She and Daniel went down to the car.

Don't get in.

She got in.

Daniel liked to drive, but she'd always only half liked to ride with him. It was an activity in which another side of him came out. You would have thought that Daniel would be a cautious, sober, defensive, old-man-ish driver, but instead his driving was caffeinated and aggressive. It always felt a little chancy to her, but he'd never had an accident, and she'd had three.

As they passed under the George Washington Bridge and breasted the Cloisters, he started to pick up speed. She didn't like going this fast, but she didn't say anything. Then he started weaving through the traffic, going twenty miles an hour faster than anybody else.

"Hey, cowboy. Let's get me there in one piece."

"You'll get there in one piece. Precious cargo."

The Henry Hudson Parkway is a narrow highway. He zigzagged around four cars, changing lanes so quickly she started to feel ill.

"Come on, Daniel. What are you doing?"

"This is how I drive in New York. You have to drive different out here."

"You don't have to drive differently. You drive fine the way you drive at home."

"Fine for Seattle isn't fine for New York. Fuck."

The car in front of them had braked abruptly and he had to shoot into the right lane.

"There's a different pace out here," he said. "The thing about New York is that everybody on the road thinks of himself as a star. And they drive like stars. Maybe they *are* stars. A lot of dentists are stars around here, you know. They think you have to get out of their way."

"What the hell are you talking about?"

Now they were on the Saw Mill Parkway, and he must have been pushing ninety miles an hour.

"I believe they still have speed limits in New York," she said.

She would have been yelling at him but she was feeling too guilty. She didn't think she had the right.

He took an envelope from his jacket pocket and pushed it into a slot in front of the instrument panel so that it blocked their view of the speedometer.

"Don't you want to see how fast you were going before we died?" she said.

"Don't need to look. You just have to trust the force."

"So what are you doing? Are you making a point?"

"I'm not making a point. I'm driving."

"Do you want to kill us?"

"Why would I want to kill you?"

"That's not what I asked."

"I'm just driving."

"If some coked-up superstar dentist swerves out of his lane while you're going ninety, what'll happen to the kids? Don't you care?"

"You're going to be fine. Don't worry about that. But you're right. I respect the sentiment. It's important to treasure the things you have."

"Daniel! Slow fucking down!" She *was* yelling now, guilty or not.

"Don't be a nervous Nellie," he said.

They reached the conference center more quickly than she would have thought possible. She was comfortably on time for the Angela Duckworth talk; she might even catch the tail end of the welcome reception.

"Okay," she said. "Thanks."

But instead of letting her out and driving away, Daniel was taking the key out of the ignition.

"You know what?" he said. "I've never really met any of your colleagues."

And he got out of the car.

The reception room was just past the lobby. She was almost trotting in order to keep up with him.

He stood in the wide vaulted doorway and scanned the crowd.

Lev was in the middle of the room, talking to a man she didn't know.

"That must be your boss," Daniel said. "I want to tell him what a great job he's doing."

Daniel walked quickly toward Lev. How did he even know which one Lev was? Maybe because Lev was obviously the person who radiated authority? Maybe because Daniel had some weird sixth sense? Maybe because Daniel had looked him up on the Internet?

Unlikely. Daniel never looked anything up on the Internet.

She saw herself throwing her body between Lev and Daniel to make sure no one got hurt. Alternatively, she saw herself sprinting out the door and leaving them to their fate. She chose a middle course and just stood there. She wasn't sure she could have moved even if she'd wanted to. She had the odd feeling that she was watching something that had already happened.

Daniel had joined Lev in the middle of the room. The other man was gone. Daniel was pumping Lev's hand, and Lev was regarding him with what looked like the usual Levian friendliness. It was impossible to tell if he was in the least uneasy.

Daniel was boring into Lev with a smile the intensity of which Janine wouldn't have been able to describe. He was standing too close, like someone who lacked the usual social boundaries.

A bearded server blocked Janine's view, holding out a tray of crackers with dabs of pâté. Janine smiled and shook her head and he moved on, but a moment later someone else appeared—a woman named Greta, a zestful apostle of "learned optimism" whom Janine had met in Pittsburgh.

"You again?" Greta said. "We have to stop meeting like this!"

Janine tried to make conversation with Greta while watching Daniel and Lev.

Daniel normally liked to keep his distance from everybody, but he seemed to be crowding Lev, forcing him back. Lev was taller than Daniel but somehow Daniel was dominating the space.

Daniel was so unlike most of his colleagues on the force that sometimes she liked to tell herself that he was a police officer only in name. But now she was reminded that he had at his disposal a physical vocabulary that was foreign to her own professional world.

Lev was moving backward, but so gradually that she wasn't sure he was even aware of it. As they spoke, Daniel would move up slightly, and Lev would step back, and then, when his weight was on his back foot, Daniel would move a little closer, so that Lev had to step back again.

A million years ago, Daniel had taken her to a SuperSonics-Bulls game. Everybody went crazy when Michael Jordan dunked the ball and Dennis Rodman snatched rebounds, but Daniel pointed out the more subtle things they were doing: obstructing the path of some hapless SuperSonic before the Sonic even knew where he wanted to go, closing up a lane to make sure that a Sonic had to take his shot from a bad angle. He showed her how good players make lesser players move in the direction of the good players' choosing.

Off in a corner of the room, there was an upholstered yellow chair.

He's going to make him sit in it.

The two men were still ten feet away from it, but as soon as she noticed the chair, she knew.

Somehow Janine was still talking to Greta. Remarkable how you can nod at the right places without listening to a word a person says.

She felt as if she should rescue Lev, but she didn't know what she'd be rescuing him from.

She didn't want him to sit in the chair. Somehow, sitting in the chair seemed like an awful fate.

Lev had taken two crackers from the server and was holding one in each hand. Now he transferred one of them so that he was holding both in his left hand. With his freed-up right hand he pulled out his wallet.

What the hell was going on?

He was holding out his wallet and trying to take something out of it at the same time, until Daniel finally took the wallet, removed whatever it was, and gave the wallet back. She felt as if she were witnessing a mugging, except that both of them were smiling. She had no idea what was happening until she realized that it was a photograph. It must have been a photograph of his daughters.

Daniel, still smiling, still seeming to be the most pleasant person you'd ever met, was holding the photograph out to Lev, as if he were showing Lev who Lev's own children were.

For a moment she felt sure he was going to stuff the photograph down Lev's throat. It was so vivid a premonition that she could see him doing it. It was almost as if the sight of the two men was less vivid than her imaginary picture of them.

Lev was now holding one cracker in each hand again, and you could almost have thought that he was trying to ward Daniel off with them.

Greta had finished saying whatever it was she'd had to say—or so Janine assumed, since Janine hadn't heard any of it. Now Greta was talking to someone else, and Janine moved over to the bar and ordered a soda so as to appear to be engaged in something while she observed the two men.

They were still—slowly, gradually—moving.

Daniel was still holding the photograph near Lev's face. She remembered some spy movie she'd seen, where the bad guy slit someone's throat with a credit card.

They were all the way in the corner of the room now. Lev was standing against the chair. Daniel took one more . . . No, he didn't take a step. He just leaned.

Lev seemed—or was this in her imagination?—to be swaying. Then, slowly, heavily, inevitably, he went down into the chair.

He looked as if he didn't quite know how he'd gotten there. He was still holding his two crackers. Daniel was leaning over him.

She saw her husband put the photograph in Lev's breast pocket and clap him on the shoulder, as if they were the best of friends.

Daniel looked around the room and spotted her and came toward her, smiling, shaking his head.

"Great guy," he said. "Solid-gold guy. Great sense of humor."

She felt as if she were being toyed with on some Zen level.

"I'll see you later," he said. "Call me if you need a ride back."

He headed toward the door. She followed him, and once they were in the hall, she grasped his arm.

"What was that?"

"What was what?"

"You know what I'm talking about. What was that?"

"We were just chewing the fat," he said.

Chewing the fat. A solid-gold guy. He didn't even sound like himself.

"I just want you to know that I'm not impressed," she said. "I'm not impressed by your Dennis Rodman bullshit."

"What are you talking about?"

"This alpha-male bullshit. It's so juvenile. It's so beneath you. If you thought I was impressed by it, you really don't know me at all."

A stillness came over Daniel. His features, which for the last hour had been lit up by a false good humor, finally relaxed, and she saw the face of the man she knew.

"I'm not asking you to be impressed. I'm not expecting you to be."

He was looking at her directly, running his eyes over her face. She didn't look away.

What can you say about the face of the man you've been married to for twenty-three years? It was a well-lined face, and it wasn't a face you'd call handsome, but it was a strong face. Usually she thought of it as strong, calm, kind, but she couldn't see the calmness or the kindness now.

And what, she wondered, could be said about her own face? What did he see as he looked at her?

Without saying goodbye, he walked toward the entrance and into the parking lot. She ran out after him, but once she was there, standing with him at the car, she still didn't know what she wanted to say. Again they just looked at each other.

"I'll be heading back on the fifteenth," he said.

"Excuse me?"

"I've got to get back to work."

"What are you talking about? I thought we were going to talk about this."

"We're talking."

"I mean I thought we were going to talk it over before we decided anything."

He didn't say anything.

He had this habit that had always gotten under her skin. When you said something that didn't, in his opinion, merit a response, he wouldn't say anything at all. As you waited for him to respond—you kept thinking he'd respond, no matter how many times he'd done this in the past—your original remark would hang there in the air, and would seem stupider and stupider, even to you.

"When were you planning on telling me?" she said.

"I'm telling you now."

"So you're just making this decision for all of us? You're just going home and expecting that I'm coming back with you?"

"I didn't say that. Everybody's free here. You're a free woman."

He got into the car and closed the door, and then he was gone.

100

Janine got a ride back from the conference. It was almost midnight by the time she put her key in the lock.

She could hear Daniel's snoring all the way from the foyer. She'd kept urging him to get tested for sleep apnea, but he kept putting it off.

She hadn't been able to pay attention to anything anybody'd said all day, and she was still agitated and unhappy.

During much of the day, she'd been thinking that she should just get rid of both of them, Daniel and Lev, find a room of her own somewhere, and spend the rest of her days in a state of wise and noble manlessness. Fish without a bicycle, etc.

But that wasn't really her. It was nice work if you could get it, but it wasn't her.

Emily was in the living room, on her laptop.

"What are you doing?"

"I don't know. Wandering the web."

Janine sat across from her. She couldn't remember when she and her daughter had last spent time alone.

"How's your summer been?" Janine said.

"How has my summer been," Emily said.

"Yes. I'm asking you a simple question. How has your summer been?"

"It's been fine. I'm getting to know the grandma."

"Do you still think she's just an old windbag?"

"Did I say that? Yeah. No. She's not an old windbag. She's the warrior from the Bronx."

"Have you learned anything from her?"

"Have I learned anything from her?"

"Don't just repeat everything I say to make me feel stupid. Answer my questions."

"You know that saying 'If the only tool you have is a hammer—'"

"'Everything looks like a nail.' Sure."

"Grandma's a woman with a hammer. Maybe there's a lot she doesn't get. Maybe there's a lot she doesn't see. But she's not your average lady."

"Anything else going on?"

The lights in the room weren't strong enough for her to be sure whether Emily was blushing.

"I don't know. Not really."

"Not really?"

Emily was silent.

"Is there a boy?"

Emily was silent.

"Is there?"

"There was a boy," Emily said.

"I didn't even know."

"Some things are unknowable," Emily said.

"Did you end it? Did he end it?"

"I did it all by myself."

"How do people break up these days? Do you just change your status on Facebook?"

"That's right. That's how I let him know. I blocked his tweets."

"No. Really."

"You know me, Mom. I'm an old-fashioned girl. I let him know by carrier pigeon."

"Was it hard to break up?"

"Is it ever not hard?"

Janine was wondering where her daughter had acquired such wisdom. Or maybe it wasn't wisdom. Maybe it was something everybody knew.

"I'm sorry," Janine said.

"It wasn't as hard as it could have been, because I studied the master. I studied the art of the hammer."

"You watched your grandmother break up with someone?"

"I just imagined how she'd do it. I started calling him by the wrong name."

That was all she was going to get out of her daughter. Janine keenly wished her son were there with them—her voluble son, who would tell you everything that was on his mind whether you wanted to hear it or not, and whose talkativeness somehow freed everyone else to talk more. When he was seven or eight he'd sometimes come into Janine and Daniel's bedroom in the morning and say, "Can I chat with you for a minute?" and if they said yes, he would slide between them and tell them about everything that was going on in his world: the latest battles of his Lego armies; his latest reflections about *Star Wars;* his critiques of all the kids in his class.

"Well, I'm glad you're okay," Janine said. "Are you okay?"

"I am. Thanks, Mom."

At her bedroom door, Janine stopped and turned around and said, "What *was* his name, by the way?"

Emily smiled. "You couldn't pronounce it," she said.

"That's . . . what? *Star Trek? Friday Night Lights?* Jane Austen? It's from *some*thing, right?"

"You're getting there, Mom," Emily said. "You're getting there."

101

Daniel's snoring filled the room. Usually, when he was snoring like this, she prodded him onto his side, a position in which he snored a little less, but now she just let him go on.

She'd been angry at him all day, but it's hard to be angry at someone who's asleep.

She still couldn't be sure what he knew or didn't know. She wished she could just peer into his mind. It was even possible, for all she knew, that he was upset because of something he hadn't even told her about, and his antics in the morning had had little to do with her.

It wasn't likely, but it was possible.

Early in their marriage, she'd had to train herself to respect his privacy. She'd always been a snoop, so it was difficult, but she'd succeeded in curbing her impulses. It had been years since she'd gone through any of Daniel's things in search of clues about his inner life.

She went quietly to his dresser and picked up his cell phone. She scrolled through the list of calls he'd made and calls he'd received, and none of it seemed revealing. She checked his voice mail for saved messages, but there weren't any.

Also on the dresser was a stack of papers: bills, receipts, torn-out pages on which he'd scrawled whatever you scrawl on torn-out pages. The light from the street was enough for her to see by. She picked up his Visa bill. Nothing unexpected. They were still paying off Emily's braces, somehow, and they were still paying Mark's bills from Reed and Emily's from Oberlin. It depressed her to look at the bills.

Watch repair receipt, article clipped from the *Times*, taxi receipt. At the bottom of the pile was a sheet of blue paper that looked promising, but she wanted to proceed methodically. Cell phone bill, cable bill, hospital bill, car insurance bill.

Hospital bill?

Her first thought was that it concerned Mark. Mark had hurt himself again, and Daniel had covered it up again. Daniel was a pain in the ass about that. When Mark was in high school, he played three different sports, and—

But this wasn't about Mark.

There was a host of terms and items and charges, most of them giving little clue of what he'd been in for, except that it was clear that he'd received a lot of tests, and that some of the tests, at least, had involved his heart.

Each procedure was accompanied by a date. He had been in the hospital for three days, three weekends ago. When she was spending the night with Lev, he was spending the night in the hospital.

She picked his cell phone back up, to see if he'd called anyone during those three days. Nope. He hadn't called Emily, and he hadn't called Mark, and he hadn't called her.

The tests weren't tests they would have given him for something less than serious. And he had told her nothing.

It was hard for her to take this in.

Daniel, on the bed, seemed to be dreaming. His eyelids were fluttering. She had no clue as to whether it was a happy dream or a sad one.

You travel side by side through the life you share, and you come to think you know each other all too well. But if each of us enters the afterlife alone, and is asked to give an accounting, asked to speak of how one lived and what one lived for, then the accounting Daniel gave of his life might involve trials of which she knew nothing, sufferings of which he'd never spoken and that had left no outer mark.

The hospital bill had shaken her up so much that she'd forgotten about the blue sheet of paper at the bottom of the pile.

After she heard Emily close the door to her room, she went to the kitchen and made herself a cup of coffee, and stayed at the kitchen table for a long time.

102

The next evening, as it was growing dark, Emily was in the living room, Skyping with her brother, and Daniel was a few feet away from her, on the couch, reading a magazine and putting in an occasional comment or two.

Daniel and Emily had visited Bard and Sarah Lawrence that day, and driven back through a rainstorm. The storm was still fierce, and the temperature had plunged. It was August, but the evening had the bite of fall.

Janine was in the bedroom. From where she was sitting, she couldn't see Emily, but she could hear her. She and Mark were talking in their own language, a mélange of shared references and private jokes.

"The more complex the mind, the greater the need for the simplicity of play," Mark said.

She could see Daniel. He was leaning back against the cushions; he had a sort of glow of honest tiredness about him; he was taking a pure, relaxed pleasure in his children.

The rain was battering the windows. It was the kind of night when you realize how lucky you are to be warm and indoors, how lucky you are to know that your children are happy and thriving and safe.

There was something in the oven; Daniel went into the kitchen to check on it.

Janine followed him into the kitchen.

"What are you making over there?" she said.

Daniel looked up at her quickly, as though she'd said something unusual, which she hadn't. Maybe there was something in her voice.

"Just something for the girl. Nothing complicated. Are you aware that in a previous life I was a short-order cook?"

"Yes, I am aware of that. In a previous life I sampled your flap-jacks."

She came over to the oven.

"That smells good. Is it vegan?"

"No. Actually not. I've decided to play a trick on our daughter. I'm sprinkling in little pieces of bacon. Bacon bits."

"Good, good. Why?"

"I'm not philosophically aligned with veganism."

"And so you take it as a mission of sorts to undermine vegans wherever you encounter them?"

"Of sorts. Does that bother you?"

"No. On the contrary. I was hoping you'd say that. I was trembling with anticipation."

"I noticed you trembling. But I didn't know what was causing it."

"Anticipation."

"I thought it might have been because the room was too cold."

"No. It's warm as toast in here."

"I thought it might have been a sort of 'trembling before God.'"

"No. It wasn't. I do occasionally itch before God, but I don't think I ever actually tremble."

"I'm glad to hear that. God's done too much damage to the world. A little itching now and then is all he deserves."

"By the way," she said.

"Yes?"

"You're probably one of the few police officers who'd use the phrase 'philosophically aligned.'"

"Actually, that's a misconception," he said, and they both laughed.

103

When Daniel called Florence to tell her that he'd be going back to Seattle soon, she found it hard to contain her delight.

"We should get together. I want to say goodbye to you all."

"I'm not sure it's all of us you'll be saying goodbye to. I'm going home. I'm not sure what anybody else is doing."

"That's unusual," she said. "That's unusual for you and your tribe."

"Yes, it is unusual for us. But we're a modern family. I would have thought you'd approve."

"I do approve. I approve of modernism in all its forms. I'm just surprised. Is Janine planning to stay here?"

"Janine has to make up her mind. She's enjoying the work she's doing. And her fellowship, as you may know, since we've mentioned it about five times, lasts until the end of December."

"So you'll be a commuting couple? You'll have what my students call an LDR?" *Long Distance Relationship*

"We used to call it an LDR when I was in college. I doubt they're calling it that now."

"And Emily?"

Emily was the one she truly wanted to get rid of. Janine was no threat. Despite how adhesive she wished to be, Janine had not proved difficult to shake off. Emily was the one to worry about.

"Emily makes her own choices. Anyway, you'll remember that Emily's a college girl."

"Is she going back to Kenyon?"

"Oberlin. And I don't know. She's thinking about transferring to Bard."

"All your women are leaving you."

"I suppose that's my fate," he said, and she wondered if he was taking some kind of dig at her. It was so hard to know with Daniel. For a moment she felt a breath of respect for her son. He kept his feelings as tightly regulated as she did, which, she knew, was an accomplishment.

"Well," he said, "why don't we have you over for a farewell dinner anyway, even if we're not sure how many of us are actually leaving."

"I'll say farewell to anybody who's there to say farewell to," she said. To her own ear, she sounded giddy, and she wondered whether this was what the coming months were going to be like—a series of giddy leave-takings, rendered sweeter by the fact that no one would know that they were leave-takings except her.

104

"What are you doing here?" Florence said.

Emily was at her door. It was Saturday night. Their farewell dinner was about an hour away.

"You're always just turning up," Florence said. "Haven't you learned by now that that's just not done in New York?"

"I know. It's rude. But here I am."

Florence let her in. That's something, Emily thought.

"So what are you doing here?"

"I thought I'd walk you over. It's time for the big dinner event."

"You thought you'd walk me over? You think I need walking over?"

"I just wanted to see you," Emily said.

"I'm very touched," Florence said, in a voice that made it clear that she wasn't.

Emily wasn't satisfied with the conversation they'd had in the café. Something was going on with Florence, and she wanted to know what it was.

Florence put on a light jacket and picked up her purse and cane and walked toward the door, but Emily didn't move.

294 · BRIAN MORTON

"What?" Florence said.

"I just thought we could talk for a minute."

"We can talk on the way."

"I wanted to just talk for a minute. Here."

It was hard for her to stand up to Florence, but it was important to make the effort.

"Well, go ahead."

"I think there's something you aren't telling me."

"Are you supposed to be my confidante?"

"I think there's something you're not telling anybody."

"What's gotten into you?" Florence said. "Have you lost your mind?"

"I think you're going through something serious, and I think you could use some help."

"How have you been spending your time lately?" Florence said. "Watching soap operas? I'm supposed to sit down and unburden myself to you? Is that the way you think it works? You think your grandmother is going through a rough patch and you're going to help her through? Is that it? You'll be the hero? Have you been ego-tripping on that thought?"

When in doubt, attack: Emily knew Florence well enough by now to recognize that this was Florence's way.

"Let's go," Florence said. "And no more of this foolishness."

105

For a paranoid minute, Florence tried to figure out if Emily had ever spent enough time unobserved in her apartment for her to have gone through her papers or intercepted a phone call from Noah's office. But if the girl had that kind of hard information, she wouldn't be nosing around like this. So she knew, but she didn't know.

106

When they were out on the street, Emily saw that Florence's foot was dragging again. Florence was trying to compensate, but the very effort to compensate made it obvious that something was wrong. She would lift her left leg carefully, as if she were placing it in a stirrup, and then she would lower and plant it with an equal deliberation.

Their destination was north, but Florence was looking south, at the approaching stream of traffic. She glanced over at Emily, but Emily spoke before she could.

"I'd suggest taking a cab," Emily said, "but I know how much you enjoy walking."

If the old woman was going to pretend that she was perfectly healthy, Emily was going to make her commit to the role.

Florence smiled at her—a tight little smile, as if she understood exactly what Emily was doing.

"Yes," Florence said. "Yes, I do. Let's go."

They proceeded north. Florence made her way slowly, laboriously lifting her left leg as if avoiding small, invisible obstacles in her path.

"I guess that sprain is still hurting," Emily said.

"It's not hurting at all."

"Then what's the problem?"

"There is no problem."

It was early September, but the afternoon was sweltering. It was one of those New York summer days where the heat bludgeons you with every step and you wouldn't mind lying down on the sidewalk.

"Did you see that enraging article in the *Times* this morning?" Florence said.

"Which one?"

"The one about all the promises Obama's broken."

"Missed that."

They arrived at the corner of Broadway and Eighty-sixth Street as the WALK sign was beginning to flash. Florence paused, unwilling to try to make it all the way across before the light changed.

"Tired?" Emily said. "Almost there, sort of." And kept going.

Florence followed. Her face was contorted with the effort to keep up.

Emily was surprised that she had this in herself. This—what was it? Sadism? Is it sadism to try to force someone to admit she needs help?

It wasn't sadism, she decided. It was love, expressed in the only language Florence might possibly respond to.

They were now in the way of the traffic, crossing against the light. Two cabs went past them, uncomfortably close; a van paused for them, but when the driver saw how slowly they were moving, he leaned on his horn. Finally they reached the other side of the street.

"I was reading this Virginia Woolf essay that you mentioned in one of your books," Emily said. "'Professions for Women.'"

"Great essay."

"She says that in order to become a writer, she had to murder . . . what does she call it?"

"The Angel in the House," Florence said.

"That's right. The Angel in the House. The spirit that makes a woman defer to everyone else instead of taking care of herself. If there's a draft, she—"

"If there's a draft, she sits in it," Florence said. "If there's chicken, she takes the leg. You don't have to recite it to me. You learned about it from me."

She was drawing a breath after each sentence.

"The thing I was wondering about is this. If a woman needs help but she doesn't ask for it, isn't she just playing the part of the Angel in the House?"

This was her trump card. She'd been thinking about this for days, working out exactly how to phrase it.

"That depends," Florence said. "Is she trying to take care of everybody else? Is she putting everybody else's needs above her own?"

"I don't know what she's doing," Emily said.

"I'd say she's just standing on her own two feet," Florence said.

They'd stopped walking. Emily, looking at her grandmother, felt that she'd never cared about anyone more. Florence, looking back at her, gave nothing. There was no hint on her face of a wish to understand or a wish to be understood.

Florence started to walk again.

You have to hand it to the old lady, Emily thought.

At Eighty-eighth Street, with six blocks to go, Emily relented. There was no point in torturing her.

"Here's a bus," Emily said. "Let's take the bus."

"I wouldn't hear of it," Florence said, and continued grimly on.

"Jesus," Daniel said after he opened the door. "You look like you've been playing volleyball."

Florence's face was sweaty. Her blouse was soaked.

"We have been playing volleyball," Emily said.

"It was a good game," Florence said.

"Who won?" Daniel said.

Florence walked toward an easy chair, forcing herself to go slowly so as not to betray the immensity of her desire to sit. Her pulse was drumming in her ears. Janine asked her what she wanted to drink, and answering felt like a challenge.

After a little bit of rest and a little bit of bourbon, she felt revived.

There was an odd static in the emotional air of the room. Daniel kept changing the music, Janine kept scrolling through delivery menus. Florence felt as if she and Emily were the only calm ones here. They were like adversaries after a battle, joined by mutual respect.

"I'm confused," Florence said. "How many of you are leaving? And where are you going?"

"Dad and I are going home," Emily said. "From there, from thence—I'm applying to colleges. Assuming someplace accepts me, I'll probably transfer in January."

"And you?" Florence said to Janine.

"She's got work she needs to finish," Emily said. "Her thing ends in December. Then she's coming home too."

Janine hadn't said anything. She reached for her glass of wine, staring at it closely, as if it might have something to say.

Florence didn't know if Emily's version was accurate or if she was intent on preserving some idea of her family that was no longer true.

"Why don't you visit us?" Emily said to Florence.

"I'd love to visit," Florence said.

"We should set a date. We should set a date right now. You're probably pretty free this year. You have a sabbatical, right?"

"Actually, I'm not sure how free I'll be. Every time you think you have some free time, the responsibilities start rushing in."

"Like what?"

"That's the thing. You can't be sure until they do."

"But I just want to know what could happen that could prevent you from making a date to stay with us for a while."

"Emily," her mother said.

"No. I just want to know what kind of responsibilities you tend to have, when you're a big-time intellectual."

"I feel like I'm missing something here," Janine said. "Subtext."

"What's subtext?" Daniel said.

"Stop it, Daniel," Florence said. "You were under the same roof with me and Saul for eighteen years. The same roofs, anyway. You know what subtext is."

"Were you and Dad always talking about subtext?" Daniel said.

"No, we weren't talking about it. But the idea of it was always there. Like a subtext."

"Now I'm totally lost."

"I'm not," Emily said. "I just want to know what my grandmother's doing this fall. I just want to know why she won't commit to visiting us."

Emily looked enraged. She had the light of battle in her eyes.

What a magnificent girl, Florence thought.

109

It was clear that Florence wasn't going to say anything to anybody, but if that was the case, Emily thought, she was going to do everything she could to make her feel bad about it.

"I'm offended that you won't commit to visiting us."

"I have speaking engagements, I have deadlines. I'm trying to finish this book."

"You have a laptop. The point of a laptop is that you can move around with it. You can even write with it on your lap. That's why they call it—"

"I know what the point of a laptop is."

"Anything you need to do, you could do at our house. I don't know if you've heard about it, but there's this thing called the Internet—"

"Let's not get ahead of ourselves here, Emily," Daniel said. "I'm not sure I want my mother underfoot. She's very clean, but she has a lot of demands."

"Let's return to this subject by email, after you get home," Florence said.

"I just want to know—"

"Stop it."

There was a new sharpness in Florence's voice. Emily had been scolded by Florence before, but this tone of voice was something different.

Emily went to the kitchen and put on some water for tea. Her hands were trembling. Her lips were trembling.

I'm a lightweight, she thought. I thought I could get into the ring with the big gorilla. But all it took to shut me down was a little slap.

She didn't know why she was approaching it like this. She could have just told her parents that she was sure that Florence was hiding something, sure that Florence was ill. But she had too much respect for her grandmother to do that.

"I'm sorry about that," Daniel said to his mother. "I don't know what's gotten into her."

Daniel bored her. Florence didn't want any of this cottage-cheesy politeness. She loved it that her granddaughter had tried to fight with her.

"Don't you dare apologize for her," Florence said. "If I ever see you people again, she'll be the reason."

It was more than she'd meant to say, but Daniel and Janine, to their credit, only laughed.

After dessert, after coffee, after a drink in the living room, Florence said goodbye to Daniel and Janine. Emily watched her give them her usual arm's-length embrace.

"Let me get you a cab," Daniel said.

"I don't need you to get me a cab. It's a lovely night. I'm going to walk for a few blocks, and then I'm going to get myself a cab. It's touching that you want to protect me, but I've done well enough so far."

"Suit yourself," Daniel said.

Emily walked to the hallway so she could have a moment alone with her. She didn't want to say goodbye in front of the others.

"Take care of yourself, my young friend," Florence said, and she opened the door.

There had to be more. There had to be.

"I'll walk you out," Emily said.

She thought Florence would say something special to her. But she didn't know what she expected. Was it that Florence would finally tell her what was going on? Was it that Florence would boil down her entire life's message? She wasn't sure. She was only sure that Florence would say something special.

On the street Florence touched her arm and started south.

That was it. That was all. Emily never saw her again.

In the days that followed, Emily kept hoping for a phone call or an email, but she didn't get one. Three times that fall she wrote to Florence, but Florence didn't reply.

Even after Florence's death—her terrible death, so unforeseen and so foreseeable—Emily kept hoping that a letter would turn up in Florence's apartment, written for her alone.

There was no laying on of hands; there was no last word. The old lady had eluded her once again.

That was one way of looking at it. The other way of looking at it was that the teaching, the passing on of whatever could be passed on, had already been done. This was the conclusion Emily would finally reach, but it would be years before she got there.

As she watched Florence making her way down the street, Emily couldn't believe that it was over. She kept expecting her to come back and say something more.

Acknowledgments

Thanks to the friends who read early drafts: Emma Barrie, Robert Bedick, Amy Edelman, Todd Gitlin, Vivian Gornick, Liselle Gottlieb, Harvey Klinger, Mark Levinson, Ilana Masad, Howard Parnes, Ann Patty, Katha Pollitt, Marc Siegel, and Chuck Wachtel.

Thanks to Henry Dunow and Lauren Wein, for their editorial guidance.

And something more than thanks to Heather Harpham.

p. 83
  88
146
165 - haha

172
267-8 - note